Starting Back

STEPHANIE ROSE

STARTING BACK

STEPHANIE ROSE

That's What She Said Publishing,Inc.

Cover Design: Kari March at Kari March Designs

Cover Photo: © Shutterstock

Editing: Lisa Hollett—Silently Correcting Your Grammar

Proofreading: Jodi Duggan

ISBN: 979-8-88643-906-9 (ebook)

ISBN: 979-8-88643-907-6 (paperback)

012023

For Ann Marie, since this was all your idea. Who knew a sea-themed dish towel would be such an awesome writing prompt? Thank you for harassing your firefighter nurse co-worker for information and for being my found family.

And for Jessenia, for being the friend I needed these past few months. I hope you enjoy the book you helped bring to life.

ONE

KRISTINA

"**W**elcome to Turtle Bay!"

I pushed a smile across my lips in a feeble attempt to mimic the cheerful greeting from the resort clerk.

"Thank you," I said with as much enthusiasm as I could muster while I tried to keep hold of my carry-on bag and suitcase behind me.

"What is your name?"

I dropped the carry-on at my feet when she turned to her computer screen.

"Kristina Webber. But the reservation may be under my friend's name, Nicole Kent."

"Ah yes, you have the suite. And it looks like you have an upgrade?"

"We do? I mean, I do?"

What could be an upgrade from a two-bedroom suite I had to stay in alone?

"A complimentary couple's massage was added."

Guilt twisted my stomach at her elated expression, and to be this upset over disappointing a stranger spoke to the problems that followed me from New York.

"I don't think Nicole booked a couple's vacation, but I could be wrong. We're not—"

"Oh, don't worry about that." She waved a hand, her blue fingernails racing over the keys. "No one will ask if you're an actual couple."

"Well, that's nice, but only *I'll* be in the suite for the next few days. I think Nicole said she called ahead to note that. But, hey, if they can give me two massages, I can go twice," I joked, but as her lips twisted at the screen in response, I guessed I wasn't that funny.

All I wanted to do was change into my bathing suit and find some frosty cocktails, anything that would make me forget that I was at this gorgeous resort in the Florida Keys alone, or keep me from panicking over what the hell I was supposed to do with all that time to myself.

"Yes, she did call ahead to put the suite in your name. So sorry about that, Ms. Webber."

I nodded, leaning against the counter as I took in all the groups of friends and couples around me. The lobby was crowded, but the impending loneliness was already palpable.

"Can I help you with your bags, miss?"

One of the resort workers, a young man who could almost pass for my high school junior nephew's age, motioned to the large pink bag at my feet.

"Thank you so much," I said, a real smile stretching across my lips at his use of *miss*, not *ma'am*. "I just need to get my room key."

"Here you go. One and a spare." The desk clerk handed me two white keycards. "Have a wonderful stay and let us know if you need anything."

"Thank you." I took the keycards from her hand and leaned in to peek at her name tag. "Nancy."

I was too embarrassed to follow up on a substitute for the couple's massage and trailed behind the resort worker down the long path to my suite. I turned my head at every splash and laugh, and I needed to snap out of this mood if I was going to make the most of this solo vacation.

"Here you are. Enjoy."

I gave him a nice tip after he opened the door and set down my bags. Despite how tempted I was to just nap under the covers, I tore through my suitcase for my bathing suit and cover-up and changed before I called Nicole.

She'd requested a phone call the minute I checked in for me to report back on the room—and probably for her to apologize ten more times.

"I'm so sorry," Nicole sniffled over the speakerphone. "I wanted to go on this trip with you so badly." She lost her words to a hacking cough.

"I know that, but you couldn't travel with a hundred and three fever, and I wouldn't have wanted you to." I sighed and plopped down onto one of the beds in our—*my*—suite, smoothing my hand over the plush white comforter. "Please stop apologizing. I just want you to rest and feel better."

"But this was supposed to be our vacation in the Keys, and I left you all alone." Her words trailed off before the blare of a nose blowing filled the space, a space too big for only one person. "After all those months of planning, I ruined everything."

"No, you did not."

I let out a soft breath of frustration. Nicole had planned this trip for us to break me out of the funk I'd been in for the past few months. Divorcing Colin wasn't all that much different from being married to him, as we were separated long before either of us could admit it, but the finality of it all got to me in a way I didn't expect.

After months of Nicole trying to convince me a vacation would be the best thing, I agreed and almost looked forward to it until Nicole came down with the flu three days before takeoff. No one in my life could jump on a plane to Florida at that short notice, and while I'd had the foresight to book us flight insurance, we were locked into the resort fees.

Nicole had gotten us a deal on a suite with her travel points, but it was still too much money to lose. Leaving my girls was enough of a stressor, and now I had to figure out what to do for the next four days alone.

"What does the room look like?"

I scooped up the phone and rose from the bed.

"Actually, really nice." I traipsed into one of the bathrooms, the full soaker tub enticing me much more than the pool I'd passed on the way back from check-in. Well-meaning friends often gifted bath bombs for relaxation, but stuffing myself into my tiny tub at home with my knees almost to my chest didn't do the trick.

"The bathroom is nice, the tub is huge." I spotted a terrace attached to one of the bedrooms and peeked out the sliding door. There was an adorable little table framed by two chairs and a gorgeous view of the beach behind the hotel, nothing but palm trees and waves crashing onto the white sand.

"You missed out on a great terrace with a view. I don't even have to leave the room."

"But you will," Nicole tried to yell but was cut off by her hacking cough. "You are *not* going to be a recluse on this vacation. Don't make me feel even worse," she told me through more sniffles.

I sighed and cupped my forehead. I never did anything alone, not even before I married Colin, my now ex-husband, and had two daughters ten years apart. Other than family trips, I never planned any vacation, especially not with just me in mind. As I'd attempted to zone out on the two-and-a-half-hour flight from New York to Florida, I tried to recall a time when I'd planned anything for myself. It was always for the girls, my mother, or whatever everyone else wanted to do.

Nicole had pushed me to go on this trip for just that reason. After years of trying to save a marriage that I could no longer deny was dead in the water, I felt, other than my girls, life had become listless for me. I had no idea how much time I'd wasted on a daily basis trying to keep us together until I stopped.

A vacation where I didn't have to map out the daily activities or make sure the menu appeased my picky kids seemed like too foreign a notion to even consider. Nicole kept sending links to all the resorts to convince me how great it would be to get away for a few days and just be Kristina, no worries or responsibilities other than what book to read or what cocktail to have next.

It took so long to agree because without my family, who was I? I'd stopped paying attention long enough to forget.

"You don't have to leave the resort. Meals and drinks are all included. Your only worry should be tan lines." She chuckled, then lapsed into coughing again. "But you *will* leave the room. Just do me a favor. When you meet a guy you want to spend the night with, sneak a picture of his license and send it to me."

"What?" I screeched at the phone. "I have no intention of doing that, and out of curiosity, why would you need his license?"

"Just for security, in case of anything. And share your phone location with me if he takes you anywhere."

"Well, you don't have to worry about *in case of anything*. I am not ready for that yet."

"Kris, you and Colin separated a year before the divorce." Her audible sigh made the reminder sting even more. "And weren't together for a long time before that. Okay, so even if you don't want to spend the night with someone, a little flirting isn't bad, right? Chat up a hot lifeguard or sexy bartender."

"Right," I said, pushing off the bed with the phone still in my hand as I looked myself over in the full-length mirror on the bathroom door, my flowy, almost see-through cover-up teasing my black bathing suit underneath.

In the last year, when it started to become evident that Colin and I had no future despite how we were trying to force it, I'd thrown myself into exercise. I'd escape to my basement every day at five a.m. and work out until I'd collapse into a ball of sweat, trying in vain to escape the problems I'd have to face once I went back upstairs and started my day.

I still found solace in those thirty minutes every morning, and my one method of self-care granted me toned arms and legs and the shadow of abs across my abdomen. I felt confident enough to pack a real bikini instead of the tank top two-piece swimsuit I'd usually wear to water parks with the kids. I'd been waxed and threaded within an inch of my life in preparation to strut around in this new suit, but with all the much younger, perfect bodies I'd spied by the pool on my way to check in, I doubted I'd be the one to have to ward off all the attention, which was fine by me.

"Go get some rest," I said, not wanting to address anything Nicole had said about flirting or ponder once again how long my marriage had really been over. "I'm going to lounge by the pool with a piña colada and try to kick-start my vacation."

"Yes, that's the spirit! If you do meet any hot lifeguards, sneak a picture. I'll try to pretend I'm there ogling with you."

"Sure, Nic." A chuckle slipped out of me. "Get some rest."

"Get some *action*."

"Check your temperature, I think you're hallucinating. No

action other than a frosty drink and maybe some fried bar food later. Sleep."

I ended the call and snatched up my purse. Perhaps I could do this and relax enough that maybe I wouldn't be so damn tense upon my return. My sweet six-year-old, Emma, crawled into my lap several times a day because I looked "sad enough for a hug."

Chloe, my fifteen-year-old, hadn't said anything about the divorce since we'd sat them both down and explained their father would be living in his own apartment permanently, instead of coming and going as he had over the past few years. She never complained, did extra chores without being asked, and even requested that I teach her how to make simple dinners so she could give me a break some nights.

She was just a kid but worried about her own mother more than any teenager should. She'd most likely heard all the drawn-out fights and was old enough to notice every bit of stifling tension in the room between her father and me after. Forcing it for so long did much more damage than just walking away when it was time.

I'd never wanted this for my daughters, and putting them through it made me feel like the world's biggest failure.

As a mother, as a wife, and as a person.

I rooted around in my bag for the granola bar I'd picked up at the airport and took a chomp on my way down the hallway leading to the pool. I hadn't eaten anything since before I'd boarded the plane, and if I was going to day drink my problems away, passing out on the lounge chair near the pool with no travel companion to nudge me conscious wasn't the smartest course of action.

Regret stuck to me like a constant fungus no matter where I was, but if I'd made it all the way here, I'd find a way to give it a shot.

TWO

KRISTINA

"**A**re you in Disney World?" Emma asked me. I held the phone to my ear as I lounged against the pillow of my pool chair, running my finger up and down the drips of condensation on my frosty strawberry daiquiri glass next to me.

"No, baby. I'd never go there without you and Chloe. I'm just sitting by the pool."

"Oh," she said. "Are you bored? You have no one to play with."

I pictured her adorable nose scrunching up like it always did when she asked a question. At six years old, she was young enough that her lack of filter was still cute, even though her big sister would often groan in embarrassment and roll her eyes when Emma would ask a simple but maybe not-so-appropriate question.

Emma was a little pipsqueak, all big blue eyes and long dark hair that she never let me cut more than an inch off at a time. Although Chloe and I shared my mother's odd green eyes, Emma was a mini, big-mouthed version of her grandmother.

She was our unexpected joy, my precious miracle that had

appeared when I had long ago accepted that Chloe would be an only child.

Colin and I had retreated to a getaway in the Poconos in a last-ditch effort to rekindle *something* before we gave up, and to our surprise, we did manage to reconnect enough on that trip to discover a surprise pregnancy upon our return.

I had hopes that her arrival meant things would work out after all—until they didn't. Still, she ended up being the best gift to all of us, even to her sister, although Chloe would never admit it.

Emma was too young to remember the fights and frustration that came back in full force after her birth, the memories that I feared haunted Chloe. My baby girl was young enough to be oblivious through most of it, but my eldest child had seen and heard too much over the years to have the pure heart that her sister had. We all cherished Emma's innocence, and I wanted to clutch on to it for as long as I could.

"Aunt Peyton, Unca Jake, and Mike are having a sleepover here. She has a belly now."

I laughed, surprised she knew enough to whisper the last part.

"Well, she's growing a baby in there. When I had you and Chloe, I had a big belly both times."

My mother, brother, sister-in-law, and nephew were all staying at our house with the girls while I was away. While I knew they'd be happy and cared for with my family, I'd hoped Colin would have taken the girls instead while I was gone. He'd said his work hours were too unpredictable and he couldn't take off, but Colin couldn't handle more than a weekend alone with his daughters. Although I'd known that, I hoped this time he would try.

But I was done asking Colin to try anything he didn't want to do. No good ever came from it, and when I remembered all the times I pleaded with him to do the simplest of things, the memories turned my stomach and settled into my gut.

"Unca Jake brought donuts," she said after a big gasp. "I love you, Mommy. Here's Unca Jake."

The thud of a phone dropping filled my ear, followed by my brother's husky chuckle.

"How's it going, Kris?"

"Here I was thinking my kids would miss me, and my baby forgot all about me once she saw donuts," I said, feigning a heavy sigh.

"They do miss you. We're just keeping them distracted until you get back. Relax and try to have some fun."

"Hard to do when you're alone." I reached for my drink and took a long sip, the sweet strawberry taste warming and cooling my throat on the way down.

"Look, you made it all the way down there, so you owe it to yourself to make the most of it. Maybe meet some new people. Embrace being single."

"*Wow.* Did my big brother just tell me to have a vacation hookup? I think that's what the kids call it these days, right?"

"You're an adult. It's not like when I had to threaten my friends when I caught them gawking at you while you were still in high school. And how the hell would I know what the kids call it?"

"You threatened them? Way to kill my social life," I teased, smiling when he groaned.

"My teenage sister wasn't dating college guys. Dad would have lost his shit, so if I hadn't stopped them, he would have."

A laugh slipped out at the reminder of much simpler times. I wasn't too young to date *anyone* now, but I had no clue where to begin or if I even wanted to after how my marriage had ended.

Love was supposed to be worth fighting for, but after going

through the motions for all that time, I doubted if that kind of love was even possible—at least for me.

My marriage ending upset me because it meant that I failed, not that I'd lost a great love. Friends tried to comfort me by saying it was better to have loved and lost, but I couldn't remember the love to appreciate it enough to miss it.

I'd only lost.

"Anyway, I figured that since you have a young wife, you'd know the lingo."

"Peyton is in her early thirties, and with me, so she doesn't use the term *hookup*."

I burst out laughing at the finality in his voice. "Still gone for your wife, I see."

"Always." I could hear his smile. "And I know it feels hopeless for you right now. I've been there, but I'm telling you not to give up. Sometimes things don't work out because something else is meant to be. I believe that now, and you should too."

"Right," I said, blowing out a long breath as I swirled the rest of the melted slush at the bottom of my glass.

"Don't 'right' me, baby sister. Try. Open your mind. We've all got the kids covered. The only person you have to worry about is you for the next few days. And if you do *hook up* with anyone, please be careful and don't tell me any details."

A smile pulled across my lips. "I love you, big brother. Even if you cockblocked me in high school."

"Please don't ever say cockblock to me again. And I love you too."

I let my head fall back on the small pillow and shut my eyes. I resolved to force myself to relax and have fun, but first, I needed a refill, and I couldn't find the waiter who'd taken my last two poolside drink orders. I slipped my feet into my flip-flops and headed to the bar, settling on one of the stools. I twisted the stem of the empty glass with my thumb and index finger as I studied the frozen drink menu on the whiteboard behind the bar.

"Need help making a decision?"

I jumped, so in my own head I hadn't noticed the bartender's approach.

"I guess I do," I said, turning my head toward the deep timbre and then fighting not to ogle lower. His hair was black and cropped short, but long enough for it to curl a bit in the front. His eyes were an unusual mix of golden brown and green, with long, thick lashes grazing his brow bone. He held my gaze as he scooped up my empty glass, the hint of a smile lifting the corner of his full lips.

"Well, it's my job to help you out." His smile deepened, teasing a dimple on his stubbled cheek. A black T-shirt stretched across his chest, the poor cotton sleeves straining from the muscles of his inked arms. He was built, not bulky, and so damn good-looking it was almost impossible to maintain eye contact.

I was relieved when he turned around, but then I had to tear my gaze away from his backside. The globes of his ass filled out his jeans just like his arms and chest filled out his shirt. I almost had the urge to dig for my phone, as this was a prime example of the hot bartender Nicole was hoping I'd find.

"Something wrong?" he asked as he set the whiteboard in front of me.

"No, why?" I cleared my throat, holding in a cringe when my voice cracked.

"I noticed you staring." My cheeks heated when I spied the twitch of a smirk in the corner of his perfect mouth.

At forty-two, I'd seen plenty of attractive men before. I'd sometimes give a quick second glance of admiration, but they never affected me like this on sight. It was as if this guy were seeing right through me, and it made me squirm enough to forget how to speak a coherent sentence.

"Oh, I wasn't staring, just that... Isn't it hot to be in jeans? The rest of the bartenders are practically wearing bathing suits. Just thought that you were hot, or that you may be hot." I groaned as my head fell back. "Listen, I'm going to blame the way I'm acting right now on drinking in the sun, and I'd appreciate it if you did too."

His gruff chuckle settled deep in my belly.

"I've seen plenty of guests after a day of double-fisting drinks in the Florida sun. I promise you're nowhere near that. If you don't know what you want, would you mind if I picked for you?"

"Sure," I said, relaxing a little at his warm and easy smile. "There isn't much I don't like..." I trailed off when he cocked a brow. "Jesus Christ, please just pick a drink for me so the wrong words don't keep coming out of my mouth."

"You're fine," he rasped, his smile fading as his gaze slid back to mine. "I'll be right back."

When he picked up a tall glass from the shelf behind him and ambled toward the bottles at the rear of the bar, my eyes were glued to the way his back muscles worked as he loaded the blender with ice and the fluid way he switched from one spouted bottle to another.

I wanted to reason that it was curiosity not enjoyment that kept my eyes on him the entire time.

He swiveled his head around and flashed a wide grin. Instead of looking away or fumbling a denial that I'd been staring, I smiled back and shrugged. Humiliating myself right off the bat seemed to take the edge off.

My brother's voice echoed in my head, telling me again to try. I still didn't know if I had it in me to seek out anyone here or anywhere, but I could allow myself a little flirtation with a hot bartender—if I could pull it together enough to stop the word vomit.

"Here you go," he said as he set a large, pink-frosted glass in front of me. "Pink lemonade frozen margarita. I tried to keep it in the same color family as your first drink, but I can make you something else if you don't want this one."

As a tiny smile ghosted across his mouth, I spotted the dots of gray along his chin and at his temples. He seemed to be around my age, early- to mid-forties, and the possibility made me relax.

After an afternoon of feeling like the parent or chaperone every time I scanned the pool area, finding someone I could talk to who spoke the same language—once I stopped putting my foot into my mouth—would be a hell of a lot easier for me.

My daughter constantly called me out when I used the words of her generation the wrong way. My nephew, Mike, was only a year older than Chloe but would gently let me know when I said something wrong or if it was simply too *cringe* for a parent to say.

I took a sip, the bite of lemonade and the salt from the tequila hitting my tongue in all the right places. Despite the slight burn warming my chest, it cooled me off at the same time.

"This is perfect. Thank you. And sorry about...before."

"No worries," he said as a slow smile stretched across his lips. "You were cute."

"Cute?" I couldn't help but snicker. "Thank you, I guess." My cheeks heated as I finally tore my eyes away, poking at the ice in my drink. I tried to recall the last time anyone had referred to me as cute and came up empty.

Before my marriage had begun to crumble, I was confident in how I looked. I always loved to play up my green eyes and enjoyed experimenting with different hair colors and highlights. It wasn't that I felt ugly after my marriage imploded, but I'd felt invisible for so long that the notion of an attractive man even calling me cute was a sadly surprising novelty.

"Is there a boyfriend or husband or friend coming along to drink with you?" he asked as he wiped down the bar, flicking his eyes back and forth between me and the white towel in his hand.

"Nope, traveling and drinking alone." I raised my glass before taking another sip.

"Hmm." He leaned against the bar, crossing his arms over his torso, a move that highlighted his broad chest and chiseled arms. My head spun, tipsy from a fixation with both that had nothing to do with the drink in my hand or the ones by the pool.

"Then I take that back. You aren't cute."

"I'm not cute?" I squinted at him, poking the slush in my glass with the straw.

"Your fumbling was cute. You're actually beautiful, but I didn't want a husband or boyfriend to overhear me say that and kick my ass."

"Well, no one to hear you say anything but me." I motioned to the other two patrons leaning against the edge of the bar with various colored cocktails in hand, as I tried to ignore the flush creeping up my neck from both his compliment and heated stare. "And them."

"I thought you were with that group by the pool that kept moving all the chairs around."

I went to take another sip and stilled.

"Wait, you noticed me by the pool? When?"

"A few hours ago." He shrugged. "I mean, I could lie and say I was checking who was taking the poolside orders, but I'm not ashamed to admit I was staring."

I reared back when his brows jumped.

"I wasn't ashamed. I mean, I wasn't." I dipped my chin to my chest and sucked in a long inhale through my nostrils. "If I'm going to keep making a fool of myself in front of you, I should tell you my name. Kristina. With a K." I smiled and held out my hand, not prepared for the heat that rushed up my arm when he slid his palm against mine or the shiver from the scrape of calluses on his fingertips as he clasped my hand.

What the hell was in these cocktails?

"Kristina *with a K* is a beautiful name. I'm Leo, a pleasure," he said, a husky dip in his voice when he said "pleasure" that traveled right to my toes. He hadn't needed two and a half cocktails to flirt. His talent shone right through.

I pulled my hand away and wrapped it around my drink, hoping the icy condensation would cool off the heat flooding my body from Leo's stare.

"Good for you for planning your own vacation."

I had to laugh. I'd planned this vacation under duress from the beginning. Therefore, not one thing about how I would end up at a poolside bar talking to a sexy stranger felt planned.

"My best friend convinced me to go on this trip. But she got sick, and I didn't want to lose money or waste time off from work that I couldn't reschedule. It took a lot of effort to rearrange my life for this vacation."

"Ah, I see." He nodded. "But it's not a bad thing, even if you seem like you think it is." He dipped his head to meet my gaze and rested his elbow on the bar. "I've traveled alone before. For me, it was great. I made my own schedule and didn't have to consult with anyone before I did what I wanted. How are you liking it so far?"

"Well," I started, twisting my straw between my fingers, "I only got here this morning. Thanks to early check-in, I was able to change into my bathing suit and head over to the pool for the day to obsess about why I came here and if I should leave early."

Leo crossed his arms again, his golden eyes studying me.

"Why would you want to leave early if you only just got here?"

Would he be so interested in picking my drinks and why I wanted to leave early once he found out I was someone's mother —or rather *two* someones?

Simply talking to a man as a single mother was already complicated enough to give me a headache.

"I have kids at home. Two girls, one fifteen and one six. I just spoke to my little one. She hardly misses me with all the extra family she gets to see for the next few days, but leaving them created a ton of guilt that I can't shake. So, thanks for the extra tequila." I lifted my glass, cringing on the inside at telling a complete stranger all my problems that he probably had no interest in hearing.

"Taking a break isn't selfish. Your husband didn't want to come with you, I guess." He grabbed a towel and wiped the top of the counter in almost the same spot as before, regarding me with an expectant look in his eyes.

I couldn't help my wide grin as I tried not to focus on the bulge of his bicep with every swipe. The mention of my girls didn't have him retreating just yet, and that filled me with an odd relief, along with a slight uptick in my pulse at the sneaky way he inquired if I was married or not.

"My *ex*-husband couldn't take off from work, so my mother, brother, and sister-in-law all volunteered to take care of my girls so they could force me to have fun."

"Ah" was all he said, his shoulders dropping as if he were relieved, a playful lift at the corner of his mouth. "So you have to be forced to have fun?"

"Seems that way. It does sound ridiculous, right? I'm at this beautiful resort, with nothing to worry about but tan lines." I hooked my thumb inside the shoulder strap of my swimsuit and slid it up and down, jerking my hand away when Leo's gaze fell to my chest. "I shouldn't bother you on shift with my problems."

I patted his hand and shifted on the stool to get up when he draped his other hand over my wrist, another charge of electricity sparking where our skin made contact.

"You're not bothering me. Stay and tell me whatever you want."

"You probably have practice hearing sad stories, being a bartender and all, right?" I slid back onto the stool.

He chuckled and shrugged when he lifted his head.

"Sometimes, but your story isn't sad. Doing something for yourself is a good thing, especially since I get the impression you probably put yourself last all the time. Or else you wouldn't feel guilty over drinking by the pool."

"How do you know that?"

"Well, the look in your eyes when you mentioned your kids. How restless you seemed to be while lying on the chair before you came over here."

"Exactly how long were you watching me?" The notion of his eyes on me all that time sent a delicious shiver up my spine.

"Long enough. Your eyes are really green."

His eyes were so dark and intense, I had to turn away for a moment to mask the blush I was sure had singed my cheeks red.

"They're weird, or so I've been told. The only ones in my family with this color are my mother, my eldest daughter, and two cousins of mine. If they lived closer, we'd all look like a weird new species."

"Not weird, beautiful."

I didn't know what to do with the heat in his eyes as they zeroed in on me, but I liked it.

"I didn't mean to make you uncomfortable if I did just now," he said, cringing when I lifted my head.

"I'm not, you aren't," I told him honestly. "It's just...different, I guess."

"Different?"

Toward the end, I could have paraded myself around in red lace and set myself on fire, and Colin probably wouldn't have even blinked.

A man hanging on my every word as he seemed unable to take his eyes off me was sure as hell different, but I didn't want to go there with Leo or bring up anything of my old or current life for fear of breaking this weird spell between us.

It wouldn't last too much longer, but from the moment I'd sat on the barstool, I felt more alive than in...in more time than I could recall.

"Of all the women here, I'm just surprised you noticed me fidgeting on my chair."

"Tell me something, Kristina." He leaned his elbows on the bar, the flecks of green and gold in his irises shimmering as the late afternoon sun washed over his face. "Why do the most attractive women in the world never know it?"

"You're asking *me*?" I chuckled, but he didn't laugh with me.

"Hell yeah, I'm asking you." His voice dipped low and husky as he locked his gaze with mine, not backing down an inch.

After I avoided his question, I camped on that stool as the sun continued to descend along the horizon. He'd leave to fill a drink order and come right back to me, asking me one random question after another while keeping my glass full.

"Where are you from?" Leo asked as he dried an empty glass and set it back on the shelf under the bar.

"New York. Upstate, not the city. Small town, everyone in your business."

He laughed, a deep rumble that shook his shoulders.

"Sounds like my hometown in New Hampshire. Not that I've been there in a couple of decades."

"Not even to visit?"

"No one left to go see." He shrugged, his smile shrinking before he cleared his throat. "I have an aunt and uncle who live in Upstate New York too."

"Where upstate? My town is near Albany."

"I think that's a couple of hours from where my aunt and uncle are in Fulton County. Small world, I guess." He shrugged, holding my gaze. "I visit a few times a year. Not as much as I should. I'm too tan to be a Northerner now."

He extended his inked arm, twisting it back and forth and showing off the sinew of muscle.

"Have you lived in Florida all this time?"

He shrugged and nodded.

"For a few years. I lived in Las Vegas before the Keys, but it was a little too much for me."

"I can see that. I was there years ago on a girls' weekend, and my liver wouldn't survive living there."

Life before my kids seemed so long ago, it was as if it hadn't happened.

"I've seen some things." He rubbed the back of his neck and laughed. "Whenever we got a call at the fire station, we never had a clue what to expect."

"Fire station? You're a firefighter?"

"I am." He nodded. "I work the bar here and there on my days off."

"Wouldn't you want to relax on your days off? I know I would. Although with kids, I hadn't experienced a true day off until..." I tapped my chin, trying to think of the last time I went a full day without Chloe and Emma, a piercing sting cutting through my chest when I realized this was the first time I'd left Emma for an entire day since she was born.

"Until now?" he asked, lifting a brow.

"Until now." That realization made me gulp my drink long enough to give me a second of brain freeze.

"Another reason why you shouldn't go home yet. Everyone needs a day off. This"—he motioned behind him—"doesn't feel like work to me. I like to get out of my apartment and people-watch. Never know who you may meet passing through."

His mouth blossomed into a wry grin that made the tiny hairs on the back of my neck stand up.

"Working as a bartender when you should be home relaxing means that you have to deal with despondent tourists like me who can't even pick their drink."

A small smile ghosted across his lips.

"It doesn't feel as if I'm *dealing* with you at all. In fact, you've been the highlight of my day so far."

"You're very sweet." I poked at the rest of my drink with my straw. "So far, you're the highlight of mine too."

His eyes danced as his smile grew wider. Maybe I wasn't so bad at flirting after all, even if it did take three servings of alcohol to muster up the courage to try.

He came closer and opened his mouth to say something when a throat clearing behind us interrupted.

"Hey, Reyes," a man wearing a Hawaiian shirt and board shorts said as he came toward us, regarding Leo with a smirk. "Can I tear you away from your new friend for a few minutes to give me a hand with the crowd at the end of the bar?" He tilted his head toward the cluster of women with almost identical string bikinis who, judging by how loud they were laughing, appeared to be a few more drinks in than I was.

That used to be me in my college days, but I wasn't so old that I shouldn't have been able to just enjoy a drink by a pool. I could reason it was from missing my girls, but there was more to it than that, more than I liked to ponder or acknowledge.

Fun shouldn't have been something I had to learn. Talking to

Leo was effortless fun, and although I'd expected it to, I was sad to see it end.

"I'm sorry." I pushed off the stool and fished my wallet out of my purse. "You're busy. Thanks for the drinks—"

He grabbed my wrist as I was about to drop cash for a tip onto the bar.

"Stay. I won't be long. Other than them and you, the guests are fading for the day. I'll be right back. Sit. Please."

"Well, since you asked so nicely," I teased and slid back onto the seat. As much as I'd been afraid to speak to him at first, he didn't have to twist my arm to stay.

I watched Leo pour drinks and hand them to the women, a few of them giggling when he turned his back, probably commenting to one another about how hot he was.

If Nicole were with me, we'd have done the same thing. But had she been here, I probably wouldn't have spoken to him other than my drink order. Traveling alone made a person do crazy, impulsive things.

So far, I didn't hate it.

I was so into what Leo was doing that I jumped when my phone buzzed against my lap.

Chloe: *Having fun? Are you okay there alone?*

I peered down at the screen with a smile. Emma was easily distracted, but my firstborn still thought about me.

Me: *At least one of you misses me. Your sister forgot all about me when Uncle Jake showed up with donuts.*

Chloe: *Can I call you now?*

Leo was still pouring drinks with his back turned. Tearing my eyes away from him was a greater struggle than it should have been as I slipped off the stool and dialed my daughter.

"Hey, are you okay?"

My heart squeezed at the concern in her voice.

"I'm fine, sweetheart. It's nice weather, and I was just sitting by the pool."

And now maybe looking back to the bar to see if the bartender noticed I was gone.

"I could have come with you. Then you wouldn't be alone."

"This isn't a resort for kids, or I would have brought you with me. I promise I'm fine, and I'll come back nice and relaxed."

I leaned against the wall next to the bar, unnerved by the long silence.

"Are *you* okay?"

"Yeah. I keep telling Emma to stop touching Aunt Peyton's stomach."

I smiled at her huff.

"I'm sure Aunt Peyton doesn't mind. Why don't we make a deal? I'll promise to relax and have fun if you do. How does that sound?"

My heart broke a little at her resigned exhale. I loved when people commented that Chloe and I looked like twins. Same color hair and eyes, almost identical nose and cheekbones, and sometimes a slight resting bitch face even when nothing was bothering us.

But when I was her age, I laughed all the time and lived for fun on the weekends with my friends.

Since Colin and I'd decided to officially end it, I'd fallen down a miserable rabbit hole of self-doubt, burning the candle at both ends for my kids and going without the little things for myself. It was what prompted Nicole to plan this trip, and while I waved off her concerns about why I needed to get away, I finally got it.

Treating myself badly in front of my kids was setting a detrimental precedent for all of us. I'd get the most out of this break and work on being a better example upon my return.

"Uncle Jake wants to take us to the lake tomorrow."

"Perfect, you love the lake. You and Mike can have a diving contest again, which I'd much rather than the all-night video game sparring I know you'll do the whole time. Go and have fun. For me, okay?"

I cupped my forehead, wishing I could see her face right now. I watched her as closely as she watched me lately, constantly trying to decipher if she was still adjusting or if this was becoming a more serious issue.

There was no playbook for divorced parents. Therapists, family, and the internet all had different opinions, and it was hard to know who was right or what to do when your kid was struggling.

"I love you. I hate that you're alone."

I let out a long sigh as my gaze wandered back to the bar. Leo stood over my now-empty seat, his brow knitted together as he scooped up my glass. When his eyes met mine, I couldn't help the smile on my face after his shoulders dropped as if he was relieved.

"I found a friend to talk to for the moment. I'm the adult and you're the kid. I worry and you don't. And I love you very much. Go annoy Mike, and don't give me another thought."

I pictured her reluctant nod as the call ended.

I needed about ten drinks to forget that conversation or the urge to fly home and scoop both my daughters into my arms and make them believe that we would all be just fine.

Which would be easier if *I* believed that.

"Everything okay? How about a refill?" Leo's hopeful smile triggered an odd pinch in my chest. For the past hour or so, the conversations we'd had made me feel, even for a moment, as if I were someone different—not a divorced mom still trying to navigate her way through a new life.

Reality had wormed its way into my attempt to escape it.

"I had to call my daughter, and I didn't realize it was past dinnertime. I should probably eat after all this day drinking." I motioned toward my empty glass. "Thanks for spending most of your shift with me."

"Of course. What a good bartender does or should do." He flashed an easy smile as he leaned closer. "My shift ends in an hour. I can help if you still need to be forced to have fun." He lifted a shoulder before clearing his throat. "I assume since you're alone, you don't have set dinner plans."

I chewed on my bottom lip, too surprised and tongue-tied at first to give him an answer.

"That's a sweet offer, but—"

"They're showing a movie on the beach tonight. They put up a big screen on the sand and set up a mobile bar and grill. If you're staying here, you wouldn't have to travel anywhere. You wouldn't even need to change." He raked his eyes down my body, heat searing my skin in their path. "Fun doesn't have to be difficult. Could be easy, if you give it a chance."

He made it seem too easy, and that made me *un*easy as hell.

I nodded, blowing out a long breath. I could go back to the room, sit on the terrace, and worry about my kids all night, or I could keep my promise to my family and make the most of it.

This was what I was here for, right? Fun, relaxation, meeting new people. Being this affected by a man I'd just met confused me, especially after forcing it with Colin so many times in more ways than I could stomach to recall.

"I actually don't have dinner plans. Movie on the beach sounds fun, as long as it's not *Jaws*." I let out a nervous chuckle, giving Leo a smile I hoped didn't look forced and would give away the flutters in my stomach.

"I don't think so. Meet me back here at seven."

His lips stretched into a megawatt, panty-melting smile that took my breath and my voice away for a moment as I nodded.

"Sounds good."

He grinned, holding my gaze until I waved and turned around, leaving the bar and pool area on shaky legs that had nothing to do with alcohol.

For God's sake, was I this out of practice? I had boyfriends before Colin, sex too. It was just so long ago I couldn't remember who or how. I went to the bar for a drink and wound up with a dinner date, and it all happened so fast that I agreed before I figured out how to feel about it.

I guessed this was what it was like to try.

THREE
LEO

The first rule I learned in bartending many years ago was not to date customers, and when I started shifts at a resort in the Florida Keys on random days I had off from the station, don't date them even more if they're tourists. It's a rule everybody is told but usually breaks anyway—and then relearns each time *why* it's a rule.

Dating customers was messy, especially if there were hard feelings and they kept coming in to cause trouble. Dating tourists was pointless since nothing could come of it once they left. Staying amicably polite but distant was the way to go if someone caught my eye, and it was never an issue.

Was never an issue until I spotted a woman by the pool and couldn't tear my eyes away from her even if my life depended on it.

Beautiful women breezed in and out of here all the time, but there was something about Kristina that drew me in and wouldn't let go. Maybe it was the way she crossed her long, toned legs, or how her back arched when she stretched her hands over her head in the lounge chair, that gorgeous body she seemed to have no clue about on full display as her head fell back against the chair as if she were surrendering to some kind of defeat.

After I'd met her, the odd frustration creasing her brow every time she lifted her drink for a sip made sense. She was a tired single mom who believed that having fun for herself wasn't allowed.

And, for whatever reason I couldn't figure out, I'd resolved to make it my mission to prove to her just how wrong she was.

I'd expected her to argue with me when I suggested the movie on the beach, but she'd agreed. And here I was, leaning against the bar at 6:55, trying and failing to ignore how excited I was to see her again after only spending a couple of hours with her.

This made no sense.

I'd never believed in instant connections. Instant lust, sure. I'd seen and experienced plenty of that, and I wouldn't have tracked Kristina's every move from the pool to the bar if she weren't sexy as hell. Those green eyes trapped me the second she sat down, staring at the frozen drink menu as if she were searching for a solution beyond what she should order.

Maybe that was it? She seemed confident but unsure at the same time, compelling me on this quest to solve whatever it was that was bothering her.

A firefighter's need to rescue even when off the clock was a sometimes-occupational hazard, but it had never applied to a woman I'd just met and was never this strong, this fast.

"What are you still doing here?" Jimmy, my boss, asked me as he looked me over and shook his head. "Bad enough you work on your days off. Go home and sleep, for fuck's sake."

He slapped my arm with the towel in his hand when I turned around.

"I'm not here to work. I have a da— I'm meeting someone for movie night."

His brows jumped. "Is it that green-eyed beauty from this afternoon?"

"Maybe." I shrugged, rolling my eyes when his shoulders shook with a chuckle. "She's here alone, and I thought..."

What did I think? I still wasn't sure. Only that I couldn't let her leave without trying to see her again. Maybe Jimmy had a point and working too much was doing crazy things to my head.

"You'd keep her company. How noble of you." He snickered when I glared back at him. "I need no explanations. You're the one who always made it a point to steer clear of tourists. That's why I was surprised when you camped out on her side of the bar the whole time she was here."

All I could do was shrug again, as I still couldn't explain or deny it. When I'd almost leaped over the bar to stop her when she'd said she was leaving, I'd known then she was different, even if I had no clue as to why.

"Hey," a sultry voice said from behind me before something tapped my shoulder. "You said I didn't have to change, but it felt weird being in a bathing suit at night."

Kristina wore a short white dress with thin straps that didn't quite fall on the tan lines of her shoulders. My gaze traveled down her body before I could help it, spotting all the freckles along her arms and what I could see of her thighs. Up close, her tan was the result of those freckles clustering together, and I wanted to trace a pattern with my tongue over the ones I spied across the neckline of her dress.

Maybe I couldn't identify what was brewing between us, but it was trouble. I knew that much.

"You two have a good night. Enjoy the movie."

Jimmy's lips twitched as he greeted the new customers who'd just sat down at the bar next to us.

"Something wrong?" she asked as she glanced down her body. "Is this okay? I packed five sundresses for four days, so I figured I might as well break one out for tonight." She grimaced when she lifted her head.

"Not at all," I said on a hoarse whisper with a slow shake of my head. "You're gorgeous. You just overwhelmed me for a minute."

She pursed her lips, a blush bleeding into her cheeks as she rolled her eyes.

"I bet you say that to all the tourists." She crossed her arms, pushing up the swells of her breasts.

"I actually don't. I don't ask to see any of them again after hours either." I laughed and held out my hand. "I'm just going with it. Want to come along with me?"

She eyed my hand for a minute before she took it, the same spark igniting my blood when her skin grazed against mine.

"Sure. It's vacation, right? It's okay to have fun and go along with the unexpected—at least that's what you told me this afternoon."

"And I still mean it tonight. We can grab a towel and find a spot on the sand." I nodded toward where guests were already settling into spots in front of the screen toward the beach.

"That's a nice setup," she mused, still holding my hand as I grabbed a towel from the pile next to the mobile bar and grill on the beach.

This was the first time I'd been to a movie night and not had to manage the main bar or assist the waitstaff on the beach, but now that I had the time to take it in and appreciate it, it was a pretty sweet setup.

The large screen was well secured on the sand, and the scent of tacos and tequila wafted along the beach. There were no barriers between towels, but sharing one with Kristina seemed intimate enough, like a true first date. A date I asked for so damn fast I made my own head spin.

"I guess they have to pay attention to high and low tide

when they plan this." She chuckled, tucking a lock of hair behind her ear as it blew in the breeze. "What are they showing?"

"*Dirty Dancing*," I said, finally dropping her hand to smooth the towel along an empty spot I found on the sand. "They usually show older, summer-themed movies, and it's an adults-only event so they don't have to keep it that PG."

"Appropriate." She shook her head, laughing to herself.

"Why, you don't like that movie?" I tried to give her a smile despite the sting from the intrusive memory floating through my head. My mother had always pushed my father to dance with her whenever this movie came on TV, my father playfully grumbling before he eventually agreed, and both of them laughed every time he'd dip her.

I shook my head to try to erase the picture and the sadness that inevitably came along with it whenever I thought of my parents.

"I do, but it's a little poignant for me at the moment. Baby let loose on vacation like I'm at least trying to do. Except it's with a handsome firefighter slash bartender at my vacation resort and not a dance instructor in the Catskills, which is fine since I can't attempt any of that." She tilted her chin to the blank screen before plopping down onto the towel.

"So, you're saying you want to let *loose* with me tonight?" I teased as I settled next to her.

"I didn't mean to get your hopes up terribly high, so apologies for that. But trust me. Just being here with you right now, besides being here to begin with, is me letting *very* loose." Her smile was bashful as she slipped off her sandals and dug her feet into the sand. "Thanks for the push."

"You're welcome." I inched closer to her. "So, I'm handsome?"

Her eyes narrowed as she shot me a glare. "Like you don't

know. I imagine you own a mirror. And thank you. I haven't heard gorgeous since...since a while."

"I can't believe that, but you should." My voice took a husky dip. "You should hear it all the time."

Her head shot up, and I spied another blush fill her cheeks before they dimmed the lights to start the movie.

"I think you're trouble, Leo," she whispered.

"I *know* you're trouble, Kristina." I pushed away the lock of hair that blew across her cheek and tucked it behind her ear, both of us sucking in the same breath when our eyes met.

Like the pull I couldn't understand and the rush from being in her presence that I couldn't figure out, this was the start of something. It would end either tonight or before she left, but I had a strong feeling—to go with all the other feelings clouding my judgment over the past couple of hours—neither of us would be able to stop it.

FOUR

KRISTINA

"**I** actually think I caught you relaxing there for a bit," Leo said, his mouth twisting into a smirk as he folded the towel.

"I always loved that movie. This is the first time in a long time I was able to watch it without worrying if one of my kids would burst in during a good part." I picked up my sandals and followed Leo off the sand. "Not that it's terribly racy when they show it on TV."

"See, your solo vacation is working out already." Leo tossed the towel on top of the pile, placing his hand on the small of my back to lead me off the beach. "Still hungry?"

I turned my head to the sexy smile playing on his lips. Why did a man's hand on the small of your back always seem so intimate? Every time we touched, there was an actual spark, a jolt when our skin made contact that caused both of us to leap back on instinct. But this time, I let myself enjoy the rush, while still fighting the urge to lean back against his palm.

"No, I'm good." I took a quick look down, relieved that my white dress wasn't stained. "A taco bar on a beach is pure genius, with or without the movie."

"I'm glad you enjoyed it. Maybe even had a little...fun?"

I laughed at the quirk in his brow.

"Fine. I admit it. I had fun. And it wasn't too painful."

A wide grin split his mouth. It *was* fun and invigorating to worry only about myself and enjoy the moment. I hadn't felt that relaxed—at least as relaxed as I could be this close to Leo—in years.

I'd sat with my legs stretched out during the movie to prevent the hem of my dress from riding up, even though the beach was dark. Leo sat with his knees to his chest. I rested my shoulder against his for the last half hour, sneaking glances at him during the movie and spotting a few from him in my periphery as he leaned back into me.

His arm was like a long, muscular brick, and being this close to him was comforting and exhilarating, not at all weird like it should have been.

It was inappropriate, not because it was too fast to be sitting on the sand like a couple, but because it didn't *seem* wrong or fast.

"Thanks for this. I'm sure you want to get home and get some sleep before starting your shift wherever you're working tomorrow."

"It's not even ten. I can stay up if you can." He shoved his hands into his pockets as we made our way back to the resort area. He seemed jumpy, as if he'd slid his hands in his pockets because he didn't know what to do with them.

I flexed my own hands back and forth into fists at my sides for the same reason.

"I can. I left Nicole in charge of what to plan at night, and when she got sick, I only focused on whether I should still come, so I never investigated the nightlife."

Or ever planned on truly participating in the nightlife in the first place.

"What else is there to do here?" As we walked, I gathered the hair at my neck and lifted it off my drenched nape. "Besides sweat."

"Florida in July is Satan's backyard." He chuckled. "You can go for a swim if you want." He motioned toward the crowd in the pool, drinking and splashing and not enticing me in the least.

"I'm sure if I go in, they'll feel like their mother is crashing the party." I snickered, peeking at the small crowd thrashing around and throwing one another into the pool. They all seemed only a few years older than Chloe, enough to be of drinking age—I hoped.

While I cringed thinking of her as a young adult taking shots poolside like the group, I wanted to see her carefree and not full of worry at that age.

But to get her there, I had to work on me first.

"Well," Leo started, tilting his head to the side. "I know of a more private pool. Around the back."

"You mean staff quarters?"

Leo chuckled when I batted my eyelashes. "Do I need to carry a watermelon in?"

He laughed at my silly reference to the scene in the movie we'd just watched where Baby carried a watermelon into a private staff party of debauchery.

"No, no private dance party. Just a place to cool off. If you want to go change and meet me back here, we can take a dip if you'd like."

A little air drained from my lungs when I spied the heat in Leo's eyes. I still didn't know much about him other than small talk, but I yearned to know more and didn't want the night to end yet.

Being alone with him wasn't a good idea for a lot of reasons. But what unnerved me the most about going off with him wasn't that I didn't completely trust him yet. I didn't trust *myself*. I had no reason to believe he was asking for anything other than a quick dip in the water, but I was considering things I shouldn't have been with someone I'd only just met, and that was dangerous on too many levels.

"There is always someone back there, and while it's more private, it's still out in the open because that's where the seasonal staff stays for the summers," Leo assured me as if he could read my mind. "I promise I'm harmless, but we won't be completely alone if that's what's bothering you."

"It's not bothering me. I know you're harmless. I mean…" I draped my hand over my eyes and groaned. "I would love it if I could just stop making an idiot out of myself in front of you. I had a nice two-hour streak during the movie when I didn't have to speak."

I laughed, but Leo didn't laugh with me or smile. His gaze was serious and intense as he came closer.

"You have this line right across here." My eyelids fluttered when he dragged his finger across my forehead. "I managed to get rid of it for a while this afternoon and tonight, but it looks like you're thinking too hard about something. We'll go in and cool off, nothing more."

"Okay." I sucked in a long, slow breath. "You can't jump in with jeans on."

"I keep a bathing suit at the bar and usually change when I get here. Today, I was…distracted."

The sudden urge to kiss the bashful smile off his face made me take a half step back on instinct.

"I'll change and meet you back here. I'll find a watermelon for you to carry."

A nervous chuckle bubbled out of me.

"Sure. I'll be quick." Our gazes stayed locked as I backed away.

"No rush. I'm not going anywhere."

This didn't seem like the reckless scenario that formed in my head when he first suggested a swim in a private pool, but even if he didn't offer the safety caveats, I would have agreed anyway.

I jetted back to my suite, my heart thudding in anticipation but unsure of what. The air was charged with possibilities, as if something big was about to happen. Even if we did just take a dip and then part ways for the night, or for good, this was the most excitement I'd had in a very long time.

I'd already gotten much more out of this vacation than I ever expected.

FIVE
LEO

What the hell was I doing?

I was fixated on a woman I hardly knew, and I had a good feeling she was just as into me. Maybe she wasn't as forward or flirty as other women I'd dated, but that drew me to her even more. I'd spent the last few hours high on every smile and laugh I'd earned from her, and each one was like a drug, making me already crave the next one.

I craved *her*, and keeping myself in check to not come on too strong was an exhausting battle that I kept losing, but how did she not realize how gorgeous she was? I was hell-bent on convincing her, and if I didn't cool it, I would scare her off.

I leaned against the wall and scrubbed a hand down my face as I waited for Kristina for the second time tonight. Stuffing my hands into the pockets of my swim trunks while I was in the water would be awkward as fuck, but how else was I going to fight the urge to touch her?

"Hey. I'm ready for the secret pool now."

I turned, blinking a few times as my gaze slid to Kristina's. I'd seen her in a bathing suit all day, but with her hair piled on top of her head, loose pieces falling down her neck and cheeks, and a cover-up that was see-through even under the dim lights, I almost swallowed my tongue.

Just standing there, regarding me with a puzzled yet excited gleam in her eyes as she adjusted the strap on her shoulder, she was the most gorgeous woman I'd ever seen. I wanted to make her believe that, but I had no clue as to how in such a short amount of time.

"What's wrong?" she asked, her brows knitting together as she stepped closer. "If you don't want to do this, we can call it a night and I'll go back to my room—"

"Nothing's wrong." Before I could help myself, I let the back of my hand graze along her cheek. "A semi-private pool suddenly became a little dangerous with you looking like that."

I spotted another blush staining her cheeks and running down her neck. I'd bet she was flushed all over, and I was too eager to find out.

"You're very kind, but—"

"No, I'm not," I interrupted. "I'm honest. You're a gorgeous woman and I'm trying to be a gentleman, but I may not be so good at it once we're alone. The last thing I want to do is make you uncomfortable, so—"

She smiled and pressed her index finger to my lips.

"You're not making me uncomfortable. Maybe a little over-whelmed, but it's been a while for me. For a lot of things." She slid her finger down my chin and pressed her hand to my chest. I was sure she felt my heart strumming against her palm. "I don't know where tonight is going to take us, but I don't want it to end. Not yet." She pressed her hand deeper and clenched her eyes shut. "But you've convinced me to make sure that I didn't come all this way for nothing. Didn't you tell me that you were just going with it? Can't we just see what happens?"

I covered her hand with mine, the air so thick between us that it was hard to breathe.

This was more than just new to me. It was as exciting as it was terrifying. I wasn't a jumpy teenager when it came to women, but this one already had me on the verge of losing all sense and control.

"Yeah," I agreed, yearning for the relief of the cold water to calm me from the waist down. It was easier to hide my reaction to Kristina in jeans, and I'd have to stay underwater so she wouldn't see how hard I'd been in her presence the entire afternoon. My body ached for her in more ways than one.

"Come on." I took her hand again, holding on to it all the way to the gate leading into the staff area.

"This is where the pool is?" she asked, scanning the place with her adorable nose scrunched up. "My suite is right over there." She pointed to the back path leading to the guest rooms.

"Suite, huh?" I glanced at her over my shoulder as I opened the gate to lead her into the completely empty pool area. I smiled despite the stirring in my gut.

It was a fairly large pool, three feet to eight feet deep with a handful of chairs lining each side. I expected one or two people in the pool or lounging around, enough to keep both of us in check. Other than the fence, the pool was out in the open. All that surrounded us was the dim glow of the outside lamps and the lights illuminating the bottom of the pool.

"Nicole got a deal with her hotel travel points. We each would have had our own room and bathroom, but it's too big for one person to spread out." Kristina let go of my hand to lay a towel on her chair. "I almost packed sunscreen, which is silly, not like I'll get a tan from those." She motioned to one of the lamps.

"Nope, night swimming is different." I laughed until she pulled the cover-up over her head. Her breasts were full and heavy against her bikini top, and drifting my eyes lower didn't help. The bows of the bottom resting against the curves of her hips made my fingers tingle. It was the same suit she'd worn today, but now she was close enough to touch.

When she said she wanted to just go with it, I doubted she meant to go along with my urge to pull her into my arms and crash my mouth against hers, right before I untied those knots and traced my tongue along her hip.

I peeled off my shirt and tossed it onto one of the chairs.

"Jesus," Kristina hissed, her eyes wide.

"Now it's my turn to ask *you* what's wrong," I teased.

"You're... I mean... Wow." She dropped her head to her hands as she pinched the bridge of her nose. "I just...never knew a man in real life with that many abs."

I chuckled and pulled her to me before I could stop myself.

"I'm following your lead, but I don't want to be anywhere else but here with you—whatever happens. Which makes no fucking sense, if I'm honest."

"No, it does," she whispered, brushing her hands down my arms and tracing the lines of one of my tattoos with the tip of her finger. "It makes no fucking sense to me either, but I actually get it."

"I think we need to cool off." I sucked in a deep breath, my chest pressing into hers as it heaved up and down.

"Do you think the pool will do it?" Kristina laughed.

"No," I said, shaking my head. "Unless we dive into some ice."

"Are we using the ladder or jumping in?" She cleared her throat as she craned her neck around, probably noting how very alone we were and how this was even more dangerous than either of us expected.

I dove into the deep end without replying. Would the water douse the heat between us enough to grasp on to a little self-control? I was doubtful but had to try.

I found her standing on the edge when I popped my head up

out of the water. I held her tentative gaze as I smoothed my wet hair back and swam over to the shallow end.

"Don't tell me after that awesome speech, you're hesitating now."

"Well, I just realized," she started as she folded her arms and cringed, her breasts now straining even more against her top. "Are you going to get in trouble for bringing me here?"

My head fell back as I laughed. She worried her bottom lip between her teeth as she looked from me to the empty rows of chairs around the pool.

"Trouble is a relative term. From my boss here? No. In general?"

I let my eyes trail down her body and drank her in, the soft curves and toned legs, and the shy smile I wanted to taste.

"In general, fuck yes." I crooked my finger, my heart kicking up again when a grin split her mouth.

She lifted a brow as she placed a foot on the ladder. "I'd jump in, but the last thing I need is to bust out of this on impact." She motioned over her bikini top, laughing until she looked back at me. The image of what she described in her nervous joke was enough for my cock to tent my shorts underwater. At that moment, I lost all hope that the cold would help even a little at bringing my dick back to its resting state.

I wasn't only in trouble. I was fucked.

SIX
KRISTINA

I stepped right into the pool, not allowing my body to acclimate to the water in steps like I usually did. I needed relief and to gain back the sanity I felt slipping away with every minute spent in this guy's presence.

The water sloshed around my neck as I submerged myself from the shoulders down, trying to both get rid of the cold sweat that broke out along my skin when Leo's gaze caressed my body and not be any more tempted than I already was if I caught him staring again.

Leo treaded water along the opposite side of the shallow edge of the pool, both of us respecting an invisible barrier between us that, as we moved around in the water, we were careful not to cross. He was almost up to the same level as I was, although the water lapping around his shoulders was just as enticing as when he peeled off his shirt. He was tempting enough with a T-shirt on, the cotton stretching tight enough over his chest and arms, but I lost count of the ripples of muscle along his chest and down his stomach, abs framed by that V I'd seen in photos and on romance novel covers but never on any man I knew in real life.

Not that I knew Leo, but I'd been all too aware of him the entire night, and now we were all alone, wet, and half naked. My heart thrummed against my rib cage as I took slow breaths in and out. This could just be casual, two people going for a night swim and nothing more.

He stood, slicking his hair back before he rested his elbows along the edge of the pool. The dusting of hair down his chest stuck to his skin as I tracked a lucky drop of water over his pecs.

Nothing about this seemed casual to me. Maybe people did this all the time. Random, hot encounters with almost strangers who made parts of their body tingle, parts that were thought of as long dead.

My life was not a steamy story. Reckless and random were never really on the table for me.

Until now. Tonight, an attraction to a man I'd met only hours ago seemed to grab hold of me, pulling me to him with a strong and inescapable hold.

"Cooled off yet?" he asked as a wry grin tugged at his lips.

"Yes and no." I lifted a shoulder.

His smile grew wider as he nodded.

"Same."

"That's why I'm keeping to my side of the pool."

Those sexy shoulders shook with a chuckle as he tilted his head.

"I won't bite if you come closer."

"You won't?"

Where had that come from? Who knew brazen would be just on the other side of terrified?

"Well, I would if you asked me to. I'd never refuse a beautiful woman anything."

He made his way toward me, and I froze, inching back against the wall before the current from the filter made me jump.

"What's wrong? There are no fish to nip at you in here." His throaty chuckle settled into my chest.

"I backed up against the filter, and it just scared me for a minute."

But it didn't scare me more than the lust in Leo's eyes as he stepped closer, boxing me in by putting his arms at my sides.

"It's only water, see?" He framed my waist, pressing his fingertips into my thighs as he positioned me over the front of the jet, the flow of water now hitting against my back and fluttering between my legs, unneeded encouragement for the sudden throb in my core. "Could be relaxing if you let it."

My head fell back as I searched the night sky for an answer or guidance on what to do. "I can't relax around you. Especially not now." My hands slid up his arms of their own accord, and if I wasn't mistaken, he trembled under my fingertips, which only excited me even more. "When I'm home, I'm actually more or less put together. With my kids, with my job, and with the rest of my family. But around you?" I breathed out an audible sigh. "I'm not used to this."

"Not used to what?" His voice was low and husky as his hands stayed on my hips.

"The way you've been looking at me. It's been a long time since anyone has regarded me as someone other than a mom or a friend."

"I call bullshit." He quirked a brow. "I think you're just not looking hard enough."

A laugh escaped me as I shook my head. "Believe me, I spent years trying to get my ex-husband's attention and—"

"I don't know your ex, but I can't understand how anyone wouldn't notice you. You've distracted me all damn day."

"You only just met me. I'm far from perfect."

"You're a beautiful woman, yet you have no idea how to respond when someone notices you like I'm sure they always do.

Yes, I hardly know you, but..." He trailed off as he slipped his wet hand onto the nape of my neck, my skin still slick but not from the pool. Another cold sweat had already spread over me. "Attention shouldn't feel so new to you that you don't know what to do with it."

"You're right, I don't." I swallowed, trying to get a hold of my breathing as my throat worked. "But that being said, I'm enjoying it anyway. Too much." My gaze fell to his mouth, those full lips parting slightly when he noticed. His beard was cropped short, and I wanted to see how soft his mouth was as his stubble scratched against my lips, or my chest, maybe the insides of my thighs.

The path back to my suite was twenty feet away. I could climb out of the pool right now before the inevitable happened, slip into my flip-flops, and tell Leo goodnight.

"I could show you that too," Leo said with a low and deep rasp that zinged down my spine. "I think I helped you have fun already." His eyes fixed on mine, both of us forgetting how to blink.

"You did," I squeaked out, my pulse too fast to push out my voice.

"So fucking beautiful."

I gasped as a low moan, almost a growl, erupted from his throat. "Tell me to back away. Tell me to take my hands off you."

"Why would I do that?" I tried for a nervous smile as I gulped my next breath.

"Because once my mouth is on yours, I won't know how to make myself stop."

I did crave attention. I wanted a man who wanted me, not one going through the motions because it was too inconvenient to admit we were over.

I'd fought against my instincts then, but they were always right. I'd chased a man who slept beside me each night, even though he'd made it obvious more than once, in so many ways, that he didn't want me anymore.

Leo was a stranger, but my instincts now were just as strong as they ever were, and even if I didn't know much about him, he saw me. Kristina. Not someone's sister, someone's mother, or someone's estranged wife. Just me.

It was a drug too intoxicating to resist.

Before I knew what I was doing, I grabbed the back of Leo's head and crashed my lips against his. He still tasted like tequila and salt from the margaritas he'd ordered us during the movie, and I whimpered against his mouth as he slid his tongue along the seam of my lips.

Despite all the lingering looks and teasing for the past few hours, the kiss was slow. Slow and deep and wet, his tongue making long strokes inside my mouth and quenching a thirst I didn't realize I'd had. He dug his fingers into my hair, grabbing hold of the elastic around my messy bun and tugging at it gently until my wet locks fell over my shoulders.

"Fuck," he murmured against my lips as he backed me against the pool's concrete edge, his thick, hard cock pressing against my core under the water's surface. Instead of backing away, I let my hands wander along the ridges of muscle on his back and pulled him closer, groaning when his cock swelled against my stomach.

I whimpered into his mouth when he slanted his head to deepen the kiss. I pressed my body against his, the taste of him doing things to my mind I couldn't keep up with. I wanted more, and I didn't care how or why we got here. I just needed to relieve the blinding ache pulsing between my legs.

He lifted me out of the water by my underarms and set me down on the edge. My legs fell open almost on their own as he stood between them.

"I need to see you," he panted, his eyes wide and full of lust as they roamed down my body.

My swimsuit was still on, but I might as well have been naked. Goose bumps prickled my skin as chills traveled up and down my spine.

"I'm following your lead, baby. I'll stop whenever you say." He skimmed his hands down my arms, the pads of his thumbs sending sparks along my skin on their descent.

"I'm not ready to stop." I wrapped my legs around his waist as his mouth came back to mine, our kisses now sloppy and desperate as he looped his arms around me. He ran his lips down my neck and across my shoulder, nipping then sucking at the skin along my collarbone. When his tongue traced along the edge of my top, I arched my back to push the swells of my breasts against his mouth. I writhed under him, gasping when I looked down and noticed a nipple had broken free.

Instead of racing to cover up, I held his fiery gaze. A couple of long minutes passed between us, Leo's eyes growing wide when he realized I wasn't moving or trying to adjust my top. That was the biggest danger sign of all. I didn't care how exposed I was. Not only didn't I care, I *wanted* him to see me, *all* of me. Even in my early twenties in college when I'd done dumb things with guys I shouldn't have even spoken to, I'd at least known them for more than twenty-four hours. Hell, even more than ten hours.

I was running on pure need and desire without thought of consequences. All that mattered was Leo, his mouth, and relieving the growing ache in my core. Would I regret this tomorrow? Most likely, but I'd worry about that later.

His gaze held mine as he captured the rigid bud between his teeth before sucking it into his mouth. I whimpered, the wet warmth of his tongue soaking my already wet bikini bottom. He cupped my other breast, teasing my other nipple with his thumb before he kissed across my chest and pulled at the wet material until I spilled out of the other cup.

I laughed to myself, trying to remember the last time I didn't have to rev myself up for sex. Sex had become as clunky and forced between Colin and me as conversation when I'd tried to trick my mind into wanting to be in the moment.

With Leo, I had to hold my orgasm back instead of searching for it. He was right. I had no idea what to do with attention from a man anymore, but I quickly acclimated to all the attention he was giving me with his lips and hands. More than acclimated, I reveled in it.

My top was half off as Leo licked a path down my stomach, my body quivering as he peppered kisses around my navel. Instead of checking around the pool to make sure we were still alone, I found that the little sense I had left was drowned out by the pure need humming through my veins.

I was aware enough to know that I was supposed to care about someone seeing us, but so caught up in Leo's mouth and hands that I didn't.

Instead of slowing down, I spread my legs wider, losing what was left of my mind as I pulled the scrap of material between my legs to the side.

"Yeah?" Leo asked, a plea evident in his eyes despite the dim lighting.

"God, yes," I begged, not recognizing my voice or even who I was.

Leo didn't waste a second and dropped his head between my legs, kissing me long and deep before sucking my clit hard enough for me to see stars and then inching it out of his mouth. His lips and tongue were everywhere, devouring me as he slid two fingers deep inside, pumping slowly as his mouth kept moving.

I'd never had a man go down on me in public. Just because I

hadn't spotted anyone around didn't mean that they couldn't see, but I detonated like a bomb, coming hard as I bucked my hips against him, riding out wave after wave of white-hot pleasure across my lower body until I slumped over, dizzy and spent.

"Holy shit," I whispered, pressing my hand to my naked chest.

"Are you okay?" he asked with a soft chuckle, framing my face and lifting it until our eyes met.

"I don't have the brain cells to answer that yet." I grabbed his wrists as I chased my rapid breaths. "Give me a few."

He smiled and kissed my forehead, weaving his hands into my wet locks before the muffled sounds of laughter grew closer in the distance.

We broke apart as I shoved my breasts back into the cups of my bathing suit top. Leo pushed against the edge, almost leaping out of the pool.

"Oh, hey, Reyes," a man's voice said. I turned and spotted who I guessed were three resort workers, two men and one woman, passing the gate of the pool and nodding to Leo.

Leo tipped his chin at them as they passed, while I wrapped a towel around my body, my hands shaking from the aftereffects of the adrenaline running through me and the strongest orgasm I'd had in years, maybe ever.

"Can you walk me back to my room?" I asked, my voice small as what we'd just done—what *I'd* just done—finally barreled over me. "If you don't mind." My legs wobbled as my knees almost liquefied.

"Of course." He nodded, concern wrinkling his brow. He bent to pick up my flip-flops and placed them in front of me before handing me the flimsy dress I'd used as a cover-up.

"Thank you for...everything tonight," I told him as we walked the quiet, dark path back to the guest suites. "You did say you'd help me have fun, so you can rest assured you delivered." A nervous laugh fell from my lips.

"I'm glad. You deserve it." His smile widened when we arrived at my door.

"Are you working tomorrow?"

"No." He shook his head. "Jimmy has a full staff tomorrow, so he doesn't need my help. Still no plans?"

"Nope. I'll relax and see where the day takes me." I fumbled for my keycard and held it up when I found it.

"I really want to see you again, Kristina." He grabbed my wrist. "As crazy as it sounds, I want to get to know you before you go."

"I think you got to know me pretty well tonight, a lot faster than most men ever have." I smiled, but he didn't smile back. "I would like that. Maybe since we got this"—I motioned toward the path to the pool behind us—"out of the way, the conversation will be easier."

"Do you really believe that?" He dipped his chin, raising a brow.

"No, not at all." I chewed on my bottom lip as his eyes bored into mine. "But I want to see you again too. So, if you're not busy—"

"I'm not," he whispered and took my face in his hands, brushing my lips with light kisses, lingering longer with each peck. When I tasted myself on his lips, a thrill, not shame, ran through me.

"Give me your phone."

I plucked my phone out of my bag, unlocking it before handing it over. He punched a few buttons until his own phone rang in his pocket.

"I'll pick you up at ten tomorrow morning. Maybe you can wear another one of those dresses you said you brought too many of?"

I grinned at his hopeful smirk.

"I'll see what I can do." I tapped the card against the door-knob until it beeped. "Goodnight, Leo."

"Goodnight, Kristina."

I watched as he shifted to leave, an odd longing stirring in my belly and tempting me to ask him to spend the night with me, but I shook it off and opened the door.

I'd probably never see him again after I went home, but I wanted to know Leo too. One night with him had already high-lighted how much and how long I'd settled, and how long I'd let myself get by with scraps of forced affection.

Leo was still a stranger, but he seemed to know me better than I knew myself.

SEVEN

KRISTINA

My eyes flew open when my phone blared. As I popped up with a jolt, my heart leaped into my throat until I realized it was only my seven-a.m. alarm. I'd meant to mute the alarm for the next few days, but I was too busy, first, second-guessing why I was here, and then enjoying myself too much to remember anything else.

I scrubbed my hand down my face as everything from last night came back to me in a rush. When I'd awoken during the night, I was sure Leo and everything we'd done were crazy-sexy figments of my imagination. I still felt the scratch of his stubble across my chest and along the insides of my thighs, the memory triggering flutters in my core.

And I'd agreed to spend an entire day with this man. A man I'd just met who made me feel more alive in hours than I'd felt in years.

As I held my phone, a text came through from Nicole.

Nicole: *It's early, but I was too stuffy to sleep. When you wake up, let me know how your first night was! Is the place as awesome as it looks on the website?*

I threw my phone across my bed and laughed out loud. I

doubted hot bartenders slash firefighters with bodies of sin and magical tongues were listed in the amenities.

Me: *First night was great. The place is definitely nice.*

Nicole: *What aren't you telling me?*

I squinted at my phone, reading over what I'd said and searching for what tipped her off that I was hiding something.

Me: *All I said was that the first night was great and the place is nice. Why do you think I'm hiding something?*

Nicole: *When I spoke to you last, you said you were killing time by the pool and had no idea what you'd do for dinner. You sounded bored and annoyed. Now your night was "great." OMG did you meet someone?*

I groaned, deciding whether to tell her about the man and the night I never saw coming, when a text came through from my brother with a photo of Emma and Peyton. Emma was on her aunt's lap, both of them giving Jake duck lips. Chloe was probably still sleeping after staying up too late with my nephew.

Jake: *Sorry, I know it's early, and I hope I didn't wake you. Emma said to send you the picture right now, and you know we all do what she says.*

I smiled even with the unraveling of my stomach. After living an alternate life for a few hours last night, and planning on heading back there at ten a.m. today, it felt strange to be reminded of my real one. The one that I spent scheduling play-dates and activities around my work schedule, and arguing with both girls over one more toy or a little more lip gloss.

After revolving my life around my kids all this time, partly because I wanted to, but also because it was easier to focus on them than my miserable marriage, I'd ignored myself to the point I didn't know or remember who I was or what I wanted.

The type of woman who let a man she'd just met run his mouth all over her body in public was not who I expected to find on my vacation of self-discovery.

Nicole: *Well, tell me. I see you read my message and are just ignoring me. Praying for hot, meaningless sex for the win!*

Me: *Fine. I met a bartender named Leo. He's also a firefighter with bedroom eyes, muscles, tattoos, and a magic tongue.*

While I waited for my phone to explode as Nicole's brain short-circuited, it buzzed in my hand.

Jake: *Jesus, Kristina. While I'm glad you're having fun, I didn't need to know that.*

I gasped, thanking God I didn't add *how* I'd discovered his magic tongue.

Jake: *My wife says she wants a picture, but I'll deal with that in a minute.*

I burst out laughing, picturing his narrowed eyes at his wife after he rolled them at me.

Me: *Sorry, big brother. That wasn't meant for you.*

Jake: *I kind of figured that.*

I shook my head and dialed Jake, compelled to explain my accidental text but without a clue as to how.

"Tell me everything," Peyton said, probably bouncing in the chair after she answered Jake's phone. "Starting with how you know his tongue is magical."

"I can't believe I just told my brother that." I cupped my hand over my eyes as if they could see my humiliation.

"He's fine and not important right now. I need a picture... for...safety reasons."

"Really, Peyton?"

I cracked up when she shushed my brother.

"We met at the bar by the pool. He picked my drink for me when I couldn't decide. Then told me he was watching me the whole afternoon and wanted to know why I looked so against having fun."

"Ah, I love a good meet-cute." I cringed when she squealed. "Go on."

"You and your romance novels." I sighed before I continued. "I'll give you the short version. We saw a movie on the beach, followed by a dip in a sort of private pool, and he's picking me up at ten to take me out for the day."

"Sort of private pool, huh?"

"Yes," I sighed. "And if you want to keep talking about this, please go somewhere my brother isn't."

"Say no more. I'll head into the bedroom if you give me one minute."

I smiled, picturing her still-thin arms and legs with that little pudge of a belly. Now that she was starting to show, Peyton was the cutest pregnant woman I'd ever seen. I'd been such a horror show with both girls, the older women in my family would pat my hand and assure me that beautiful girls always stole their mother's beauty, as if that would've made me feel better.

"Hot and heavy in the pool. This is a great story already."

"Well, on the side of the pool. We..." I trailed off, cringing at all the details flooding my mind but halting on my tongue. "Peyton, I think I've officially lost my mind."

"Kristina," she chided back. "This is what vacation is supposed to be, right? An escape from life."

"And then when I get back, I can look forward to all the remorse from the memories."

"Okay, I'll infer all that could have happened poolside last night. I can wait on details. But tell me this, do you regret any of it now?"

"No," I said, surprised at how my answer fell from my lips with no hesitation. "I've never clicked with anyone so fast. It was pathetic, really. I had no idea what to do when a man seemed interested in me, or how to respond. I know I'm severely out of practice, but—" I raked my hand through my hair as if I could sift out what was really bothering me. "Even now, I can't believe it's real."

"I really hate that you feel that way. You're beautiful and deserve all the attention. Do me one favor while you're there. Instead of worrying about what happens when you come home or whether you should be doing this, if it feels right, just go with it."

"Are you trying to guidance counsel me?" I teased.

Peyton had a way of making you feel better or at least believe something wasn't as awful as you had originally thought. She was like the wise younger sister I never knew I needed.

Throughout the divorce, I'd leaned on both her and my brother more than I'd planned or wanted to. But she was the one I'd told the ugly parts of what I was going through, as my brother would go into fixer mode and simply want to kick Colin's ass. Her high school students loved her as much as we did.

"Just a little sisterly advice. Because I love you. And really want you to come back with an amazing story for me."

"Love you too. And I'll do my best." I pushed off the bed and eyed the dresses I'd hung up in the closet. "Tell the girls I'll call them later."

"They're fine. They miss you, but we're all keeping them busy until you get back."

My phone vibrated with another text after we ended the call.

Unknown: *Still on for 10?*

I assumed it was Leo and keyed in his name before I responded.

Me: *Still on.*

Leo: *Good. How did you sleep?*

I glanced down at the king-sized bed and its layers of fluffy comfort.

Me: *Good, actually.*

Leo: *Why is a good night's sleep a surprise?*

What a loaded question that was. There were a lot of reasons why I never had a full night of sleep. The main one, I supposed, was my brain not giving me a reprieve from the turbulent thoughts in my head about the present that would bleed into fears for the future. I'd fixate on what we'd done to the girls by splitting up, even though, for us, there was no other right choice, what Chloe was really going through since Colin left and was holding back from me, and if Emma having only fuzzy memories of two parents living together under the same roof was a good thing or a bad thing.

On weak nights when I'd feel really sorry for myself, I'd fall into a pity spiral. My kids were my life and I had no regrets, but I'd watched my brother fall in love after a horrible divorce, and I couldn't help but want that. I never entertained it as any kind of real possibility. And when I would allow myself to daydream about it, the guilt over the complications that could arise from even thinking about it would overpower any whimsical feelings about what could be.

What happened between Leo and me surpassed my most indulgent fantasies, and making them a reality in such a public place should have made me take some kind of pause then or in the cold light of the early morning after, but the regrets still hadn't come.

I was sated on a level I wasn't ready to face but couldn't deny. I'd slept so well that for the first few minutes after I woke, I'd forgotten where I was.

Me: *Too many to list. I guess the night wore me out.*

Or he did, and the stirring in my belly had me up for more.

Leo: *I slept like a baby too, but I was up early.*

Me: *Firefighter's occupational hazard?*

Leo: *Sometimes. But today, the reason was a woman I couldn't stop thinking about and couldn't wait to see again.*

A smile blossomed across my face as my cheeks heated.

Me: *You've been on my mind too. Mostly because I only half believe you're real. This wasn't the vacation I was expecting.*

Leo: *I'm going to make sure you have a hell of a vacation. Pack a bathing suit. I'll come to get you at 10.*

I wasn't sure I could handle more of a vacation than last night.

EIGHT

LEO

W hen I'd left Kristina at her door last night, I had to almost pry myself away from her. From her lips, her body, and those goddamn sounds she made when she came. I fell into a deep sleep when I arrived back home, but I dreamed of her all night long, starting with what else would have happened by the pool if we weren't interrupted.

I'd always believed that instant connection was bullshit, but I had no other explanation for us—for this. I'd only known her for an afternoon, not counting how long I'd tracked her by the pool from the beginning of my shift. But aside from being gorgeous, she was warm and sweet, with a guarded edge that I'd managed to get around from that first conversation. Even with a blush bleeding into her cheeks when she'd fumbled her words that first time, she owned who she was, and that was sexy as hell.

It all made me want more of her, even though she'd be on a plane back to New York in a few days, back to her kids and her real life that I was pretty sure didn't have room for whatever we were doing right now.

If I hadn't met her last night, I probably would have headed to the station to pick up an extra shift or asked Jimmy if I could help out around the resort. I didn't do well with time on my hands and was just as clueless as anyone else why I didn't take a damn full day off once in a while.

Over the past year, something had made me restless. I always had to be doing something and didn't know what to do with any time alone.

One of the guys at the firehouse suggested I was lonely, and while I laughed him off and hated to admit it, he was right. I'd been a nomad for more years than I wanted to recall, my five years in Florida the longest I'd spent anywhere after I'd left my aunt and uncle's house.

I was overdue for a visit back home to see my aunt and uncle. While I tried to visit often, I never stayed longer than a couple of days at a time. I loved them and they were the only parents I'd had for most of my life, but visits home brought back old and painful memories.

The odd pull to this woman wasn't just me trying to fill the empty hours. From the moment my eyes opened, all I wanted to do was come back here. I almost asked if we could start the day earlier, but while being with me was something Kristina agreed to, she still seemed hesitant. The last thing I wanted to do was scare her off for the little time I'd get with her.

"Hold on a second," Kristina said before opening the door to her suite. She cradled her cell phone in the crook of her shoulder as she waved me in.

"Your kids?" I mouthed to her as I stepped inside.

She wore a black sundress that stopped midthigh, treating me to a perfect view of those legs. The sight of her collarbone along the strapless neckline made my cock twitch, triggering the memory of dragging my tongue over it as her head fell back, her wet body quivering under my hands and mouth.

I cleared my throat and rubbed the back of my neck to calm the fuck down.

Get it together, Reyes.

"No, my friend Nicole," she said with her hand covering the phone. "She's nervous about me going off with a stranger and wants me to ask for a picture of your license." She rolled her eyes and held up a finger. "Give me a few."

"Give me the phone." I stretched out my hand. "I'll talk to her."

Her brows knit together before she brought the phone back to her ear.

"He says he wants to talk to you. Hold on."

I opened the camera and pulled Kristina to me, holding the phone up over our heads before I snapped a picture. I stepped back and dug into my wallet, taking a shot of my license.

"Hi, Nicole. A photo and my license are heading your way. My badge number for the Fire Department is 3295. Kristina is lucky to have a friend like you to worry about her, but she's safe with me. I promise."

Kristina bit back a smile when I handed the phone back to her.

"There. I just sent both," she sighed into the phone. "Happy?"

"Holy *fuck*, he's hot." We both jumped at Nicole's loud voice over the speaker. Kristina grimaced and covered her eyes with her hand.

I shook my head, a laugh escaping me before I could help it.

"Tell him not to bring you back to the room until sunrise."

Kristina winced and shook her head.

"I put you on speakerphone by mistake. But we both heard you."

"Good. I'm so glad I'm sick. This is the vacation you were

meant to have. I'll expect a call from you tomorrow. Not too early, of course."

Kristina's eyes narrowed at Nicole's giggle.

"Goodbye, Nicole." She jabbed the screen with her finger and tossed it onto the small table next to the door.

"Once, just once, I'd like to not make a total fool out of myself in front of you." She dropped her head into her hands, pinching the bridge of her nose.

"Stop," I said, grabbing her waist and pulling her to me. "You have not made a fool of yourself at all, so please don't think that. So, do you agree with Nicole?"

"About what?" she asked after she lifted her head, her brow furrowed. "Sending her your license? I agreed to do it when I got here because I didn't think I'd actually meet someone, but asking you for it now seemed ridiculous. I'm usually suspicious of people, but...I trust you. I'd have to, to let you—" She clenched her eyes shut and let out a long exhale. "Just take it as a compliment, okay?"

"Okay, I will. But that's not what I was asking." I dragged my hands down her bare back, stopping right before the sweet curve of her ass. "Do you think I'm hot too?"

She pursed her lips, exhaling a soft and fucking adorable groan.

"After everything in and outside of the pool last night, why are you asking me that?"

I shrugged, smiling when she shivered against me as I ran my finger up and down her spine.

"I'm needy and soak up validation from a beautiful woman like a sponge."

"I wouldn't think a man with all this ink would be a sponge." Now it was my turn to shiver as she brushed her soft hands down my arms and over my torso. "Yeah," she whispered as her gaze fell to my mouth. "If you need your ego stroked, then yes, I think you're pretty hot. That's why I've lost any semblance of rational thought since you picked my drink for me yesterday."

I brushed her lips, stealing another quick kiss when her eyes fluttered shut.

"Well, if it makes you feel any better, you have me all out of sorts too." I stroked my knuckles over the curve of her jaw. "Again, I'm just going with it."

"Me too," she said before burrowing her head into my chest. "God, you smell good."

I chuckled and pulled her tighter, bending to bury my head in her neck. I breathed her in, already high on the scent of vanilla and roses, and couldn't help running my lips across her shoulder.

"Ready?" I whispered when she pulled away.

"Probably not." She flashed a wide grin as her throaty laugh reverberated through me. Every move and sound Kristina made had me hypnotized and hooked...and already dreading whenever what we were starting would end. She'd be gone before either of us knew it, and it would be best to keep this as casual as possible.

Except when she slid her hand into mine, triggering a jolt up my arm before she squeezed, my visceral response to her was the complete opposite of casual.

"So, where are you taking us?" Her sexy grin made me not want to take her anywhere except her unmade bed behind us.

"Oh. I know it's a mess, but I'm embracing being on vacation and letting housekeeping make the bed, even though it's making me twitchy." She craned her neck when she saw me staring. "I guess I could just sleep in the other bedroom tonight, get my money's worth and all." A smile stretched the soft lips I'd dreamed about since I left her last night.

"I wasn't staring at the bed because it wasn't made, Kristina."

A blush bled into her cheeks and traveled down her neck.

"But small steps." I smiled and rubbed her shoulders as they relaxed under my fingers. "We'll start with breakfast. I know a place that has the best iced coffee, then I figured we'd drive down the coast and see where the day takes us. You aren't one of those who has to make a schedule on vacation, right?"

"I'm not one of those who *takes* a vacation, so that all sounds perfect." She raised a brow and pressed a kiss to my cheek. "Thank you."

I wanted to thank her instead. When I saw women, I didn't ponder whether we would last beyond the moment or worry if we did or didn't. Being this excited to spend the day with her knowing she was just passing through in my life was a warning sign I didn't want to acknowledge or decipher.

But right or wrong, weird or not, for today, she was all mine.

NINE
KRISTINA

"Is this like a prerequisite in Florida?" I pointed to the open sunroof of Leo's truck, attempting in vain to hold my hair back as the wind whipped it across my face.

"No, it's usually too damn hot to keep any windows open." The corner of his sinful mouth twisted into a smirk. "I thought driving up the coast would be nicer with a breeze while it's still early and not that hot yet. I never use my sunroof."

"So, I'm special," I teased and nudged his shoulder. "That's sweet."

I caught a smile ghost his lips as the truck rolled to a stop, gravel crunching under the tires.

"Yes, you are. I wanted to show you the Keys beyond the all-inclusive." Leo shut off the engine and turned to me.

"Where are we?"

"This is the beach I usually come to on the rare days I'm not working. It's quieter."

"Like the quieter pool you took me to?" I laughed but stopped when his smile faded.

"I didn't bring you here for that. I mean, it's not that I don't want that, I just—" He rubbed his eyes as a groan rose from his throat.

My heart swelled when I spotted the red tinge of his cheeks against his olive skin. I rubbed his back after I burst out laughing.

"It's nice not to be the one to fumble the words this time. You've been the suave one up until now."

His shoulders shook before he lifted his head.

"Suave?

"The one without their foot in their mouth." I slurped the rest of my iced coffee as I took in the beach and swaying palms. The closest thing we had to this back home was the lake. A beach was at least an hour's drive from us, and I hadn't made a trip to one since Emma was a baby.

Getting lost in the waves crashing onto the shore always filled me with a calming peace, even if present company excited me too much to stay still.

"Was I right?" Leo asked as he nodded to the plastic cup in my hand.

"About what?" I asked, all that inner calm evaporating at his crooked grin.

"Best iced coffee you've ever had, right?"

"It's good," I conceded. "Simpler than what I usually get, but yes, very good."

Leo's question triggered another sour memory. Colin used to pick up iced coffee for us on his way home from work every day, until one day he told me that he didn't feel like stopping and giving them my complicated order because it took too long.

When I attempted to pinpoint the day everything started to deteriorate from good to tolerable and then awful, I found little things like that were to blame for chipping away at our marriage over time before resentment blew up on both sides.

The fading affection wore away at us little by little, like when

Colin stopped kissing me hello or goodbye anymore, then rolled his eyes when I pointed it out, which I never did again after that one time.

He didn't hesitate to book a reconciliation getaway at the suggestion of our therapist but stopped caring for me in tiny ways that grew bigger over time.

To me, proof of love was always in the smallest details, and when I looked back and tallied them up, my heart always sank when they added up to nothing.

"I can take you to Starbucks on the way back if you like that better."

My chest squeezed at the simple offer. Leo was right. I had no idea how to accept attention or even consideration from a man because I'd learned not to expect it. Maybe my attention-starved and bruised ego were responsible for this crazy thing going on between Leo and me.

It was hard to simply enjoy how Leo made me feel without my suspicious brain trying to pick it apart. Years of therapy and being forced to tune in to how I felt and why made it an annoying knee-jerk reaction.

"No, this is perfect." I cradled his cheek, brushing his lips with a light kiss before I could help it. "Breakfast was great, too. This is all very sweet of you to do on your day off."

He took a lock of my hair and sifted it between his fingers as he chuckled to himself.

"Buying an iced coffee and an egg sandwich for a beautiful woman who agreed to let me take her out for the day isn't a hardship." He traced my jaw with the tip of his finger. "That's you I'm talking about, in case you were wondering."

A smile snuck across my lips.

"And right back to smooth."

He leaned back, squinting at me.

"I thought you said I was suave?" He arched a brow at me.

"I said you were hot too." I eased closer, sliding my hand to the back of his neck. I laughed when his brows jumped. I didn't expect such a brazen response to come out of me either. I was surprising myself left and right this vacation.

His chest rose with a deep inhale before he breathed out a slow groan.

"Let's get out before the only part of the Keys you see is my truck." He skimmed his thumb over my lips. "That mouth..."

He shook his head, shooting me a playful scowl before he stepped out of the cab.

I sucked my bottom lip between my teeth as it tingled from Leo's callused finger. I shoved the empty cup into one of the holders and shifted to get out, almost falling over when the door opened as I reached for it.

I eyed Leo's extended hand.

"This is sweet, but I can get out by myself—" My words faded at the heat in his eyes as they locked with mine.

"The cab is high, and I don't want you to slip on the rocks. Maybe letting someone look out for you a little bit could be part of your vacation. I mean, I know trying to have fun is already taxing for you, but..." He trailed off, lifting a shoulder.

"Not taxing," I said, a smile breaking across my face as I slid my palm against his and climbed out of the passenger seat. "It's hard to get used to something that you know isn't going to last."

His features softened as he kept hold of my hand.

"Or you can just enjoy the moment," he said, bringing our joined hands to his mouth and pressing a light kiss to my knuckles, pausing long enough for the warmth of his lips to travel down my legs. "Believe it or not, I'm having the same struggle."

I thought his panty-melting grin would be my weakness, but his shy smile killed me.

How miserable was my life that I was mooning over

someone buying me breakfast and offering me a hand out of a truck?

I'd be sad whenever this ended between us either way, so why not enjoy every moment for all it was worth?

"Where are we headed after this? Not trying to take the fun out of it, just curious."

His mouth curved up, a plan to drag him into the back seat of his truck and devour his mouth right before I ran my tongue along the ink trailing his glorious arms blossoming in my brain.

"To see all of the Keys takes a few hours, but I thought I'd show you my favorite beach and we could stop at a good seafood place on the way back." He stilled as he made his way to the back of the truck and swiveled his head toward me. "If you don't like seafood, we can stop somewhere else."

"I do, sounds like a good plan." I bit back a smile. Leo was proverbial sex on a stick, but I'd caught a couple of cracks of vulnerability last night and today which made him even more irresistible.

The more time we spent together, the more the attraction grew, but I liked Leo. Granted, I hadn't known him long enough to learn any of his habits, but it was easy to spot a nice guy. My father and my brother had set that standard for me early.

Colin was sweet when we first met, which seemed so long ago it didn't even feel like part of this lifetime. I'd gotten too used to a man who grumbled more than smiled.

I guessed simple consideration was my new kink.

I let my gaze fall on Leo's back as he rooted around for something in the trunk. His muscles worked under his T-shirt as he leaned forward, tempting my eyes lower. Every inch of him was toned and rippling, as if his body was photoshopped to be that perfect, but I'd touched and felt enough of him pressed against me to know he was all real.

If I weren't preoccupied with keeping my tongue inside my

mouth, I would have snapped another picture for Nicole and Peyton, but I liked keeping him to myself. For the little time I'd have Leo, I didn't want to share him.

"Ah, here it is," he said before straightening and turning back toward me. "This should have enough room for both of us." He held up a beach towel that seemed huge even folded up. "Ready, or do you want to stare at my ass for a little longer before we head to the beach?"

I shrugged. "I was just appreciating all the beauty the Keys have to offer like you're supposed to do when you're on vacation."

He burst out laughing before he slammed the trunk shut and came back over to me.

"Yes, very good." He dragged the tip of his finger across my brow. "The line is starting to fade. You look more relaxed already." He pressed a kiss to my forehead and picked up my hand like we'd done it a million times before. I followed him toward the beach, ogling him once more as he set the towel down near the shade of a palm tree.

"It's nice not to have a schedule or anywhere to be." I hugged my knees into my chest. "I'm in for a shock when I get home." I chuckled, but he only nodded when I lifted my head.

"This day is all up to you. I'll take you wherever you want to go."

I folded my arms and rested my head in the crook of my elbow.

"I'm happy where I am for now. I can see why you like living here."

His features tensed for a moment. "It's good. For the time being anyway."

There was a noticeable pinch in his brow when his eyes came back to mine.

"I'm always fascinated by people who've lived in so many

places. It makes me sad for myself, as I've never moved out of the town I grew up in."

"How come?"

It was my turn to stare into space. Why did I never leave?

"I met Colin in college, and staying in town seemed natural. My family was there, all my friends. It never occurred to me to move. Sometimes..." I sighed, digging my heels into the sand. "Sometimes I wonder what it would be like to move somewhere new, where no one knows me or my family or what I looked like in high school. This is the closest I've come to doing that."

I shifted toward Leo, careful not to bunch up the towel under me.

"So, in a way, I know a side of you others don't." My breath caught when he feathered the back of his hand down my cheek.

"What side is that?" I asked, not recognizing my own breathless whisper.

"Well, you're right. I don't know you as anyone's mother, sister, or as a woman from town. I just know the beautiful woman who deserves so much more than she seems to let herself have, and ever since I met you, I have this strange urge to give you all I can for as long as I have you."

He ran his lips over my jaw and down my neck. I'd become familiar with strange urges since we'd met too, the most overpowering one to take whatever Leo had to give. The guilt I had over taking a solo vacation was gone, evaporating into the salty sea air as Leo's mouth covered mine. I whimpered into his mouth as he delved his tongue across the seam of my lips. I exhaled a happy sigh as I let him in, licking into his mouth with long strokes and savoring his taste to lock it into my memories for *after*. When I was back to my old but still new life and didn't know how to want things for myself.

We leaned back on the towel, my legs falling open as Leo settled between them. I dug my fingers into his hair as he moaned into my mouth, his erection hot and heavy against my core as he pressed us into the towel.

His groan reverberated against my chest before he buried his head into the crook of my neck.

"I did want to get to know you today, but I can't keep my lips off you."

He smiled, his mouth still wet from our kiss.

"I'm not complaining, but okay, what else do you want to know?" I wrapped my arms around his neck, my back arching off the sand a few inches on instinct to stay as close to him as possible.

"What's your last name? Only fair since you know mine."

I leaned my head back on the sand, the eager sheen in his golden eyes squeezing my chest.

"Webber. I was considering going back to Russo, my maiden name, but I don't want my girls to feel weird."

He brushed the hair off my forehead, regarding me with such rapt attention, I didn't know whether to squirm or melt into the towel.

"Italian?"

"Yes. Although my father and my brother are the ones with the rich olive skin that always tans so well. My mother and I are fair and get connect-the-dot freckle tans."

"I definitely notice the freckles." He skimmed his finger along my collarbone where a large cluster of freckles had already bloomed after only a day in the sun.

"Chloe gets freckle tans too. She's my eldest. She worries about me, more than any other girl her age should about her mother, but I haven't been able to make her stop. Emma is still little." I circled my finger around the dimple hiding in his stubbled cheek. "Her only concern when it comes to me is where I hide the cookies and candy."

A tiny smile lifted his lips before he rolled off me and leaned on his side.

"I don't know why I brought them up just now."

"Your face lights up whenever you mention your kids. You miss them, and it's okay to talk about them to me. In fact, that's why I took you out today. I want to know you."

"You want stories of a moody teenager and a kindergartner?" I sat up on my elbows. "You're a heat-induced mirage, aren't you? Like, you can't be real."

"I assure you I am." He leaned in and kissed the corner of my mouth.

"What about you? I know Reyes is a Spanish last name, but where is your family from?"

"The Dominican Republic. Well, my father is—was. He was born there and came to the United States when he was five. My mother was born in Washington Heights in Manhattan, where they grew up together."

"That's sweet that they grew up together."

He nodded as he turned his gaze toward the ocean. I caught his quick correction from present to past tense when he spoke about his father, but he didn't seem like he wanted to elaborate, and I didn't want to push.

"Hey, are you okay?" I scratched my fingers along the short hair at the back of his neck.

"Yes, I'm fine." He peeled my hand away from his neck and pressed a kiss to my wrist. "I have a cooler in the back with water. You seem to make me forget everything." He narrowed his eyes at me before standing and heading for the truck.

I resolved to forget his rapid change of subject and surveyed the mostly empty beach, a few umbrellas dotting the sand in the distance. As I rolled up to sit, my phone buzzed in my purse.

Nicole: *So he's a decorated firefighter, tons of pictures of ceremonies and with kids. His social media is private, but he doesn't look* *like he's full of himself in his profile picture. Still a total smokeshow, though. I hope you're too busy being naked and satisfied to read this now, but I am so excited for you!*

"Everything okay?" Leo asked as he sat down next to me and handed me a cold bottle of water.

"Yes, just Nicole checking on me."

"I'm guessing she gave Google a good workout." He raised a brow as he took a long pull.

"She did. She found pictures of awards, kids, and a hot but not douchey profile picture."

"Nice to know. That was the exact look I was going for."

I chuckled at his wink.

"What did you tell her?"

"Nothing. She said she hoped I was too busy and satisfied to read and reply." I held his gaze as I took a sip from my water bottle.

"Satisfied, huh?" He clicked his tongue with his teeth, the smolder in his eyes kicking up my pulse. I couldn't add "naked" to that since we already had trouble keeping our hands off each other. The power of suggestion was unneeded and dangerous.

"I'm supposed to come home with a good story for both Nicole and my sister-in-law."

"No pressure," Leo huffed, a smile pulling at his lips.

"Trust me, I have plenty to tell already." I stilled when his brows jumped. "I mean... God, here I go again." I groaned and dropped my head into my hands.

"Stop," he said, wrapping his hand around my ankle before he skimmed it up my calf. His light touch soothed me even when it shot straight to my core.

"I didn't tell Nicole much about you other than how we met and that we had plans today. Peyton, my sister-in-law, is the one who usually drags things out of me. She knows more, but I didn't tell her everything either."

Leo nodded, still running his hand up and down my calf, skimming my knee as he inched higher.

"Mostly, we talked about what you said. Having someone's undivided attention is something new to me—too new—and I didn't and still don't know how to handle it. But I'm trying. Because it's nice."

A slow grin spread across Leo's face.

"Really nice," I whispered as I leaned forward to graze my fingers over his stubbled chin. "You're raising my standards by a lot, which is going to suck when I land back in New York," I joked, but he didn't laugh. Goose bumps trailed down my back when he cupped my neck.

He brushed my lips with a light, lingering kiss that kicked up my heart rate. "I only have a little time to give you a good story."

I fell back with Leo on top of me, not caring who was on the other end of the beach or how fast this was all going. As I melted into the sand, it all seemed too right to worry about what should or shouldn't be.

"So then, we need to make this count."

TEN
LEO

"Can I ask you something?" Kristina squinted at me from across the table.

"I told you, you can ask me anything. That's the whole idea for today. I'm an open book."

"I see," she said, pursing her lips as she bit into a coconut shrimp, my eyes following her mouth and tongue as they had all damn day. The beach had started to fill up after an hour, putting a halt to where we were headed as we lay tangled up in each other on the sand.

Every part of me wanted to be near her or on her, and it was becoming near impossible to think about anything else. I'd hoped a lunch break would help me recalibrate my brain.

"It's a little personal, so you can still feel free to tell me to mind my own business, but why do you move around so much?"

My beer bottle stilled right before I took a long pull. I brought it to my lips, gulping a long swig before setting it back down.

"I haven't moved in a while. I've actually been in Florida longer than any other place I've lived since I left New York."

"Hmm" was all she said as she traced along the rim of her cocktail glass.

"That sounded like a loaded 'hmm,'" I said, leaning back in my chair as I searched her gaze. "Any reason why you're asking?"

"Well, you didn't answer my question. You said something earlier about Florida being good for the *time being*. Do you have plans to move again?"

I shrugged. "Right now, no. I've only lived in a few places."

"How many?" she asked, lifting a brow.

"I don't know, four, maybe five. I'm not a nomad if that's what you're thinking."

Just always felt like one.

I had no real roots here or anywhere. I could pack up my apartment in a day and move on tomorrow if I found a job somewhere else without much hesitation or breaking a sweat. I'd miss some of the friends I'd made here and liked the guys in my firehouse, but nothing and no one compelled me to make this home.

It was a problem I liked to ignore, but Kristina didn't seem like she would let it drop.

She rested her elbows on the table and leaned forward. "I have a tiny confession to make. When you were in the restroom, I may have checked out some of the screenshots Nicole sent me of you." She let out a long exhale before turning back to me, a frown pulling at her lips. "What you did in that fire, all those kids you helped save."

"That's my job. Some fires are easier than others, but we always go in with the same purpose."

"You don't get awards for just doing your job."

"I did, so the award wasn't necessary." I realized how clipped my tone was when she reared back. "I'm sorry, I didn't mean to snap at you." I reached across the table and grabbed her hand.

"Can I make an assumption that you may get a little mad at me for?"

"Go for it," I told her, flashing a smile to hide the dread over whatever she was about to tell me.

"I know it's silly to think I know you, truly know you, after only a day. But the Leo I know so far is warm and considerate and open. And maybe I'm naive in thinking that's not something a person can fake. You don't seem like someone who moves from place to place without a second thought. What's making you so unsettled?"

I set the bottle down on the table, taking in a slow breath before lifting my head. It wasn't that I didn't know why. In fact, I'd spent most of my life avoiding the answer. But for some reason, Kristina's kind green eyes gave me the first inclination I'd had maybe ever to confess to someone, and myself, why I never liked to stay in one place.

"My parents died when I was sixteen. A car crash on an icy road."

She pressed her hand to her chest, her eyes widening as she fell back in her chair.

"I'm so sorry, Leo."

"My mother went right away, but they were able to get my father out. Once they told him what happened to his wife after he was stable, he had a heart attack. I moved in with my aunt and uncle until I turned eighteen."

She picked up my hand and covered it with both of hers.

"I'm a nosy asshole, and I'm so sorry I pushed you."

"You aren't and you didn't push. It's not something I talk about, but I'm okay with telling you."

"Where did you go when you turned eighteen?"

"College. I completed the credits I needed to become a fire-fighter and an EMT. When I graduated, I followed a couple of friends to Chicago and lived there for about a year. So that's one." I shot Kristina a crooked grin and held up a finger.

She shook her head. "You don't have to tell me any more. I lost my father when I was thirty-five and it was awful enough, but losing them both so young must have been terrible."

"I guess I moved around so much because it was easier to stay distant and detached. Which is fine when you're young, but since I just turned forty, I need to settle somewhere, right? Florida is pretty easy living. The weather is mild, I have a good routine with both jobs, and I can keep busy easier."

"You don't seem distant or detached to me."

"Because you have been my big exception on most things since we met. Well, since I noticed you scowling at your drink by the pool."

A slow grin spread across her lips.

"Back at you." She let go of my hands and took a sip from her water glass, jerking her head to me after she set it down. "Wait, you just turned forty?"

"The spots of gray and the lines around my eyes should have been a clue. Is that a problem?"

"No, not at all. I just didn't know your age until now. I'm forty-two. If you Google the meaning of life, it comes up as forty-two. But so far, I have more questions than answers."

Her smile was warm and patient, without any judgment. I'd taken her out today because I wanted to know her, and the more I knew, the more I liked, and the more screwed I was.

"I think you may have more answers than you realize."

She leaned forward, resting her elbows on the table as she held my gaze.

"I can honestly tell you, I have no clue about anything at all from where I'm sitting right now. But oddly enough, the one thing I am sure of is wanting to be here with you."

"Good vacation, then?" I asked, a smile pulling at my lips despite the ache in my chest.

"Leo, this has been one of the best, and one of the strangest, trips of my life so far." She sat back, squinting at me. "So you're a firefighter, but are you like a captain or lieutenant or something?"

"Nicole didn't find that out for you?" I teased. "Lieutenant."

"Oh, wow. No, she didn't tell me your job title, but I haven't looked at my phone since the beach. That's impressive."

"And I just got my RN degree last year."

She squinted at me over her water glass.

"When did you have time for that?"

"It took me a while. On days off from the station, I'd go to class and whatever clinical hours I had to make."

"Are you switching jobs?"

"No. I was trained as an EMT when I first joined the fire department and was thinking about doing that full time, but I like helping at the scene and after, if that makes sense."

I'd often wondered what the crash scene had looked like when my parents died, but I was too young to be told any details. I wanted to believe that emergency services and the doctors at the hospital did all they could, but that was always in the back of my mind on any call—to do better and save everyone.

"I can find a per diem nursing job and split my time between that and the fire department, which I'll eventually do."

"I think that's awesome. A good friend of mine is an ER nurse, and he always said that it's the hardest yet best job there is. It doesn't surprise me that you want to help as many people as you can. As I keep saying, I haven't known you for very long, but I can see that pretty clearly with you."

"Thanks, and since I didn't get a chance to Google your job, what do you do?"

"I'm a vascular technician. I work at a doctor's office doing scans, and one or two days per month on call at the hospital. I can be home for the girls at night and feed them at a reasonable hour. Not as cool as your job, or *jobs*."

My stomach fluttered when we shared a smile, and I got lost in those damn green eyes again.

"Hey, you have an important job. I bet you're great at it too."

"What about me says that I'm great at giving ultrasounds?" She narrowed her eyes.

"You're sweet and soothing. Direct but gentle hands."

She laughed before giving me a slow nod. "Direct, gentle hands. First I've heard that one."

"You're smart." I shrugged. "And since I've met you, you've been direct with me."

"Yeah," she said, scrunching her nose at me and bobbing her head in a slow nod. "Direct around the foot in my mouth."

"You're honest. Genuine. You draw people in. At least that's what I'm blaming for not being able to stay away from you since the bar."

A shy smile tilted her mouth.

"Well, thank you. That's actually very sweet."

"It's the truth. Why I'm sure you put a lot of nervous patients at ease." I reached over and slid my palm against hers. "Easy touch, smooth skin, soft lips."

Her hand stilled against mine as her grin shrank.

"I don't think my lips have anything to do with how well I can perform ultrasounds."

"I don't know about that." I brought her wrist to my lips and kissed across her knuckles. "Staring at that mouth is so distracting, you could do anything you want to me right now and I wouldn't stop you."

The urge to pull her into my arms and cover her mouth with

mine, not giving a single fuck if we were in a crowded restaurant or not, barreled over me.

"Tourists don't stand a chance against you, do they?"

"As I've told you," I said, keeping hold of her hand, "I don't take tourists out, especially not for a whole day. I'm breaking all my rules for you."

She coughed out a laugh.

"I'm breaking rules I never knew I had since I met you. Still not sick of me yet?"

I smiled when she squeezed my hand.

"I'm still working on giving you the best vacation story that I can. I'm only warming up."

I grabbed her hand when she tried to slip it away.

"And no. Not sick of you. Not even close."

Instead of my usual cracking a joke or shutting down when anyone brought up my parents, she made me want to tell her more. She made me forget about that agitation I always had when I didn't know what to do or where to go next.

A woman like her made you want to stop and stay—even when you knew she couldn't.

ELEVEN
KRISTINA

"**C**an I ask you something else?" I leaned my elbow against the inside of the passenger door as I turned toward Leo.

"You can just ask, Kristina." He laughed, lifting a shoulder. "At this point, we can leave pretense at the door, right?"

The side of his mouth curled, and I almost forgot my question. He sat with his arm stretched out, shifting it as he kept the wheel straight. My eyes followed the swivel of muscle covered by lines of black ink from his bicep to his wrist. I fixated on his fingers against the steering wheel, how they flexed as he held it steady, the same fingers that twisted inside me last night until I came apart in his mouth.

"Are you okay?" He angled his head to squint at me.

"Fine," I squeaked out as I turned the AC vents toward me in a futile effort to bring down my body temperature from the hot as hell memory.

"You look a little flushed, babe. Want to jump in the pool and cool off when we get back?" He flashed a cocky grin as his gaze slid to mine.

"I'm not flushed." I scowled, my attempted denial pointless

since the heat rushing up my cheeks had to be turning them a bright red.

I ignored the rush of warmth in my chest when he called me babe—and the confusion over how natural it seemed—and cleared my throat.

"What's your story? Like, I'm divorced, so I assume people our age have some kind of history..." I trailed off. I wanted to ask if he was ever married or engaged, another question that was absolutely none of my business but couldn't help asking him anyway.

"Are you asking if I have a girl in every city? No, since that's a lot of work," he joked, smirking as he kept his eyes on the road.

"I know you don't. I mean, you could, no judgment, just...curious."

He nodded as he turned his truck into the Turtle Bay parking lot.

"I was almost married once. In Vegas, as cliché as that sounds. We were dating for a while and ended up at one of those chapels as a joke. I asked if she wanted to just do it, and she got very angry with me and said no before breaking it off for good."

"In her defense, that doesn't sound like the most romantic proposal. Not that the proposal gives you any real clue about what marriage would be like."

Colin proposed on the big screen at a Buffalo Bills game in front of all our friends. It was a big show that took a lot of planning, but even then, it felt like just that—a show.

Maybe proposals were a good indicator of what you were in for if you said yes, but I was too naive to notice.

"I think that was my subconscious giving me an out. I had a good feeling she'd be pissed enough at the suggestion to end things. We were at a place where it was either move forward or stop."

"What if she called your bluff?"

"Well, then my answer to you would be divorced instead of almost married."

I burst out laughing at his shrug.

"Quite the chance you took."

He chuckled when I nudged his arm.

"As I said, distant and detached was how I rolled. I dated but nothing that serious."

"For when you would leave again?"

He shut the engine off after he pulled into a spot, gazing out the front window for a long minute.

"Something like that, I guess."

His eyes bored into mine with a sadness that I didn't want to notice or find so damn familiar. Maybe in another life, we could have given this a real try, but in the ones we had, all this could be was fun.

It seemed too soon to be disappointed about that, but the sting from the thought felt very real.

"Are you sure you want to come back here tonight since you work here?"

Something about coming back to Turtle Bay felt final, and I wasn't ready for the day to end. We'd gone on a long drive after lunch, talking about everything and nothing. I expected a moment of awkward silence to come along eventually, but it didn't. In fact, the easier it was to be with Leo, the sadder it was that when this awesome vacation ended, so would we.

Not that we were anything real now. He was a single man in Florida—for now—and I had two kids waiting for me in New York. I couldn't and wouldn't do a long-distance relationship, as this one trip away from my kids was taxing enough on all of us.

Plus, he never said he'd even want that. We were living in the glorious chemistry of the moment. He'd promised me a good story to take home to my friends and family and nothing more.

There was no after, just a stop—if only my mind would stop jumping ahead and cut it out with the what-ifs.

"It's a different experience when you aren't on the clock and with a beautiful woman for the night."

He flashed a sweet, almost shy smile.

"I had a great time with you today. Now that we're back at the resort, you could probably stop sharing your location now."

"How did you know I was doing that? And I only did it to shut Nicole up so I didn't have to deal with a thousand texts about where I was."

"I would tell a friend of mine going off with a strange guy for a day to do the same." He stretched his arm around the back of my headrest. "But I told you, I'm harmless." He brushed my lips with a light kiss, lingering longer with each peck until I grabbed the back of his head and attacked his lips. Leo leaned over the console, his hand gliding up my bare thigh and skimming the edge of my already soaked panties as he plundered my mouth.

"Harmless, right," I joked, panting when we broke apart. "I know where we could go if it's okay with you."

His brow furrowed as he cradled the back of my head.

"I'll go anywhere you want."

I swallowed as my throat worked, revving up the courage I wasn't sure I had to make the most of this unexpected but temporary gift I'd been given.

"My suite is much too big for one person. I never liked wasting a huge king-sized bed on just me." I smoothed the collar of his T-shirt, pinching the cotton between my fingers instead of meeting his widened eyes in my periphery.

"I'm divorced, as you know, and I haven't been with anyone in longer than I'd like to admit." I sputtered out a nervous laugh. "I haven't been tested or anything, but it's been long enough, I'm pretty sure that I'm clean."

"So am I. Not divorced but unattached and confirmed clean."

He weaved his hand into my hair and grabbed a fistful. "And I want inside you more than I want to breathe right now. So, if you're asking me what I think you are—"

"Come home with me. I mean, the suite isn't home."

None of this was home or would last past a matter of hours, but I was diving in headfirst anyway.

"Spend the night with me." I grabbed his face, the words falling from my lips like a desperate plea. "This is all fucking crazy, but I don't—"

His lips crashed into mine, impatience and desperation igniting the kiss even more. Leo groaned into my mouth as he gripped the inside of my thigh.

"Yeah, it's all fucking crazy," he said between kisses. "But I don't want it to end either. I already hate thinking about it."

"Me too," I whispered as he kissed down my neck.

"I did promise I'd give you everything while I had you."

A chuckle slipped out of me, despite the anticipation pumping through my veins. I was dizzy enough to almost forget the dread over how I'd feel when this was all over, but I pushed that as far out of my mind as I could.

This moment was too short not to enjoy every second.

"So I'll take you to that big" —he kissed my jaw before running his lips down my neck— "messy bed." I felt his smile against my skin as he trailed his tongue along my collarbone. "The minute you close the door, I'm peeling this dress off you and giving you all the fucking attention you deserve."

He leaned his forehead against mine, clenching his eyes shut.

"And when I'm done, you're going to feel me all the way back to New York."

We fell into another kiss. What the hell was my life these past twenty-four hours? I had no doubt I'd feel him all the way to New York, and that whatever would happen tonight would live rent-free in my head for a long time to come.

Vacation was supposed to be an escape from reality, but this was a realm in another dimension.

I wanted Leo in every way I could have him, and I couldn't care less about any consequences or regrets because I was too busy reveling in the here and now.

"I'm ready, let's go." I broke away from his hold and almost leaped out of his truck, grasping the door handle for purchase as I climbed out on shaky legs. I grabbed his hand when he made his way to my side and almost jogged to the path to the suites, not looking back for fear of breaking the spell or in case reason and logic wanted to creep into my head.

I had no time or interest in either.

As cocky and distant as he played himself off to be, Leo seemed lost. We were both searching for different things without ever expecting to find them, and although fleeting and temporary, whatever this was between us felt exactly like what we both needed.

Even if we'd have to give it back.

TWELVE
KRISTINA

I almost tripped over my flip-flops as I kept stepping out of them on the sprint back to my suite. I didn't turn around as I pulled Leo behind me, not wanting to risk the temptation of chickening out or spotting the looks we'd get from the people he worked with at Turtle Bay when they noticed a strange woman dragging him somewhere.

I fished the keycard out of my purse, my gaze still straight ahead as I swiped it over the door handle until it beeped.

"I didn't know we were running a race," Leo said, his deep chuckle reverberating through me as he shut the door behind him. The suite was silent other than the faint buzz of the air conditioner.

I exhaled for the first time since stepping out of his truck as I kicked off my flip-flops and finally turned to face him.

"I..." I started, raking a hand through my hair, the sweat on my forehead dampening my already clammy palm. "I both wanted to get here as soon as possible and was afraid I'd lose my nerve."

His wide grin shrank as he nodded.

"I get it, and listen," he said, framing my face. "We don't have to if you don't want to—"

"Oh, I do. Trust me." I slid my hands up his arms until they met at the back of his neck. "It's all I've thought about since last night. I almost pulled you inside then."

"You have no idea how hard it was to leave." He glided his hands down my back, his touch making me shiver and burn up at the same time. "I had to fight the urge to come back here at the crack of dawn this morning, but I didn't want to scare you off."

His eyes were dark, boring into mine with a feral gaze as if he was holding himself back and losing the battle for control.

"I wish you had." My voice was nothing but a crackling whisper. "Today was wonderful, but finishing what we started has been on my mind all day," I confessed, my heart pounding in my ears. "Now that I've gotten to know you and like you, it's just made it so much worse."

"Yeah?" He ghosted his lips over my jaw and down my neck. "I know what you mean. Spending the day with you only made me want you more, want this."

He dragged openmouthed kisses over my shoulder and along my collarbone. I slumped against him, lost in the warmth of his mouth and the delicious scratch of his stubble.

"Well, I *finished* last night, I suppose. But you..." I coasted my hand down his shirt and over the hard bulge of his shorts. He groaned against my skin when I squeezed, moving my hand up and down his hardening length in a slow enough motion to feel him jerk against my palm.

"I think I owe you," I said in a breathless whisper as he trailed kisses over my throat and then down my chest, running his tongue along the neckline of my dress.

"Owe me?" He straightened, narrowing his eyes at me before he shook his head. "I loved every minute of last night. Your lips..." He kissed me, dragging his tongue along the seam of my lips until they opened on a needy moan. He slanted his head, going deeper and harder, the kiss going from sweet to dirty in seconds. "All of this," he murmured against my lips as his hands roamed my body, cupping my ass before he fisted the hem of my dress. "So warm and wet and fucking sweet."

I fell back onto the large mattress, landing with a whoosh against the fluffy blankets as Leo climbed over me, hooking his thumbs into my panties and dragging them down my legs.

"You have something, I hope." I coughed out a nervous laugh as the cool air hit my drenched core.

He nodded, lifting me up by my underarms and setting me down against the pillows.

"I do, but not yet." He made his way down my body, his gaze roaming over me like a caress before he dipped his head, dropping light, torturous kisses along my clit until he sucked it into his mouth. "First, I need to taste you again. But this time, you won't hold back. You'll scream as loud as you want while you come all over my tongue."

"Leo," I cried out as I clenched my eyes shut, stars already bursting under my eyelids. He spread my legs wider, pressing his hands on the insides of my thighs as he kissed, licked, and sucked until I lost all control and words. I whispered his name between mewls and moans and other sounds I'd never heard fall from my mouth before as he slid two fingers inside, curling them as he twisted them deep inside me and then out, all the while never taking his mouth off me.

I was so close it was painful, the tremors between my legs beating to a sharp pulse.

"Come on, baby." He lifted his head, his lips and chin soaked with me as a dirty grin pulled across his mouth. "Let go." His voice was husky and strained as he swiped his tongue across his bottom lip. "I've got you."

He covered me with his mouth again, this time sliding his tongue all the way inside as he drew circles around my swollen clit with his thumb. My legs flailed back and forth as I drowned in sensation, my orgasm barreling over me so hard and fast I fisted the blanket on either side of me for purchase as I came back down to earth.

"Wow," I croaked out as I dropped my head back and pressed my hand against my throat. When I tried to clear it, my throat was dry and scratchy like spent sandpaper.

"Loud enough?" I opened one eye and peered down at Leo, his chest rumbling with a laugh as he stood and peeled off his shirt. My eyes went to a small line of ink peeking out of the waistband of his shorts that I didn't spot when we were together in the pool. I'd get to see all of him now, and my mouth watered at the thought.

"I thought you said you'd make sure I had a good vacation, not try to kill me," I teased and propped myself up on my elbows, ogling the gorgeous sight in front of me without a drop of shame, only an undercurrent of regret that I couldn't take it home with me.

I'd expected sex after my divorce to be much further into the future, and when it finally did happen, it would be awkward as hell no matter who I was with. After being with only one man for almost two decades, I couldn't fathom intimacy being comfortable or even pleasant that first time.

Instead of awkward and forced, so far, it was glorious and everything I didn't know I needed.

Or maybe I knew what I needed and just learned to live without it for so long that I'd forgotten all about it. Leo was making me remember so many things. Too many things.

The bare minimum wouldn't cut it anymore—with anyone.

"Sit up," he crooned, crooking his finger at me until I complied. Before I knew it, my dress was over my head and strewn across the carpet, leaving me in nothing but a flimsy strapless bra.

For the first time since I'd met Leo at the bar, trepidation slipped through me. The lights by the pool had been dim enough for me not to overthink the imperfections that having two kids left behind on my body. The stretch marks on my abdomen that never went away no matter how many sit-ups I did or creams I slathered on and the C-section scar that changed the contour of my stomach as it healed never bothered me or even occurred to me. The bikini I'd bought for this trip covered those places fine, but I'd be totally bare for Leo, and my shoulders tensed at the sudden need to cover up.

"Don't do that." Leo shook his head, his eyes holding mine as he unbuckled his belt and let his shorts and boxers drop.

"Do what?" I breathed out, forgetting to be embarrassed as my attention went to Leo's huge cock bouncing against his stomach as he ambled back toward the bed. It was long and thick, and I wanted to trace the vein along the side with my tongue after licking all his tattoos.

"Cover yourself." He slid his hands to my back and undid my bra one hook at a time. "You're so damn beautiful that I'm about to lose it, so please don't hide from me."

He caught my mouth in a kiss, curling his tongue against mine and drawing another whimper out of me. I arched my back off the bed as he sucked a nipple into his mouth, delving my hands into his hair as he grazed over it with his teeth and kissed his way across my chest before taking the other nipple the same way, just as he'd done next to the pool last night, causing the same blinding heat to build between my legs.

Every part of my body was fired up. Even my fingers and toes tingled as he raised his head to kiss me again, sloppy and desperate with a passion I couldn't recall with anyone else and still didn't understand.

He wasn't only trying to kill me. He was ruining me.

The kiss kept going as I heard the soft tear of foil, my back hitting the mattress again as he climbed over me.

"Still yes?" he asked as he came back on top of me, the dusting of his chest hair against my rigid nipples making me gasp, more intimacy between us that I didn't expect, and stealing what was left of the air in my lungs.

I nodded, trying hard to find my voice while still so damn breathless. I wanted to reason that the intensity between us was from being out of practice, but I couldn't deny there was more to it. I didn't know why or how it was there, but it was too strong to ignore.

And too impossible to stop.

"You? Still yes for you?"

A smile broke out on his perfect mouth before he pressed it against mine.

"I'm a hell fucking yes."

He sat up on his knees and began to roll on the condom when I grabbed his wrist.

His head shot up, his eyes smoldering as they held mine, the air thinning between us even more as I slid the rubber up his length, taking my time as I inched it on and biting back a smile as he jerked against my hand.

He hovered over me, the same intensity in his gaze as he thrust inside me, slowly but easily, stilling when he spotted my eyes grow wide.

"I'm fine. Just more, please."

I dug my nails into his back until he started to move.

Every minute of last night and today reminded me just how long I'd been alone. Maybe I was never physically by myself very often, but truly being with someone was such a distant memory that I couldn't tell if it was real or not.

I'd been a robot forcing myself to go through the motions

while feeling nothing for too many years to count, but why did I feel so much with a man who should have been a stranger?

It was like waking up after being in a full body and mind sleep, and my eyes were wide open, appreciating every noise he made and every wince on Leo's face as he inched in and out, going deeper every time.

"So good," he whispered, sliding his arm under my waist to bring me closer.

"Yeah?" I hooked my leg over his hip, meeting him thrust for thrust.

"Yeah." He cracked a smile, his hooded eyes searing into mine as he nodded. "Like fucking heaven."

I crashed my lips against his, clutching the back of his neck as he groaned into my mouth. This did seem like heaven, or at least far enough outside of this world to be wonderfully surreal.

What this didn't seem like was the meaningless sex Nicole told me to have. But making love didn't seem right either—not with a man I'd known for a day. Maybe I'd been so damn affection-starved that my emotions didn't know what to make of what was happening, but as much as it confused me or didn't make logical sense, this entire day had been more.

But I had to keep in mind that *more* had an expiration date.

He shifted angles, the new spot he found inside and the new friction he created sending me right over the edge.

I roped my arms around his neck, shuddering against him as my climax rocked through me, my body still sensitive from the aftershocks of the first. Twice in one night, never mind so close together, I'd thought was a myth found only in fiction.

I guessed this was fiction too, as real as it seemed.

I dug my nails into Leo's back until the tremors subsided, wiggling my toes as the sensation came back to my limbs. I held him tighter as he quivered over me, his body going rigid as he dropped his head into the crook of my shoulder.

"Go ahead," I whispered into his ear. "I've got you."

"Fuck, Kristina," he called out in a half moan, half plea as he rode out his release, slowing down until he collapsed on top of me.

As Leo chased his breath, I scrubbed a hand down my face before I opened my eyes.

Pink hues of light filtered through my window as the sun set, but that wasn't the reason everything seemed different. I lifted my head and kissed Leo's shoulder, still scanning the space around us as I acclimated to what had just happened.

I smiled, almost laughing as I recalled the pep talk I'd given myself when I first arrived to at least be a little social even if it was the last thing I wanted to do.

I glanced at the pile of clothes next to the bed and my dress spread out alongside Leo's shorts and shirt.

"You okay?"

Leo lifted his head, peering down at me with a furrowed brow before he eased out of me.

"I...I honestly don't know what I am right now." I cupped his neck and brought him closer, pressing my forehead to his. "But if you're asking if I regret any of it, no. I loved every second." He relaxed his shoulders when I let out a long exhale. "I'm just not sure what to do with it."

He kissed me, slow and sensual, as his breathing slowed. Although I was physically spent from the waist down, a thrill shot through me.

"Then you and I are on the very same page."

THIRTEEN
KRISTINA

"Are you hungry?" I asked Leo, grimacing as I shifted next to him. It had been a long time since I'd had sex, but the sore pain between my legs was a sobering indicator of just how much time had passed.

I rolled up to sit, hissing at the sting in my core.

"I am, but what's wrong? Why are you making those faces?" He chuckled as he cupped my chin.

"Because when I told you it's been a long time for me, I meant a *really* long time. Not complaining." I leaned in to kiss his lips. "Just need to acclimate a little bit."

"I should have been more...gentle. I'm sorry. I've been lost in you since yesterday and got carried away." He chuckled and sifted his fingers into my tangled locks. "But I'd never want to hurt you. Are you sure you're okay?"

"I'm great. I'm sore, but it's a good sore."

I lay next to him and roped my arm around his chiseled waist. "All my meals are paid for, from what Nicole told me, but I'm not sure if it counts for room service." I cuddled into his side as he ran his finger up and down my spine, tangled together on the bed as if we'd always been just like this.

"Do you want to go out to dinner?"

"Hmm. Dinner, yes, but I'm good where I am if you are." I laughed but stiffened when he didn't laugh with me. "I mean, you don't have to stay if you don't want to. We can do whatever you want—"

He pressed a finger to my lips and cocked his head to the side.

"Am I hungry? Yes. Do I want you to put your clothes back on? That's a hard no. I'm down with room service if you are." He kissed the tip of my nose. "You have no idea how sexy you are when you ramble."

I slammed his stomach with the first pillow I could grab.

"I only ramble around you. Back home, like I said, I'm more or less put together. Boring." I crinkled my nose. "The tongue-tied thing only happens with you." I traced the swirl of black ink across his chest. "I blame these."

He laughed and rolled on top of me.

"You are definitely not boring."

My legs fell open on instinct as he settled on top of me, arousal tingling at my core, a new kind of ache building despite the pain.

Pain was probably the wrong word, as it didn't really hurt. It was more like a special souvenir, reminding me of everything we'd done together every time I moved.

You'll feel me all the way back to New York.

I was sure I would, as one day with Leo was more unforgettable than years with someone else. That both thrilled me and stung like hell.

Our lips were about to touch when my head swiveled toward a familiar buzz coming from inside my purse. I'd been removed from reality since this morning, and guilt wormed its way into my gut.

My breath caught when I spotted Colin's name on the screen.

"Colin? What's wrong?" I did a quick scroll of my phone screen to see if my mother or brother had tried to contact me, panicking for a moment that something had happened with the girls, but there were no texts or missed calls.

Colin and I were amicable but not friendly. We spoke when needed and learned to communicate without spiteful jabs back and forth—most of the time. It was unlikely he was contacting me for a social call, and my stomach tensed on instinct before he even said a word.

"Why are you in Florida alone?"

I padded back to the bed, grabbing the duvet and draping it over me as I sat on the edge, my back to Leo as I didn't know how to look at him and hear Colin's voice at the same time.

"You knew I had a trip planned to Florida. What's the problem?"

"Yes, with someone. Not going off alone for four days."

I reared back and squinted at the phone. Being scolded by my ex-husband from thousands of miles away was an unexpected and unwelcome surprise.

I took in a deep breath, as I always did when Colin started to get under my skin, and squared my shoulders to give a calm and even answer.

"Nicole came down with the flu and the room was nonrefundable. I had the time off and couldn't reschedule it or I'd lose it. I'm fine," I added, even though I knew that wasn't concern slicing an edge into his tone.

My body tensed up, a muscle memory reaction from fighting with Colin for so many years until it was finally enough.

"I know that. Emma told me when I called. What is the matter with you? You left the girls to go on vacation by yourself, vulnerable and alone, where something could happen to you. Kris, I really didn't think you were this irresponsible."

Heat rose up my neck as I gripped the phone, wishing he were close enough to throw it at his face.

"I don't know what makes you think you can speak to me like one of our kids, but we aren't married anymore, and my vacations are my business."

"Look," he sighed, that dramatic, audible blow out of air I was all too familiar with. "If you want to be reckless, that's your business, but you should know better."

Where the hell was this coming from? Colin hadn't cared what I did or where I went for a long time. His only concern would be if there was someone to watch the girls. It didn't make sense for him to be so upset with the idea of me in Florida alone.

"First of all, this is a safe five-star resort. I'm not the first person to ever go on vacation alone. Hell, I never go at all unless it's with our kids, and I wanted to get away and try to relax for once. Like you do with all your fishing and hunting trips. So, if that makes me irresponsible to you, again, that's your problem, not mine."

Those trips took him away on Thanksgiving every year and a weekend a month every summer. Even while we were married, I'd mostly taken the girls away alone while he went with his friends or had some excuse for not being able to go. But I could only blame him so much as I'd kept my mouth shut and let the resentment fester until it spilled out at all the wrong times.

"And they're with my mother and brother because you thought it would be too much to take them for four days since a day and a half is your limit as a full-time parent. You aren't inconvenienced at all by my irresponsible trip, so whether I'm with someone or alone, it's none of your concern."

I felt the bed dip behind me as the mattress creaked. So much for the lust bubble that I'd thought Leo and I were nestled into for the night. Nothing like hearing the woman you just had sex with argue with her ex-husband to kill any kind of mood.

"And here we go again. I was a terrible father and husband, you never got a break. I've heard this song before. This is taking a selfish risk when you have kids depending on you. Act your age, for Christ's sake."

"Ah," I said, a humorless laugh falling from my lips. "Are you afraid something will happen to me, and you'll actually have to be a full-time father? I'm sure my brother would step in should anything happen to me from being so reckless, so you have nothing to worry about."

"Stop putting words in my mouth. I never said that."

Divorce was supposed to end this cycle. The constant gaslighting, accusing me of taking things the wrong way, or over-reacting so often that I pulled too many punches and held too much in, accepting scraps from my own husband because I thought it was all I deserved.

"Whatever your reason for calling, I don't care. My vacations are none of your business, and you aren't ruining this one. Goodbye."

I stabbed the screen to end the call and dropped my head into my hands, clenching my eyes shut as I took slow breaths in and out.

"I'm sorry," I told Leo without turning to face him. "My ex called to tell me how reckless I'm being by going on vacation alone, which I'm sure he only cares about because if something happens to me, he may have to take care of the girls full time. It's a lot of bullshit and why I'm divorced."

"So, I was right."

My head jerked to where Leo now sat beside me on the bed.

"Right about what?"

"I figured he was an asshole. And from what I overheard,

probably a big reason you think doing anything for yourself is a crime."

"Probably," I allowed, forcing a smile across my face to lighten the rotten mood shift. "Anyway, we can stay in, go out, whatever you want to do—"

Leo grabbed my wrist when I stood.

"Talk to me. I think I've proven to be a good listener." The corner of his mouth lifted as he motioned to the edge of the bed. "Sit for a minute."

I plopped back onto the bed, cupping my forehead and digging my thumb and index finger into my temples.

"As I told you, I'm far from perfect. But with Colin, anything I asked or did grated on his nerves, to the point where I had to tiptoe in my own home. Wears on a person."

"I bet" was all Leo said, his patient golden eyes disarming me enough to continue.

"No one knows all the details of what happened with Colin and me. They knew we were having problems and that we were in and out of counseling with constant short separations. My parents had this *beautiful* marriage," I mused as I pinched a fraying string from the blanket between my fingers. "In love until the very end, and I wanted that. I didn't want my older daughter to have to go back and forth between us, so I held a lot in. The right thing to do would have been to just divorce, but then I wouldn't have my Emma, and she's the sweet little distraction we all didn't know we needed." Talking about Emma always made a smile run across my lips.

"It's obvious when someone is only nice to you because they feel like they have to be. And that was Colin for many years. If I pushed anything, it was me being petty or selfish. I can only blame him to a point, as I took more than I should have for a long time. And he did try sometimes, or I think he wanted to try.

But when we'd fall back into the same fights, he'd give me nothing but resentment, and then it would be that much worse."

I lifted my head, Leo's gaze still fixed on me as I continued.

"I almost thought we were finally getting somewhere when he asked to date me." A laugh escaped me when I spotted the deep furrow in Leo's brow. "Like, he lived somewhere else, but we'd go out on dates and try to rekindle whatever got us together in the first place, which at that point was pretty damn hard to remember."

I groaned and rubbed at the back of my neck.

"It wasn't bad. We didn't fight. For once. But it felt less and less temporary as the months went by. Whenever I'd suggest moving back in, he'd ask why couldn't we keep things the way they are?"

"That," Leo started, pressing his hand to my knee and gliding his thumb back and forth over the blanket, "sounds shitty, to be honest. Stringing you along like that."

"Felt like it. I finally said either you move back in or we stop this. He said I was pushing him again, and this was why he didn't want to move back home because he couldn't take it."

I heaved out a long sigh, recounting the story I'd never told to anyone in its entirety.

"This was in a restaurant, by the way, with everyone's necks turned toward us because he was getting loud. I got up, left a twenty on the table, and told him I was officially releasing him from the torture of being married to me. And that the next date we went on, he could bring his lawyer and I'd bring mine."

I traced the vein along Leo's forearm with the tip of my finger.

"Not sure if he expected that, but he didn't follow me. Instead of being upset or disappointed, all I felt was relief. It was like running around in a circle for years and finally stopping to catch my breath. I stayed in our house, he takes the kids on weekends, but four days was above his parenting pay grade, so my mother and brother have them now."

"No one knows any of that?"

I tilted my head from side to side.

"Some, but not as much as I just told you. My brother would kill him, and then his police chief best friend would help cover it up," I said, a snicker slipping out. "But the girls have been hurt enough, and I just want to move on with no more arguments or trouble." I shrugged. "I admit, this was a bit of a surprise." I nodded to where I'd thrown my phone onto the bed. "It's been a minute since he came at me like that."

"You gave it right back from what I heard." I smiled when he squeezed my knee. "You sounded pretty badass."

"I don't know about badass. But yes, I can go back at him now. And I've learned that a lot of his problems with me were his issues and not mine. But if I hadn't met you"—I scratched my nails up and down his arm—"the inclination to book an early flight home right now would have been pretty damn strong."

"I rocked your world, I guess."

I burst out laughing when his brows jumped.

"That." I gave him a slow nod. "But it's more the little things. You were right when you said I had no idea how to accept attention or relax and have fun. It's embarrassing that it's so weird to me now, but you've made it fun to learn again."

He picked up our joined hands and brought them to his mouth, planting a lingering kiss on the inside of my palm, his eyes holding mine.

"You shouldn't have to relearn what should be natural to you, but I'm happy to help."

"You've been teaching me all kinds of things over the past day." I let my nails graze along the stubble on his jaw before I pushed off the bed. "Right now, I'd like to forget all that aggravation and get something to eat since I just revved up a pretty good appetite."

I tried for an easy smile despite the residue of bad memories Colin had dredged up.

"I'll go find a menu. I think I spotted one on the desk inside—"

I yelped when Leo dragged me back onto the bed, taking my mouth in a bruising kiss that robbed me of all thoughts and words.

My anger faded enough to kiss Leo back with the same urgency, scratching my nails up his back as I hooked my leg over his hip.

"This was gone until...before." He grazed his finger across my forehead. "But I can get rid of it again." He coasted his hand down my torso, stopping right before the scar on my lower abdomen I'd tried to cover earlier. Instead of being repulsed by it, Leo painted kisses along the raised white line of skin before his breath fanned hot against my core.

He dragged his finger up and down my slit, already drenched with need. His eyes held mine as he slid one finger inside and thumbed my clit, moving his hand back and forth in a painfully slow motion.

"So fucking wet, baby. That's a good girl. Forget everything but me."

I'd thought consideration and attention were my official new kinks, but Leo calling me a *good girl* almost made my eyes roll into the back of my head.

My journey of odd self-discoveries continued.

"This is okay?" His voice dipped to a husky rasp as he continued his delicate but exquisite torture. I couldn't possibly come again. I'd orgasmed more in one day than I had in five years.

"Good, really good."

He slid next to me, still playing my body like no one else ever had as the pressure built again. He covered my mouth with his, his lips moving as slowly as his fingers as he drove me out of my troubled mind.

I dug my heels into the mattress as number three hit. Quieter but sharper, a jolt running through my body from head to toe.

"You're kind of lethal, Lieutenant Reyes." I melted into the mattress as my hazy eyes met Leo's.

"I told you." He kissed my forehead and drew me to his side. "I'll give you all I can while you're here." He pressed his lips to my forehead, then rained kisses over my eyelids, down my cheek, and across my jaw. I heaved out an audible sigh as I melted against him.

"How's the vacation story coming along?"

I laughed at the arch in his brow when I opened my eyes.

"Like a goddamn fairy tale."

FOURTEEN
LEO

"**I**f we put some clothes on, we can move out to the terrace for a little while."

Kristina sucked chocolate frosting off her finger as she jerked her chin toward the sliding door outside the bedroom. I was too jealous of her finger to register what she was suggesting for a few minutes.

"Define 'some.'" I grabbed her hand after she popped another icing-covered brownie into her mouth and sucked her finger clean.

Her hooded eyes fluttered for a minute before she smiled.

"Well, I definitely don't want you to put a shirt on." She pulled the fluffy comforter wrapped around her tighter, but it still hung low across her chest, tempting my hands and my mouth to memorize the slope of her cleavage along with the rest of her. I had a double shift starting tomorrow, so our goodbyes would have to be in the morning, but I couldn't bring myself to tell her yet.

I'd gone into this knowing it wouldn't last past her stay, but I was the one who had to leave first. And for some reason I didn't know, or I did know but couldn't understand, I couldn't admit it or accept it.

"How about," I said, leaning over the bed to grab my crumpled-up shirt off the carpet, "you wear my shirt, and I guess we'll both put underwear on." She chuckled at my reluctant shrug. "Here, I'll grab my shorts and the brownies and meet you outside."

She beamed back at me, so relaxed and beautiful that I had to force a smile. My stomach turned as I prepped to tell her about our impending time limit.

Although we hadn't said it out loud, I had a good feeling we were in agreement that this could only be a vacation fling. She couldn't go back and forth to come to see me down here with two kids at home, and although I wasn't sure if I'd stay in Florida long-term, I wasn't able to make the long trip to New York all the time with my schedule.

Or was I, and I was just too afraid to make the offer?

It wasn't a surprise or something we didn't know was coming, but saying exactly when this amazing and strange thing between us would end wasn't something I could bring myself to do.

And this was only the second day I'd known her. The thought of leaving her shouldn't have gnawed at my gut so much to the point I couldn't even tell her that tonight would be it for us.

I opened the sliding door, placing the plate of brownies on the tiny table before heading back inside for the bottle of wine and glasses. Our dinner was finger foods, plus all they offered for dessert, with a bottle of Pinot Grigio on the side.

We ate in bed, talking so easily for hours about everything but what we'd do after Kristina was back in New York and I was back to my empty, fly-by-night lifestyle that now seemed even more hollow.

I dreaded any double shift. While I kept myself fit, I wasn't getting any younger. I'd worked for so long to get my RN degree so I could split my time between the department and nursing, but I hadn't applied to any hospitals yet. It was almost as if I was afraid to make the dual commitment.

Or it was exactly like that.

I was fully aware of my issues, but they never bothered me as much as they did now. A stranger had shone a spotlight on what I never wanted to see about myself and how lost I'd always been.

Kristina joked that she didn't have any answers, but it made me uneasy how hard she seemed to push me toward the ones I didn't want to find.

"So how private do you think this is?" she asked me as she came up to the railing, leaning over as she swept her gaze along the beach. The hem of my shirt fell halfway down her thigh, treating me to a nice view as she bent over. I liked her in my shirt as much as I liked her.

Too much.

"And why do you ask?" I came up behind her, wrapping my arm around her waist as I swept the hair off her shoulder to nuzzle her neck.

"I don't know," she said, leaning into me. My dick and I should have been exhausted after being inside her so much for most of the night, but when she brushed the sweet curve of her ass against me, we were both ready for more.

"Maybe the pool brought out the exhibitionist in me." She reached back and looped her arm around my neck. "I did want to get our money's worth in the suite. How many rooms can we tackle in a day?" She chuckled as she pulled me in for a kiss.

I kissed her back harder than she was expecting, spinning her around in my arms and backing her against the railing. I swallowed her sweet whimpers as I kept going, exploring and tasting her as our tongues tangled, so easily lost in each other once again.

It made no sense to miss someone before they were gone, and it was even more insane to miss them after only knowing them for thirty-six hours.

"I had no idea terraces made you this hot or I would have suggested it earlier." She grabbed my face, but I stilled before she pressed her lips back to mine.

"I have a double shift tomorrow. So I have to leave in the morning to get ready. I work the next two days."

"Oh" was all she said as her smile faded. Her gaze broke from mine for a minute before she lifted her head, a sad smile pulling across her lips instead of the playful one from a minute ago. "I didn't realize—"

"I didn't say," I said before pressing a kiss to her forehead. "Asking you to spend the day with me was a spur-of-the-moment thing. I hated leaving you last night and needed to see you again, and I didn't want to think about saying goodbye. Still don't."

"I actually get that." She laughed and shook her head. "I guess I'll have to sort out fun for the next two days alone."

I nodded and tried to smile back, even if the picture of her chatting at the bar with someone else while I was working at the station filled me with a confusing white-hot rage.

"I'm sorry. I managed to forget about it for most of the day, but..." I trailed off when she shook her head.

"Neither of us planned this. Or expected something beyond this week. So why don't we..." she said, pausing to feather her hands down my chest. Goose bumps followed her touch even though the air was thick and hot. "Appreciate this for the gift that it is." She shrugged. "We have until the morning, right?"

"Right." I slid my hand to the back of her neck. Those green eyes killed me as they held mine, translucent even in the soft light.

"Okay, good. There's still time to work on my vacation story."

A laugh slipped out of me. We both had quite a vacation story at this point.

"You're incredible, Kristina. Please know that and take it home with you. Don't ever let anyone make you think anything different again."

"Stop." She held up her hand. "That's a goodbye speech, and you said we have until the morning. None of that yet."

She tilted her chin toward one of the chairs. I nodded, surprised all of that had poured out of me, but it was true. I was almost tempted to leave while she was sleeping to avoid anything else falling out of my mouth before I could help it.

I dropped into one of the chairs, jerking back when she hopped on my lap.

"I wanted a cake with frosting, but frosted brownies aren't a bad substitute, I guess." She broke off a piece, licking her fingers again. "Just messy."

I grabbed her wrist and swallowed the brownie in her hand with one bite, sucking on her fingers as I pulled away.

"I may have a new appreciation for brownies after I leave this place," she said, her voice breathy and soft.

"When you leave, I may have a new appreciation for a lot of things." I tucked a lock of hair behind her ear.

"What's your favorite dessert?" she asked as she shifted on my lap, the lace of her panties rubbing across my leg with a soft scratch. My hand traveled up her thigh on pure instinct and need.

"Bizcocho Dominicano, Dominican cake. My mother always baked it for my birthday. My aunt would try, but it was never the same. Still good, though. She tried to keep things a little normal for me after...after everything. And I loved her for it."

I draped my hand over Kristina's nape, bringing her mouth back to mine with light kisses to distract from the sadness in her gaze.

"I don't think I've ever had it."

"It has a fruit filling and meringue icing. It's not a heavy cake. It tastes like..."

Home and simpler times I didn't like to think about but suddenly couldn't stop.

"Very sweet. But I never paid enough attention to how it was made. Brownies are enough to hold me over." I kissed her collarbone and brought her into my chest, trying to get my bearings from the storm of emotions swirling through me.

We were high on lust and great sex, and the endorphins were probably messing with our heads. It was the only explanation I could come up with that made anything close to sense. Still, when I thought of being at work, knowing she'd still be close enough to touch, my chest constricted so hard I had to clear my throat to breathe.

I'd go back to my life, and in a couple of days, she'd fly back to hers. Our time together wasn't meant to last. Finding Kristina was like spotting a shooting star or a rainbow. You appreciated its unexpected beauty before it faded away—like it was meant to from the beginning.

Flashes of time and vacations weren't supposed to affect daily life after they were over.

So why did nothing feel the same?

FIFTEEN
KRISTINA

Why was the thought of never seeing Leo again such a gut punch?

Friends and family had all reminded me—repeatedly—that my marriage was over long before we'd put the divorce in motion. Meaning before *I'd* started divorce proceedings because if I hadn't, I'd still be dating a husband who didn't want to treat me like his wife.

Despite how long we'd really been apart, I didn't want anything serious for a long time—if ever again—even if I decided to go on a date with someone in the distant future.

What Leo and I were doing was fun and easy—too easy. I bared myself to him, not just with my body, but I told him secrets I hadn't shared with anyone. But for some reason, I wanted to tell him.

I tried so hard to put up a good front when it was a lie that even I didn't believe. When I did confide in anyone, I left certain things out on purpose, both so they wouldn't worry about me or be disappointed in me for what I'd let continue far longer than I should have.

Our time together could still be counted in hours, but Leo made me feel beautiful and brave in a way no one else ever had.

Although it would be tough to say goodbye, I felt good about moving on with this stage of my life. Being alone was a reward not a punishment after what I went through, and I'd go home with my head held higher, even if my heart was a little heavy.

"Are you going to have time to get any sleep when you leave?" I asked as I lounged in bed with Leo, naked again with our legs entangled. If we were any closer, we'd be behind each other. I smiled at the thought before lifting my head.

"I may. It doesn't matter. I've learned to function on very little sleep. I'll probably get a couple of hours at the station between shifts." He traced circles on my back with his finger, relaxing me enough to make my eyes flutter with each swirl over my bare skin. "Are you throwing me out?" he teased and kissed the top of my head.

"No, of course not. I just feel guilty about you having to work a double shift with no sleep because of me."

"Being exhausted because I spent as much time with you as I could is a privilege, not a burden. And one I won't have past today, so I'll deal with it."

I pushed off his chest, propping my elbow against the pillow and resting my chin on my hand, spying the ridiculous yet genuine sadness in his gaze that felt all too familiar.

"What the hell is wrong with us?"

He laughed, shaking his head as he rubbed his eyes.

"I keep asking myself that same question. Since the moment I met you, I've been trying to find ways not to make you leave, and yet I'm the one who's leaving you first."

"No one is leaving anyone. We're more...parting ways. Going back to our old lives after a glorious vacation. Well, speaking for myself anyway."

"No, I had a glorious vacation, too." He shot me a lopsided grin that melted and squeezed my heart. "This is about as far from real life as I get. I've worked with some of the guys at the station for five years, and I've told you a shit-ton more than I ever told them about my past. No one's cared about my nomad lifestyle before."

"I've told you a lot too." I slid my finger up and down the vines of ink cascading over his ribs. I'd always been intrigued by tattoos, but I'd never known anyone who had this many. One arm was almost entirely covered from his shoulder to his wrist, with what looked like constellations on his opposite hip, all in black ink.

"It's cute how you can't stop touching my tattoos."

He chuckled when I narrowed my eyes at him.

"So, I'm cute again."

"I told you you're beautiful, but I can't help it if I find everything you do so damn adorable. I've just never seen anyone so fascinated before. Not that I'm complaining. Touch me wherever and however long you want, babe."

"What do these mean?" I smoothed my hand across his stomach and traced my fingernail along one of the star patterns.

"Zodiac signs. One is Capricorn for my mother, and one is Cancer for my father." His hooded eyes focused on where my fingers trailed the lines and stars connecting them. "These are just because I thought it looked cool." He lifted his arm with a laugh.

Without thinking about it, I leaned over to kiss one of the constellations, my pulse kicking up at his quick gasp when my lips lingered against his skin.

"It all looks *very* cool." I turned my head as I leaned against his stomach, running my thumb along the grooves of his abs.

He delved his hand into my hair, brushing his thumb back and forth across my cheek.

I pressed my hand into his hard stomach to hide the quiver

in my fingers. I tore my eyes away from his, the charge between us too much to take as I peppered kisses down his hip, flicking his skin with my tongue as I moved lower toward where his erection tented the sheets.

I smoothed the sheet down his legs, coasting my hand over the swell of his cock, hard and heavy against my palm.

"Don't tease me, gorgeous," he rasped, propping his hand behind his head as a wicked grin played on his lips.

"What fun would that be?" I raised a brow, inching my hand up and down. I scooted over, my mouth hovering right above what we both wanted. "Yeah?"

His shoulders jerked with a chuckle before he nodded.

"*Fuck* yeah."

I swirled my tongue over the tip before taking all of him in my mouth, the salty taste making my mouth water even more. I took my time, sucking and licking until he poked the back of my throat.

A strangled noise fell from his lips as he grabbed the back of my head, weaving his fingers around a fistful of my hair before pressing me closer as he bucked his hips off the bed.

I'd learned a lot about myself over the past two days. I was already aware of how affection-starved I was, but I'd forgotten what it was like to have someone crave my touch and my body and revel in how I made them feel. Every moan and curse Leo muttered as I worked him over with my tongue filled me with an intoxicating high.

I promised myself I'd never settle again, but after Leo left tomorrow morning, it would be impossible not to.

He not only gave me a great vacation story, but he'd become both an amazing memory and an unattainable standard.

"Kristina." He growled and sat up, pushing my shoulders back until he fell out of my mouth with a wet pop.

"Something wrong?" I asked, my breaths coming quick when I lifted my head.

"No, it's all very right, but come here." He sat up, leaning over to lift me up onto the pillows.

"As much as I love your mouth, I want to come inside you instead of down your throat. I need to feel you." He reached over to the nightstand, patting around before he found a condom and ripped off the edge of the foil, gliding it on before I could even offer to help.

"Jesus," he hissed when he swiped his finger across my core. "My cock in your mouth made you this wet? This is so fucking unfair."

I almost laughed when he grabbed the back of my head, hauling me to him and plundering my mouth before thrusting inside me. I pushed against him until we rolled over and I was on top, shifting my hips back and forth as Leo's eyes bored into mine.

"This okay?" I asked, biting back a smile at the deep furrow in his brow.

"Okay? You're ruining me, beautiful. I'm yours. Do whatever you want to me."

Something scratched at my throat at Leo saying he was mine. Maybe at this moment, but we were passing ships as the old saying went, no matter how much it would hurt when I couldn't see him in the distance anymore when this was all over.

The mattress squeaked under me as I pressed my hands against his chest for balance.

"Let me meet you halfway, baby." Leo sat up, clutching the back of my neck as he met me thrust for thrust. We fell into a sloppy kiss before my legs started to shake.

He groaned, swallowing my screams until my legs almost gave out under me. Before I knew it, I was on my back with Leo driving into me until he shuddered with his own release.

He kissed my cheek and plopped his head down on the pillow beside me.

"This is a bitch."

I laughed when he groaned into the pillow, hoping that would stop the burning in my nose. Getting choked up made no sense, but nothing about us made sense. Yet nothing had ever felt this right.

And nothing was more fucking unfair.

SIXTEEN
LEO

Considering the hour and a half of sleep I'd managed to get, I had no business being up this early. I pushed off the bed with a soft grumble and trudged over to the window.

I was just in time for sunrise. I pulled on my shirt and shorts as I peered out the window. The sky broke out into a dozen shades of pink and purple, the horizon stretching across the ocean and reflecting it all.

It was beautiful, but not as gorgeous as the woman behind me in bed, the one I couldn't look at when I opened my eyes, much less wake up to say I had to leave.

I never stayed long enough with anything or anyone to be upset over a goodbye. The loss I'd had as a teenager made me avoid attachments like the plague I grew up thinking they were. I hadn't been with Kristina long enough to become attached to her, explosive chemistry and amazing sex aside. Then why was I so damn hesitant to leave her?

Maybe it was the possibility of what could have been if things were different. My life was only my own. I had family and a few close friends who loved me despite how I didn't see or speak to them as much as I should. But at the end of every day, I was my only consideration.

Kristina had two kids and a life filled with friends and family back in New York. From what she'd shared with me, it was a life new enough to still be finding her way through it.

I liked to think that maybe crossing paths with me would make that easier when she went home. She deserved the best of everything, despite what her tool of an ex-husband made her believe.

I truly hoped she'd have that, even if I couldn't give it to her.

After the past hour of staring at the stucco ceiling over the bed, a dumb idea flashed in my mind. What if I asked to see her again? Flights to New York weren't that long. I had clusters of three to five days off sometimes, and it wasn't like I had to manage anything in my absence. I didn't have so much as a gold-fish to miss me if I decided to travel back and forth on a regular basis.

As much as the thought of giving whatever this was an actual chance tempted me, something stopped me. I couldn't expect her to drop everything for whenever I'd be able to see her, and after watching her come alive whenever she spoke about her girls, I knew she wouldn't want to. Putting her in that position would be selfish and as inconsiderate as her dick of an ex.

I knew there was an easier way, but even if I had nothing keeping me here, I couldn't move for a woman I'd just met. That was plain batshit crazy to even consider.

The thought of a hypothetical real chance with her both thrilled and scared the shit out of me.

The notion of loving someone so much that your body gave out because they were no longer in this world wasn't just terrify-ing, it had paralyzed me for my entire life. The chasm was sharp, instant, and irreparable, or so I'd believed until now.

Kristina was the first person to make me wish things were different. That *I* were different. It all came so easy with her, and from the moment we'd met, it was so damn difficult to let her out of my sight. She'd broken through an important wall before I even realized it, but getting too close would only end up hurting both of us. She deserved a man who could love her full time without years' worth of barbed wire around his heart.

As much as I hated the fuck out of it, that man couldn't be me.

"What time is it?"

I clenched my eyes shut at Kristina's gravelly voice, smiling despite myself at her drawn-out yawn.

"Six. I'm sorry I woke you, but I need to head out."

I slowly turned, my breath catching in my throat when her hazy green eyes zeroed in on mine, wide and glossy despite the tiny curve of a smile across her lips.

"Did you get enough sleep?"

My chest squeezed at the concern in her gaze, but sleep wasn't coming to me this morning. She'd be right there when I shut my eyes, along with the new nagging voice echoing in my brain, asking me what the hell I was doing with my life.

Maybe it wasn't new and I'd just learned to ignore it, but it had become deafening over the last few hours.

"I don't need that much sleep. I'll be fine." I tried to smile back and exhale over the tightening in my chest. I needed to be alone right now, even though it was the last thing I wanted.

She grabbed a T-shirt from the open suitcase next to her bed and slipped it over her head. It was baggy and long, but I still spotted the points of her nipples through the cotton. The need to climb back on top of her, spread her legs, and devour her as if she were my last meal—like I did over and over last night—had my feet pinned to the carpet and unable to move.

But it was the sad pull on her features that distracted me most of all and kept me from reaching for the doorknob to leave.

She smiled, cupping my cheek in her hand before she planted a soft kiss on the other one. I shut my eyes and grabbed her wrist on instinct, wanting to push her away and not let her go at the same time.

"Thank you," she whispered, leaning her forehead against my chin. "It's been an amazing couple of days. Thank you for..." She sucked in a long breath before lifting her head. "It's amazing how a man I only knew for a short time made me feel more like myself than anyone else. That's you I'm talking about, by the way."

I laughed at her narrowed eyes.

"You have a lot to give, Leo. I just hope that someday you'll stop keeping it to yourself. Even though I think you gave more to me than you expected."

I wanted to reply to that, but I couldn't. Everything was so spot-on, but any words I had for her were stuck in the back of my throat.

I took her face in my hands and kissed her, light closed-mouthed pecks lasting longer each time my mouth brushed hers, but we couldn't fall into that again. Reality came up with the sun, and there was nothing to do to fight that.

"I did. I couldn't help myself. And you," I began, dipping my head to meet her gaze, "you are going to give yourself a break when you get home. Fuck your ex and anyone else who doesn't treat you like the incredible woman that you are."

"Breaks are hard to come by," she said, chuckling as she darted her eyes from mine. "But I think I have a better handle on the rest. Thanks to you." We shared a smile before a heavy silence fell over us. "Be careful at work."

"Have a safe trip home." I kissed her forehead, holding her

face a little tighter before I finally let go. "At least I helped you make use of the space."

She laughed when I nodded toward the terrace.

"That you did. I was hoping to hit that big soaker bathtub, but maybe later. I'll see." She blew out a heavy breath before grabbing the back of my neck and pulling me in for another kiss, both of us stilling and probably afraid to ignite anything we couldn't, or shouldn't, see through.

"Goodbye, Leo."

I smoothed a lock of hair behind her ear and nodded.

"Goodbye, Kristina."

I didn't look back when I shut the door behind me. I ambled over to the parking lot, my footsteps on the ground the only sound other than the noisy chorus of cicadas.

That feeling of jumping out of my own skin was so potent, I almost itched.

I avoided planting roots for my entire life, but I'd never felt this lost.

"YOU'RE QUIET," ANDY, ONE OF THE PROBIES, SAID TO ME, GIVING me the side eye as he cleaned up the truck after our last call. I never was very chatty on shift here, but other than a grunt of hello and what I needed to say on the calls we set out on today, I was basically mute. I'd kept as busy as I could since I'd come in, but I was starting to crash.

"It's been a long day, and I'm exhausted. Sorry if I seemed rude. If I'm getting through the rest of this shift, I need some sleep. Come get me if you need anything." I slapped his arm and headed for the beds in the back of the firehouse.

Bartending at Turtle Bay was a hell of a lot easier than this, but that wasn't why my mind was fixed on my side gig today.

Wondering what Kristina was up to occupied most of my head-space when I let my mind wander, and I needed to stop.

I collapsed onto one of the beds, too tired yet too wired to shut my heavy eyes when I jerked my head toward my buzzing phone on the table next to me. I scooped it up with my heart in my throat, half hoping maybe it was Kristina reaching out even though our goodbyes today were final.

I groaned when I spotted my cousin's name on the screen. If I didn't pick up, he'd just keep calling, and if I wanted to snag even a little sleep, I had no choice but to answer.

"Hi, Gabe," I yawned into the phone.

"I guess you're on shift if you're yawning at five p.m. When you didn't text back this weekend, you had me worried. I'm the one responsible for making sure you stay on the grid."

"You did?" I held my phone away and went to my messaging app. Sure enough, three unanswered texts from my cousin stared back at me from the other night and yesterday.

I'd forgotten I'd put my phone on do not disturb the entire day to get the most out of every minute with Kristina, and the night before I had been too into her to care about anyone texting me, family or not. I'd probably missed other calls too, but I didn't feel like fishing around to find out.

"Sorry about that. I was out all day yesterday and had my phone on do not disturb."

"Out?"

I held in a groan, picturing the sly grin across his bearded mouth. Gabe was ten years older than me, already grown and out of my aunt and uncle's house by the time I moved in, but he was the closest thing I had to an older brother.

When I was finding my way after my parents' death, he was the one to set me straight whenever I'd stumble, kicking my ass when needed, while my aunt and uncle would step back to give me space.

It was a three-person job to handle me for many years, and all this time later, he was still the pain in the ass who reeled me in when I needed it.

"I met someone and took her out for the day. I turned my phone off so we'd have no interruptions."

"You're shitting me."

"I see women, Gabe. I'm not a monk."

"Oh, I know that, but being that into one to ignore everything for two days, she must be something extra special. Good for you."

"She *was* something special. She'll be on a flight back to New York the day after tomorrow. We had some fun, and then I had to go to work. Don't make it a big deal."

"I wouldn't," he scoffed, chuckling like the smug bastard he was, "if you didn't sound like someone ran over your puppy. If you liked her that much, why didn't you ask to see her again?"

"Because she has two kids at home. Long-distance wouldn't work, and after two days, it was ridiculous to even suggest it."

"I'm not saying propose marriage. But if you like her this much, it wouldn't hurt to chat back and forth after she leaves, no?"

"I can't give her anything real. And after what she's been through, that's what she deserves."

"Can't or won't? Come on, primo. All right, I won't press on that, but if she's leaving soon, why waste time at work? Stay with her until she leaves if you're so attached to her."

I groaned and sank my head deeper into the pillow.

"Well?" Gabe pressed as I tried to come up with an answer. With him, it was always too damn pointless to lie.

"Because why delay the inevitable and make it worse? Plus, I can't just blow off the second half of a shift."

"How many times have I heard you say that you're covering

for this one or that one? Cash it in. If you don't, you'll regret it. Fight me on it, but you know I'm right."

"Fuck off, Gabe," I muttered as my cousin's hearty laugh filled my ear.

"Thought so. A woman who can get you this out of sorts isn't someone you just had fun with. Stop worrying about what makes sense. Just go with it."

Just go with it. It was what I'd asked Kristina to do when we first met, but fear was holding me back now.

"Are you really okay with never seeing her again?"

"No," I answered so fast I surprised myself. "But it can't work when she goes home."

"But she's not home yet, primo. You can look back on these past few days with fondness or regret. Up to you."

SEVENTEEN
KRISTINA

"I love coming to the Keys. I can't believe you've never been here."

I nodded at Alex, the man sitting next to me at the bar who didn't take the hint that I wanted to eat and drink in peace. He seemed about my brother's age, late forties, but while Jake had a full head of hair, the sun's rays bounced off this man's bald head and right into my eyes.

Bald could be sexy, and my friend Buck had been shaving his head from the time we were in our mid-thirties since he found that less depressing than monitoring a growing circle on the top of his head. If this guy would let me get a word in edgewise, I would have asked if he brought sunscreen for his scalp as it looked red and raw.

"Hard to plan vacations with kids at home." I shot him a tight smile and took a sip of the fruity drink I'd ordered with my sandwich.

It was difficult not to mope around the resort after Leo left, but I was determined not to ruin what little time I had left here. I missed my girls and, although I'd only known him for a short time, missed Leo, but I fought to make the best of it.

I'd almost tried to book an early flight home but decided to enjoy the solitude and break from real life while I could, even if it drove me a little crazy at first.

I'd lounged on the beach and steered clear of the pool, not wanting to get sappy or sad from the sweet and hot memories I'd made on this trip. I even took a spur-of-the-moment snorkeling class this morning, mostly to snap photos of strange and different fish to show Emma when I got home.

I couldn't wait for her to climb in my lap and chew my ear off, and I hoped to convince my eldest daughter that I had fun and was relaxed and okay, maybe lessening her constant concern for me for at least the rest of the summer.

Until I went home tomorrow, all I wanted to do was relish the calm and quiet, and I would be if Alex would only move on to someone else.

The back of my neck burned, and my shoulders were crisp from a little too much sun. I took a quick glance down my body and laughed. I was a cluster of freckles from the neck down, which I supposed could pass for a Florida tan for a few days when I got home.

Alex laughed and I smiled, the man still oblivious that I wasn't listening. My heart had leapt three times tonight when I'd sworn I spotted a familiar pair of massive shoulders, but my stomach sank each time I noticed the absence of ink on their arms.

I picked up my phone and scrolled, not wanting to be rude, but I didn't want to make a scene by telling Alex to back off. Maybe the passive-aggressive way would work before I had to go loud and direct. I randomly clicked on my texts with Nicole, my heart seizing at the selfie Leo had taken of us before our day together.

I finally understood the saying don't be sad that it's over, be happy that it happened. I wasn't there yet, but I would be.

The chords of classic Madonna had played since I'd sat down. I enjoyed the music and watching the tipsy tourists sing off-key with drinks sloshing in their hands. I was no longer jealous of how much fun they were having or how carefree they seemed.

I'd had my own adventure. And I wouldn't trade it for anything.

The beat slowed to "Crazy for You," and I smiled at all the strangers making the most of the almost dark as the song suggested. One guy gave the girl in his arms a sudden and deep dip, and she let out a squeal.

I looked away in case they caught me staring. My plan was to slurp the rest of my drink and retreat to my suite balcony and Kindle for the rest of the evening, maybe calling room service one more time for memory's sake.

"Well, good night, Alex. Have a safe trip back home."

"Hey, what's the rush? We could dance too if you want. I saw you watching."

My meal threatened to come back up when I spotted the slimy grin on his face.

"No, I don't want to." I jerked my hand away and didn't muffle the huff falling from my lips.

"Hey," he said, holding up his hands in mock defeat. "I was just trying to be friendly since you were alone."

"She's not."

My heart dropped into my stomach at a familiar voice I had been sure I'd never hear again.

"She's with me." Leo grabbed the drink out of my hand and set it on the bar with a loud thump before pulling me in for a kiss. I stiffened, still in shock that he was here, but I melted against him after a few long and eager strokes of his tongue against mine.

Alex muttered something behind me, but I didn't turn or

care what he said or where he was. Finally grasping on to a tiny bit of my senses, I pressed my hands into Leo's chest and pushed him back.

"Wait, what..." I trailed off, breathless and clutching his shoulders. "What are you doing here? I thought you had to work."

"I found someone to cover for me." He picked up my hand and laced our fingers together as his arm roped around my waist. "I've done a lot of favors over the years, covering everyone's shifts when they needed it because I had nothing special going on. You, pretty lady, are very fucking special. And I won't leave you until I absolutely have to."

He flashed me a crooked grin as he pulled me closer.

"You didn't strike me as the jealous type." I jerked my head to where Alex had retreated behind me, biting back a smile at the scowl twisting his face.

"I didn't like the looks of that creep. It seemed like he couldn't take a hint, so I thought I'd just be as clear as possible that he should back the fuck off."

"Mission accomplished," I said, laughing as I wrapped my arm around his neck.

Leo laughed with me for a second before his mouth flattened to a hard line.

"So I'm with you until I drive you to the airport. That is," he said, tossing me a hopeful smile as he swayed us back and forth, "if you'll have me."

"Fuck yeah, I'll have you." I chuckled and dropped my head into his chest, breathing him in to make sure he was real.

"So beautiful," he whispered, bringing our joined hands to his chest as he studied me. "I think you caught a little more sun."

He dragged his gaze up and down my body, heating me up from the inside out.

"I see more freckles."

The air whooshed out of my lungs again. My reaction to this guy was so overpowering it made my head spin.

"I guess you aren't here to work, right, Reyes?"

Leo's boss regarded us with a smirk and shake of his head.

"No, Jimmy. I'm not," he said to his boss with his eyes still on mine. "I'm booked for the night."

"We're the only ones dancing at this end of the bar," I whispered, craning my neck to a few puzzled stares around us.

"Do you really think this is the weirdest thing we've done since we met?" he whispered back. "For the next few hours, we aren't questioning or overthinking a damn thing."

"Good point. So, what are we doing for the rest of tonight?"

"Well, I saw you had dinner already. I was going to ask if you were up for room service, maybe on the terrace? I enjoyed the last meal I had there." He raised a brow, sending more heat curling up my neck.

The last meal he'd eaten on the suite terrace was me.

"My flight is at noon," I said, hating having to inject any reality into this amazing fantasy I'd fallen back into.

"Plenty of time. Well, no, not nearly enough time. But," he sighed, cupping my chin and bringing me in for a kiss, "I'll take it."

EIGHTEEN
KRISTINA

My eyes blinked open right before my phone alarm blared next to me. My head was heavy as I lifted it up off the pillow, both from the lack of sleep and the reality of going home today hitting me.

Sex with Leo was as incredible as it always was, but I wasn't prepared for the sudden intensity. It had the euphoria of makeup sex with the undercurrent of despair for our impending goodbye.

This one wouldn't get an unexpected reprieve. I'd get out of his truck at the airport, and that would really be it.

The total time I'd known Leo was four days, rounded up with loose math. Not nearly enough time to form the dull pang in my gut at never seeing him again.

I was supposed to go home relaxed and refreshed, not confused and conflicted.

"Five more minutes?" he asked, pulling my arm toward him until I was draped over him.

"I need to finish packing. I planned to when I got back to the suite last night, but someone distracted me." A yawn stretched my mouth as I rested my head on his chest.

"So, I wore you out?" he teased as he kissed the back of my head.

"It was all that sun and snorkeling. It's a rough life down here."

His laugh rumbled against my cheek.

I pushed off his chest, flutters taking off in my stomach at his wide grin. I wrapped the sheet around me and took a deep breath.

"I know we talked about it, a little anyway. But why did you come back?"

He averted his gaze toward the gray early morning light leaking through the window.

Before Leo surprised me at the bar, our goodbye had seemed very final. There was no discussion about seeing each other again or keeping in touch, which I took as a given, considering we lived thousands of miles apart with completely different lives.

I'd resolved to file him away as a sweet memory, even if watching him walk out of the suite had hurt more than it should have. I still didn't expect anything more from him now and couldn't offer him anything after I left.

Yet, when I'd heard his voice last night, my heart was ready to burst out of my chest with joy. But as great as it was to get more time, it would still end the same way.

"Because," he started, exhaling a long breath before dragging his gaze to mine, "I knew if I didn't get as much time with you as I could, I'd regret it. If this is all I get," he said, tapping my chin with his knuckle, "I didn't want to waste a second."

"Listen," I started, pulling the sheet around me as I sat up. "Maybe we could..."

I trailed off at the pinch in Leo's brow. I didn't blame him as I didn't have a clue as to what I was about to say either. This wasn't a second chance at something more, yet a yearning stirred in my belly. But I was still clueless as to more *what*.

I was saved by the buzz of my phone on my nightstand, spotting my brother's number at the top of the screen.

I picked up the phone, my eyes still fixed on Leo as I pressed the green button to answer.

"Hey, everything okay? I know you need my flight number, but it's early."

"Mommy, it's me." Emma giggled. "Move the phone away from your ear."

"You want me to put you on speaker?" I stretched the phone out in front of me, sucking in a horrified gasp when I realized I was on FaceTime.

When I glanced at the mirror screen, my relief that I had a sheet covering me was short-lived when I realized that Leo was in the picture. I moved the phone closer to me and scooted away from him on the mattress, but Emma's puzzled gaze let me know I was too late.

"Are you having a sleepover?" she asked.

Leo buried his face into a pillow as his shoulders shook.

"Um, not really."

Shit. How did I explain being in bed with a strange man to my six-year-old? I prayed her sister couldn't see the screen because she was old enough to realize her mother was full of crap.

"I went snorkeling yesterday." I cleared my throat and moved up on the bed. "And I got lots of fish pictures for you."

"Did you see Dory and Nemo?" Her eyes grew wide. "Did you have big goggles?"

I blew out a long breath of relief, thanking God for my little girl's squirrel-like attention span.

My panic ceased enough to quell the tremor in my hands and shut off the phone camera.

"Not exactly Dory and Nemo but all kinds of fish I'd never seen that close up before. Yes, I had goggles. I can't wait to tell you all about it."

"Yay! I miss you, Mommy. Grandma, Unca Jake, and Aunt Peyton are fun, but it's not the same."

"I am glad to hear all the donuts didn't make you totally forget me."

"Nope, I'll see you later. Mommy's on the phone, and she's having a sleepover!"

"A sleepover?" I heard my brother ask.

"Yes, there was a guy sitting next to her in her bed when she answered the phone. I don't know his name, though."

I dropped my head into my hands after I heard the phone drop.

"Hello," Peyton said, chuckling. "Your poor brother looks like he just sucked on a lemon. How much did she see?"

"Enough to have to figure out an explanation before I get home."

"Oh, I cannot wait. Text me the flight number."

"I will when I get to the airport. Talk to you later."

"Oh, you absolutely will." I shook my head at Peyton as I ended the call and glowered at Leo as he cracked up, his head resting on his knees.

"This is not funny." I shoved his shoulder. "Thank God it was Emma. I would have scarred her older sister."

"Well, you still need a better explanation than *not really* before you land."

"No kidding." I pressed my palms against my eyelids. "So much for keeping this to myself."

I laughed until I spotted Leo's smile fade.

"What I meant was—"

"Stop. I know what you meant." He grabbed my hand in both of his, bringing it to his lips. "When I picked out your drink, I never expected all of this after. But I am not mad at any of it." He smiled with a sadness in his eyes I felt in my bones and shook his head. "Not even a little."

"Big same." I squeezed his hand. "What if we...maybe texted once in a while?" I shrugged. "Just a friend checking in on another friend."

"Friends?" Leo huffed out a laugh. "Is that what we are?"

"I don't know what we'd call us, or this. A vacation fling doesn't seem right. But I don't want to get out of your truck at the airport and not speak to you ever again. If that's not what you want, that's okay too—"

"I don't want to not speak to you ever again either, but I don't want to disappoint you. I'm flaky and in my head a lot. My cousin tracks me down when he doesn't hear from me, likes to brag he's in charge of keeping me on the grid."

"You're not flaky." I moved closer to him on the bed. "I think you may be a little lost, which after what you went through is very understandable. Maybe I can help keep you on the grid too sometimes. Silly meme back and forth just to check in?"

I lifted my shoulder in an exaggerated shrug.

"I think I can swing that." He cupped my cheek, kissing the corner of my mouth before running his lips down my neck.

"This is still a bitch." He groaned against my shoulder. "If we could talk without any expectations on either side, then yes, I'd love to keep in touch with you."

"I need to pack." I pulled the sheet with me, a cramp in my neck from holding it in place and not turning to a naked Leo behind me.

Sex now, after Leo drew a proverbial line in the sand as to what we could be to each other, which was nothing, seemed wrong.

As uninhibited as I'd been with Leo up until this point, it didn't come as easily now. Our impending goodbye punctured a big hole in the bubble we'd enjoyed living in the past couple of days.

We dressed in silence. I felt Leo's eyes on me as I packed, while words unspoken hovered over us. We said all we needed to say, yet it still seemed as if we were holding back.

He carried my bags out to his truck and loaded them in the back, hurrying over to the passenger side to open my door.

He shrugged, his wry but sad smile getting me right in the chest.

It shouldn't have been this hard to say goodbye or feel as if I was leaving him behind as he drove out of the parking lot.

"Looks like my flight is on time," I said, taking in Leo's perfect profile as he kept his eyes on the road. I stared at him for a few long beats, tempted to snap a picture without him noticing. I had our selfie and his license to remember him by, and that would have to be enough.

"Good, I'm sure your family is anxious for you to get home."

He didn't turn his head as his truck rolled to a stop outside the terminal. I climbed out of the cab as Leo shot out of the driver's seat to grab my suitcase.

"Thank you. For the ride and the help and…everything."

"It's all my pleasure. It was, anyway."

I nodded, darting my eyes away from the sad curve of his lips.

"We'll talk," I offered, hating how desperate I sounded but not wanting to bid him a permanent goodbye.

"Sure," he said with a noncommittal lilt to his response.

"Thanks for everything. The Keys promised an adventure, and I guess I got one." I sputtered out a laugh.

He took my face in his hands and covered my mouth with a soft kiss, lingering long enough to halt my heartbeat. He smiled into the kiss as he pulled away, sliding his hand to the back of my neck and giving it a squeeze.

"Remember what I said when you get home."

"Remember what I said after I go. Take care of yourself, Leo."

"You too, Kristina. And," he sighed, shutting his eyes for a second, "thank you. This was an adventure for me too. It's been amazing to know you."

I smiled through the sting in my chest as I grabbed the handle of my suitcase and dragged it toward check-in.

It was both the best and worst thing he could have said. We were a moment in time—moment an all too perfect term. And now that moment was over.

I didn't check to see if Leo was watching me walk away. Forward had to be my destination, and I could only hope my foray into glorious fiction would push me into a better reality.

NINETEEN
KRISTINA

"**K**ris, over here!"

I turned toward my sister-in-law's voice as I exited the airport terminal. Peyton waved her hands over her head, her round belly, slightly bigger than I remembered from only a few days ago, straining against the long tank she wore over denim shorts.

"My brother sent his pregnant wife to come pick me up?" I padded over to the back of her car to shove my bags into the open trunk.

"His pregnant wife wanted the scoop before I took you home and we had to keep it PG." She clasped her hands under her chin. "You look so amazing. Pretty and tanned and...maybe rested from your sleepover?"

I groaned when her brows jumped.

"Emma didn't let that drop, did she?"

"Nope. She said she only saw your friend for a second, but he had drawings on his arm." She brought me in for a hug after I closed the trunk. "Everyone is waiting for you, so I wouldn't be able to get any of the good details. We're taking the long way home."

I said nothing as I piled into the passenger seat, refusing to acknowledge her wide grin. When I dragged my gaze to hers, her brown eyes danced as she tapped on the steering wheel.

"All this excitement isn't good for the baby."

She waved a hand at me and started the engine.

"I can't help it if I'm excited for you. I know how hard it was for you toward the end. My husband should only know what an asshole Colin was to you."

"Oh, I heard from Colin. He called to let me know what a selfish, reckless thing it was to vacation alone when I had kids to consider."

Peyton grunted as she changed lanes.

"You should really think about letting Jake kick his ass."

"It's all over and not worth Jake's time and energy. I can handle Colin. I told him to basically fuck off. Then," I exhaled, biting back a smile, "Leo gave me my third orgasm of the day, and I was able to relax."

"Third?" She glanced at me, her eyes saucer-wide. "*Holy shit.* Now that is what I call a spectacular vacation. I have so many questions, but first, when are you going to see him again?"

My stomach twisted at her innocent question. It was hard to match my sister-in-law's joy over meeting someone special on my vacation when I was trying to get over the disappointment of probably never seeing or hearing from him again.

"I'm not. He lives in Florida. I have two kids at home and can't do a long-distance relationship with someone I just met. Plus, he doesn't do that."

"Doesn't do that? What do you mean?"

She turned to squint at me when we had to stop for traffic.

"He's moved around a lot. He had a rough past, and he's... unsettled. But..." I breathed out a long sigh and shifted toward the window.

"But what?"

"He was so amazing. Sweet and considerate and open. As you can imagine, that was a novelty for me."

"And hot," she added. "Nicole sent me the picture when I texted her to see how she was feeling." I had to laugh at her dropped jaw. "You looked good together. It was cute how he pulled you into his side like that."

I shrugged, looking back out the window. There were no palm trees or views of a sandy horizon. I was back home, and this was reality—or it would be when I saw my girls.

I couldn't help the guilt triggered by the sad pang in my gut as my mind kept drifting to what Leo might be doing now.

"It's better not to keep in touch."

"Who are you trying to convince, you or me?" Her brows shot up as she kept her eyes on the road. "What's upsetting you?"

"It's ridiculous that I miss him since I hardly knew him to begin with."

"You connected. Sometimes that just happens. It's a mix of chemistry and fate, sort of like your brother and me." Her smile turned wistful. "That inexplicable pull and the rush when you're just in the same room together."

I laughed at her audible sigh.

"I'm serious. Finding someone who makes you feel that way is everything, and there's no right time frame for it to happen. Not everyone experiences that, so even if you turn out to be right and nothing comes of it, consider yourself lucky. Instalove is like being struck by lightning."

I snickered at her raised brow.

"Love is not what happened. You and Jake are just so disgustingly in love that you force it on people."

"No. I mean, while that's true, it sounds like you had something special for however long it was, so you don't have to downplay being sad that it may be over."

"It *is* over. I asked to keep in touch, and he didn't seem all that interested. Look, let's call it what it was. He paid attention to me. I wasn't used to that, so my emotions are confused. And he was *very* attentive, with everything."

Peyton bunched up her shoulders as if she were about to scream.

"I have a strong feeling you'll see him again—somehow. I bet you're wrong that you won't hear from him."

"I'd be surprised," I said with a yawn, fatigue slamming into me thanks to the confusing concoction of feelings and lack of sleep. We had been too busy getting reacquainted and then saying goodbye to get any rest last night. The sad intensity of it all drained me.

The bittersweet memories of my time with Leo made all the unexpected and confusing heartache worth it.

"Maybe this is supposed to be like a *Bridges of Madison County* type of thing. You know, something beautiful that's not meant to be."

That movie always made me cry. Why didn't she just leave to be with the real love of her life? But now that I was an adult and had responsibilities that took precedence over epic romance, I pitied Meryl Streep's character even more.

"They were together in the end, if you remember."

"No, they weren't," I said, rolling my eyes at my sister-in-law. "Sharing the same final resting place isn't being together."

"Semantics." She shrugged as she pulled into my driveway behind my car.

An odd relief washed over me at finally being home. My boring gray shutters almost seemed vibrant, and I smiled at the new additions to Emma's rock garden along the walkway.

Everything looked the same but seemed different. Maybe *I* was different. Things didn't seem so hopeless, other than the lingering question of if I'd ever cross paths with Leo again.

I'd done something for myself, and not only did I not feel an ounce of guilt about it, I was also proud of myself for seeing it through.

Most of all, I was happy to have met a wonderful man who'd pointed out all the ways I'd been selling myself short.

Things would change, or at least I would give myself a break sometimes, and I would finally put my marriage and all the work I'd put into it behind me.

"Mommy!" Short arms wrapped around my thighs right after I almost fell over from the impact.

I turned to scoop Emma up. She was still small enough to carry and cuddle with, and as she burrowed her head into my neck, her long raven-colored ponytail draping down her back, I let my chin rest on her shoulder and breathed her in.

"I missed you so much," I told her and squeezed my arms tighter around her little torso. She giggled and squirmed in my arms.

"I missed you too! Unca Jake bought bagels. I saved one for you and one for your friend."

I glanced over her shoulder at Peyton, holding her fist to her mouth to cover a laugh.

"My friend lives in Florida, so he didn't come back with me."

"Oh," she said, her dark brow knitting together as she studied me, disappointment in her innocent face. Her hair was as dark as my mother's, only my daughter's was still naturally that way. It was a stunning contrast with the light-blue eyes she shared with her grandfather and uncle.

My baby was too gorgeous, and we were all too wrapped around her beautiful finger.

"Well," she started, those eyes narrowing at me as I braced myself for what her next question could be. "Since he's not here, can I eat his?"

I turned to my brother's deep rumble behind me.

"I'll bet that's not what you thought she'd ask."

Emma kicked her legs against my stomach when Jake tickled her neck.

"Welcome home, baby sister." He planted a kiss on my temple and headed over to Peyton's trunk.

"Thanks, big brother. You don't have to get my bags. I can do that."

"No worries." He kissed his wife, giving her belly a quick caress before he lifted my bags out of the back. They were always cute enough to be nauseating, but I was happy for them. After his own miserable marriage imploded, he never expected to want to be with anyone else, but he'd lit up ever since he met Peyton.

I'd never thought it was possible for me after my divorce. I'd written off any kind of second chance for me, but meeting Leo gave me a spark of hope. Even if that chance couldn't be with him, it was still possible.

My silly heart was still set on him, but in time, that would fade. It was something I both dreaded and hoped for.

I set Emma down, picking up her hand and swinging our arms as we made our way inside.

"Welcome back, sweetheart." My mother rushed over to me and brought me in for a quick hug, pushing back to search my face. I cringed at the smile tugging at her lips.

"What?"

"Nothing, you just look so beautiful. And relaxed. Exactly what I was hoping for."

"Glad to know you were all so anxious to get rid of me," I laughed, searching the living room for my firstborn.

"Chloe is upstairs with Mikey, yelling at that video game." She chuckled. "I told her we'd get her when you came home, in case you wanted to talk to us first about—anything."

"Mommy's friend didn't come home with her, so I can have

his bagel." Emma dropped my hand and raced into the kitchen as my mother examined me with narrowed eyes.

"If that's the *anything* you wanted to talk about, I'm sorry to disappoint you, but there's nothing. We had fun for a few days, and now I'm home and he's still in Florida. And that's all there is."

I held in a groan at my mother's slow nod.

"I see. Shame, though. He's handsome."

I was going to kill Peyton.

"Peyton showed you?"

"She did, but don't be mad at her. We were all thrilled for you. You looked happy and relaxed for once." She tapped my chin. "And that"—she patted her chest—"made me happy. Even if it was only for a few days, like you said."

She lifted a shoulder, that dismissive shrug she would give us as kids when she didn't quite believe us.

"It was."

Mom nodded again before heading into my kitchen.

I hung my purse on one of the hooks on my coatrack, letting out a frustrated breath. It would be easier to move on if my family stopped being so damn happy for me.

I fished my phone out of the bottom of my purse and turned to head up the stairs to get Chloe, jumping when my phone buzzed against my hand.

Leo: *Hey, just checking that you got home okay.*

I stared at the screen, falling back against my banister in shock. A stupid hope stirred in my belly that I didn't need, but a smile ripped across my face anyway.

Me: *I did. Thank you for checking on me. My daughter saved a bagel for you, thinking I was bringing my friend home with me.*

The minute I sent it, regret made me freeze. After feeling so free with Leo while we were together, I hated the need to dissect a text now that we were apart.

Leo: *I guess she figured that's what you do after a sleepover. She sounds sweet, just like her mom.*

"Hey, you're home!"

Chloe's voice wafted down the stairs, followed by the thunder of teenage footsteps from her and my nephew.

"I am." I brought her in for a hug, both delighted and concerned by her relieved exhale as she held me tighter.

"Hi, Aunt Kris." My nephew, Mike, waved behind her. His voice seemed to dip an octave each time I saw him, the crystal-blue eyes and sharp planes of his jaw so much like his father.

I leaned in with Chloe still in my arms to kiss his cheek, jerking back with an exaggerated gasp. "Is that stubble?"

He blushed, running his hands over his jaw. "A little, I guess. How was Florida?"

"It was great, and I'm glad to be home." I reached over to squeeze his shoulder. "Go attack the rest of the bagels or whatever else is in the kitchen with Emma, I'll be right there."

I patted Chloe's back until she let go. She was always a serious kid, but her smiles were so muted now. That was high on my list of things to work on or try to fix upon my return.

"I'm glad you're home."

"I'm glad I'm home too, kiddo." I kissed her forehead. "So glad, I won't give you any crap for staying up all night with your cousin, as I'm sure you did every night since I left."

"It's summer, Mom," she said, rolling her eyes before following Mike into the kitchen.

I tapped my finger against the screen after my daughter's departure.

Before I could chicken out, I searched for the photo I'd sent Nicole and shot it to Leo.

Me: *That's very sweet of you to say. She's a thoughtful little mush. I thought you might like to have this.*

I almost added, "To remember me by."

I threw my phone onto the hallway table and joined my family.

Florida needed to stay in Florida.

TWENTY

LEO

Two months later

"How about a little heat up in here?"

Gabe rolled his eyes at me as I fiddled with the knobs on the SUV console, leaning backward to feel the warmth running up my back from his heated seats.

"Is your blood that thin now, primo?" Gabe teased.

"I think so," I said, cramming my hands into the front pocket of my hoodie as we headed to the hospital.

Temperatures in the thirties and forties were average for late September in Upstate New York, but I'd been away from New York and any real shift in seasons long enough to get a chill from the slightest bite in the air. Florida did get occasional cooler days, and we'd all shiver and bundle up as if it were the dead of winter.

"I need you to prepare for what you'll see." Gabe's face was as stoic as his tone as he shot a quick glance at me.

I held back an eye roll. My uncle's condition was serious

enough to tell, not ask, me to find the first flight and get here as soon as possible, but I didn't need to be treated with kid gloves or condescension.

"I've taken care of enough stroke patients to have an idea of what to expect when I see tío Joe."

"I'm talking about what to expect from *both* of them. Mom's Parkinson's has progressed a lot more than she's probably told you."

I nodded, guilt and anxiety now swirling around in my gut, not because of what I was about to see, but how I should have seen it a hell of a lot sooner.

I'd never gone this long without seeing my aunt and uncle, but I'd been so in my head the past couple of months, even for me, that I hardly saw anyone outside of work, which I did all the damn time.

I'd signed up for extra shifts from both jobs to distract myself from the woman I didn't want to remember but couldn't stop thinking about.

We hadn't spent enough time together for me to miss her this much, but she ran through my mind all the time. Our time together was as amazing as it was short, and when she left, I realized how empty my life really was.

Not just because she wasn't in it, because no one was—not really. The comfortable distance I'd learned to keep everyone at from a young age didn't seem so comfortable anymore.

And although I was here on a family emergency, knowing Kristina was only a couple of hours away had gnawed at me since my plane landed.

I had enough to worry about on this trip and shouldn't have been thinking about her to begin with, the same as I should have deleted her number and the photo of us right after she sent it, taking it as the goodbye she probably meant it to be.

But I couldn't do that or stop looking at that damn photo.

An ominous hold had taken over me since the call from my cousin. I was about to pay the price for my months-long distraction.

"No, tía Lucia never said anything. She said her hands shake but she's okay."

My cousin grunted as we made our way into the hospital parking lot.

"She shakes, she falls, and she's having a harder time getting words out. Now they *both* have trouble speaking." Gabe shut off the engine and scrubbed a hand down his face. "Although at least she still can."

"Shit," I said more to myself as my head fell back on the seat. "She never told me, but she shouldn't have had to. I shouldn't have waited so long to visit."

He waved a hand at me.

"I didn't mean to put a guilt trip on you. I asked you to come, and you did without a second of hesitation. And the Parkinson's progression has been relatively fast, so it's new and tough to see, even for me."

I nodded, a little of the tension coiling in my stomach loosening, but the guilt wouldn't let up.

"They both always seemed larger-than-life."

"Happens when people get older. I'm just grateful we have them as long as we do."

His eyes darted away for a moment, a sad smile drifting across his mouth when he turned back toward me. I'd known my aunt and uncle more than twice as long as I'd known my own parents, and they'd become my mother and father in every sense of the words over the years.

I was grateful to have them too, and I should have shown them a hell of a lot more than I'd done for my entire life.

I hoped I'd have a chance to make up for it.

"Have the kids seen him yet?"

Gabe shook his head. He lived about fifteen minutes from his parents with his wife and two kids. If my aunt and uncle were as bad as he was warning me they were, it was going to be hard to take care of them and still be there for his family.

"Jessenia helps her grandmother all the time, but she isn't going to know how to react to seeing her favorite person bedridden. Louie is a lot like you, doesn't sit still but takes in all that's going on. We explained it to them last night, and they haven't said much."

After Gabe parked, I followed him to the hospital entrance. I could feel the tension radiate off him as we walked.

"I won't stay away so long again," I told Gabe when we stepped onto the elevator. "At forty, I should grow the fuck up, no?"

He shook his head when the elevator dinged on our floor.

"As I said, I wasn't getting on you for not visiting in a while. It's not a question of growing up, but we'd like to see you slow down a little so you could give yourself a chance to enjoy your life. All we've ever wanted was for you to be happy, no matter where you are." He slapped my arm and pointed to the open doorway of one of the rooms.

"Leo's here!" Tía Lucia's eyes grew wide when they met mine. She sat in a chair at the foot of the bed, her brown helmet of hair we always teased her about tucked under a kerchief. I guessed she hadn't been keeping up with the weekly salon appointments she'd always made a priority, and it already hurt to see her looking so unlike herself.

She scooted to the edge of the vinyl cushion chair to get up. My chest squeezed when she tried to hold on to the chair arms to stand but couldn't get enough of a grip to pull herself up.

"Ción, tía. Easy, I'll come to you."

I knelt in front of her, taking her thin, quivering hands in mine before kissing her cheek. "Of course, I'm here."

"D-dios te bendiga." My stomach dropped at how much she struggled through her usual blessing and the helplessness in her glossy, frustrated eyes.

I swiveled my head when the bed creaked behind me.

Gabe was right. There wasn't any training that could have prepared me for what I was seeing. Instead of boisterous and vital, the man in the bed was a shell of whom I'd always known my uncle to be.

The corner of his mouth drooped as his entire side slumped into the mattress. His eyes were glassy as he moved his head back and forth, his chest heaving up and down.

I leaned over to check where the IV penetrated his arm, an urge from the nurse in me. My eyes followed the line up to where the machine ticked and whooshed, filtering whatever was in the bag into his veins. His arm still looked strong, like he could pop up and slap me on the back as he always did whenever he saw me.

A frustrated growl erupted from his throat when his hand on his good side floundered against the mattress as he attempted to sit up.

I squeezed my aunt's hands and stood, shaking my head as I made my way over to the bed. Whereas my aunt seemed frail, tío Joe was still solid and stocky, which probably made his frustration over the loss of control over his own body even more difficult to bear.

"Hey, tío. Don't get up on my account, you lie down and rest." His eyes lit up as he peered up at me, the smile he couldn't form with his mouth reflecting in his eyes.

"You must have rushed here. Did you eat, mijo?"

I shot a look at Gabe. He closed his eyes and nodded. Her soft voice was strained as if it was taking all her strength to get it out.

"I'll eat later, tía. Don't worry about me."

"That's hard." She laughed, looking between Gabe and me. "I always worry about my boys."

Gabe smiled, a tiny chuckle jerking his shoulders. I'd always been close to them, but when they'd had to take me in, I'd felt like an intruder. I was blood, but not their own. Gabe and I always looked enough alike to pass for brothers, but I fought hard not to belong with them at first.

My anger at losing my parents had made me lash out at the beginning before I realized how fortunate I was that they chose to take care of an emotionally fucked-up and ornery teenager. They'd always treated me like a son, not a nephew.

And like any son, I shouldn't have been this far away from the only parents and family I had left—especially when they needed me.

Since whatever I'd had with Kristina, I'd felt lost. Making it a point not to settle down was my lifelong MO, but it just seemed wrong now. A woman I hardly knew grounded me in a way that I'd fought against since I was a teenager, and when she left, and I was back to being the loner I always was, it didn't seem so natural anymore—if it ever was.

In truth, I hated it. I hated the daily solitude without anything or anyone to look forward to—only drifting from day to day without a purpose beyond work. Even if I wasn't meant to keep her, Kristina showed me that living a solitary life wasn't working if I wanted to *have* a life.

My parents wouldn't have wanted this. They'd hate the thought of me always alone and would want me to take care of my family like they'd wanted to take care of me but didn't get the chance.

It was the quickest and most final decision I'd made in decades. This was where I belonged, and my next move would finally be a permanent one.

We all turned to a soft knock at the door.

"Hi, Mr. Reyes. How are you feeling?" The doctor, I supposed, came up to my uncle's bed, squeezing the wrist tío could still move.

He was tall and lanky and appeared to be young, younger than Gabe and me, at least. His wide smile, brightened by the contrast of his dark skin, seemed to make my uncle relax. Tío Joe's shoulders softened before he managed a shaky nod.

"Good. And how are you feeling, Mrs. Reyes?"

"Good, my nephew is here."

"I'm more or less forgotten now," Gabe joked as he leaned against the wall. I could only nod, still bothered by my aunt's faint whisper of a voice.

I'd only spoken to her last week. How fast was her condition progressing? Maybe the stress of my uncle's stroke was making it worse.

"Nice to meet you. I'm Dr. Walker." He extended his hand. "I'm the attending neurologist on staff."

"I'm Leo. The nephew." I mustered a smile for my aunt's sake and took his hand. "Nice to meet you."

"You as well. Gabe, would you mind stepping outside with me for just a moment?" Dr. Walker asked my cousin.

Gabe motioned for me to follow him.

"I don't think it's going to be news that Mr. Reyes will probably need extensive therapy. He was strong before the stroke, so that should work in his favor, but my recommendation is a rehab facility where he can get the most therapy and round-the-clock care."

"I figured that." Gabe rubbed his eyes. "There's one a couple of exits away that we were hoping could accept him for therapy."

I didn't like the way the doctor's mouth flattened to a line when he nodded.

"Mrs. Reyes isn't my patient, but even after therapy, your father is going to need additional care, and your mother appears to need therapy of her own. Have you ever thought of an assisted living facility for them both in the long-term?"

"Eventually, yes. But there aren't any close by. My wife and I did some research, and the only one we found with both the rehab my father would need and assisted living for them both is near Albany."

"That is actually the one I was going to suggest. I'm hopeful your father will make a great recovery, but it's going to be a long time. And if your mother's illness progresses, that's a lot for a family to deal with."

"Albany is two hours away. I can't go back and forth like I'd need to. Even if they're being taken care of, I wouldn't want them alone all the time."

"What if they had family close by?" I asked.

Gabe squinted at me. "Most of our family is still in New York City. Washington Heights isn't close."

"What if *I* was close by? Nothing is keeping me in Florida. I can transfer anywhere." I glanced back at the doctor. "This is the best solution for them both, right?"

"I believe so, yes. They'd both get the care they needed, and you wouldn't have to worry about them living alone."

"Then it's settled."

"Wait," Gabe said, holding up his hand. "Let's think about this for more than a minute."

"Of course," Dr. Walker said. "I want to keep Mr. Reyes here for the next four days so I can determine the rehabilitation he needs. You have time to consider it or even visit the facility if you'd like. I have a few patients there and I visit once per week, so I can vouch that it's a great place and my patients have thrived there. Let me know if you have any questions."

I waited for the doctor to head back into my uncle's room before I turned to Gabe.

"Okay, so let's talk about this."

"Leo, we don't even know how bad Dad is yet."

"You thought he was bad enough to tell me to book the first flight to New York. And you were absolutely right. Tía's voice was fine last week, so this could be stress or her condition is getting worse. If this place can give them the therapy they need and take care of them both, why are you hesitating?"

He crossed his arms, regarding me with a deep furrow on his brow.

"You're really going to up and move—and stay? I know you mean well at the moment, but you...get antsy in one place for too long. If we move them both to Albany, I can't always be close if something is wrong."

"And that's why I would be close. Keeping a life for only myself is a selfish way to live, and I'm ready to stop. We're family, let me do for all of you what you did for me."

Gabe let out a long exhale and nodded.

"Let's see how bad it really is at the end of the week, and while Dad is in here, we can both take Mom to her doctor and see what we're dealing with. She was only there a week ago, but things change in a week, I guess."

"They do. They change in days, primo."

"I guess I could tolerate seeing you more." His lips twitched into a smile.

"Thanks, cousin. That gets me right here." I pressed a hand to my chest. "I'll have to trade my truck for one with ass warmers if I'm going to deal with winters up here again."

"And the winters up here suck and last forever. You really want to give up all that sun and sand for this?"

"Sun and sand aren't so great after a while when it's only you."

I tried to smile when Kristina flashed in my mind again. If I moved back to New York, I'd be close enough to see her if I wanted to. God knew I did and had wanted to reach out to her a million times since I'd dropped her off at the airport. If only I hadn't convinced her that I was a flake who wouldn't keep in touch and got her to agree that we wouldn't be anything after she left.

But if I did move back to New York, I could contact her and ask to see her again, maybe even get a real chance with her. I shook my head and scrubbed a hand down my face.

I had other things to worry about before I could daydream over something and someone that would probably never happen.

"You looked miles away just now." Gabe chuckled, looking me over as we ambled back to the room.

"Just thinking of all the hoodies I'll get to wear again when I move back up to my arctic roots."

"Right. Doesn't that woman you met live upstate too?"

"Not now." I shook my head, not wanting to address Gabe's question or his smirk in my periphery.

"No problem," Gabe said, squeezing my shoulder. "One big move at a time."

TWENTY-ONE

KRISTINA

One month later

"There must be someone you've liked. At least a little." Nicole shook her head at me from across my kitchen table, the pleading in her eyes a mix of sympathy and frustration as she studied me over the rim of her coffee mug.

"Meeting men on an app isn't exactly a romantic setup."

"But it's practical. *If* you'd give it a chance." She set the mug down and arched a brow. "They can't all be hot bartenders slash firemen at the beach."

"That—" I said, taking a deep breath once I noticed the defensive edge in my tone. "That has nothing to do with anything."

"Right. Why don't you just text him already?"

"Okay, I'm not having this conversation again." I rose from my chair to put my empty mug in the sink. "It's been months. I was shocked he texted the one time. Let it go."

"I will when you do."

I groaned, crossing my arms as I leaned against the sink.

"Is this why you stopped by for coffee on the way back from the gym? To scold me about my crappy love life?"

"Not completely. I just thought that as Colin has the girls since you're at the hospital tonight, we could talk freely."

"You act like there is something juicy enough that my kids couldn't hear. The guys I've met have been fine. But nothing has felt like a real date. I know, we have plenty of friends who've met their husbands on a dating app, but I can't get into it."

"What can't you get into? I agree it's not the romantic meet-cute everyone dreams of, but it could work if you'd open your mind a bit on these dates."

"Dates that feel like job interviews. The last guy asked me how long I thought I had left in my childbearing years."

"You can't be serious." Nicole's face twisted in disgust.

"As a heart attack. I said zero since I am not interested in having any more children. I think that's probably part of the issue, dating app or not. Even though the men I've met are around my age, they seem to be in a rush to settle down and have kids. All I want is someone to have dinner and some good conversation with, and so far, I'm coming up empty."

"I'm sure every man over forty isn't using the dating app simply to find someone to knock up and marry. You've gone on four dates. Isn't there a box you can check saying that you don't want children?"

"I did check it, but the last two guys thought they could convince me otherwise. The last one even said, 'What's one more?' Like Chloe and Emma were potato chips."

Nicole burst out laughing.

"Well, I am proud of you for getting back out there, however reluctantly." She came up to where I stood by the sink. "Just good conversation, not anything else?"

I rolled my eyes at her lifted brow.

"When I meet someone I find a connection with, then I'll think about *anything else*."

"Well, I think things are about to change for you. Just a hunch."

"Sure." I plucked the empty mug from her hand and put mine and hers into the dishwasher.

"That's it. Fake it till you make it. Hope you have an easy night at work."

I shrugged. "We'll see. The last Saturday night I was there, I spent most of my time bullshitting with Buck and assisting other technicians. It's good extra money for a night. And takes the pressure off making plans."

Nicole groaned and exhaled a long breath.

"It may not look like it, but I've made some progress. I just need a little time to get used to being out there."

"You seemed to acclimate pretty well when you were in Florida." She held up her hands as if to stop my protest. "Just saying."

"Leo was different, and a moot point since this"—I motioned across my kitchen—"this is real life. The dream was nice while it lasted, but I woke up when I left."

I didn't mention how Leo still starred in every dirty fantasy I had since I'd come back in July.

And there had been plenty.

I dreaded summer and the full-body flush I'd probably get at the sight of a pool again.

But more than all the great sex we had, I missed the confusing but undeniable connection we'd made. How wonderful it felt to feel beautiful and wanted and understood. Not that my friends and family didn't want to understand me, but they couldn't comprehend what I wouldn't let them see.

My short time with him gave me the validation I shouldn't

have needed but desperately craved to be able to—finally—move on with my life and stop dismissing my own wants and needs like my ex-husband always had.

It was impossible to settle for less than perfect when I'd had a glimpse of what it was like. Or could have been like if things were different.

"I'll let you get ready for the night. Tell Buck I said hi."

"Sure," I said as I returned her hug goodbye and held open my front door. "Thanks for stopping by. Sorry there was nothing worthwhile to report."

"I mean it, Kris. Good things will come if you're open to them."

"I'm sure they will eventually. I'll take things one awful date at a time."

She nodded, the tilt of her mouth as she eyed me on her way out telling me this conversation would never be over until I gave someone a real chance.

And I would, when things felt right. The last time anything felt close to right, there was sand between my toes and an arm of inked muscle around my waist.

Silly fantasies wouldn't do me any good in the long term, but Nicole was right, I hadn't let Leo go completely. I had the temptation to text him all the time, but I never sent a single one.

What we had was perfect, and if I'd reached out, only to get no response, I'd ruin it. But holding on to the idea of him was a crutch that prevented me from considering anyone else.

It was sad to admit, but I preferred my imaginary love life over trying to make a real one.

I pondered that sobering epiphany all the way to work and through half of my shift. I was partway through my third cup of coffee when Buck's tap on my shoulder almost made me spill it all over my scrubs.

"Maybe cut down to fewer than five cups when you come in

next shift. A tap on the shoulder shouldn't give you a heart attack."

"Yeah, yeah." I glowered at my second best friend snickering at me as I patted the drops of coffee I wasn't able to stop from landing on my pants.

Buck and I had attended high school together, and everyone thought we were a thing. He was attractive, tall with dark eyes and, at the time, dark hair, but I could never think of him as anything else but a friend.

Other friends didn't believe us, always swearing we'd end up together, and I supposed we were, just not how everyone assumed we would be.

I was in his wedding party, and he was in mine, despite Colin always giving him a side eye because he couldn't fathom how a man and woman could be true platonic friends.

"I have a patient with leg pain and we think it's from an injury, but while you're here, we want to double-check it's not a blood clot."

"No problem. I'm ready when you are." I stood, eyeballing my pants for more spots.

"Awesome. A new nurse is shadowing me, so he'll be helping me bring him in."

"He? You mean we finally got a second male nurse in the ER?"

He smiled with a slow nod.

"I'm the only male nurse here because this is a tiny town with only one of everything. When I did clinical at Albany General there were more of us, but yeah, I guess I'm not the king anymore."

I laughed at his exaggerated sigh.

"Is that where he's from?"

"No, he just moved here from out of state. He'll be a per diem nurse in the ER only a couple days a week because, get this, he's a fire lieutenant too. Started at the Kelly Lakes station last week. I've never seen someone do both."

"Wow, that's funny."

Buck followed me into the small ultrasound room outside of the ER that resembled a closet. There was just enough room for me, a patient, and the equipment.

"Why is that funny?" Buck asked as I turned on my computer and gathered my supplies.

"Leo, the...guy from Florida. He was both. He had his RN degree." I took the patient chart from Buck and started punching in their information. "He was a lieutenant too. I guess maybe it's a more common thing than I thought."

I was halfway through setting up when I noticed how silent Buck had become.

"What made you get so quiet?" I glanced over my shoulder, my smile fading at the deep crease in his forehead. I was familiar enough with it to freeze with concern.

"I forgot you said his name was Leo."

"Because I'm actively trying to not repeat it and make dating these clowns from the app even sadder." I chuckled, keying in the last of the fields, and turned to Buck. My stomach twisted at his still-grim expression.

"Jesus, Buck. What?"

He still said nothing, his head falling back as he burst out laughing.

"You may want to sit down." He jutted his chin to the small folding chair next to the bed.

"No, I don't want to sit down." I moved away from the computer and approached Buck, his shoulders still shaking with a hearty laugh. "Whatever it is, just spit it out."

"Wow, you weren't kidding when you said this room was small."

A familiar chuckle reverberated through me. The last time

I'd heard it, I was naked and resting my cheek on Leo's bare chest.

I prayed I'd heard wrong, that the conversation with Nicole before my shift had dredged up memories of our days together and my mind had conjured his voice in my head.

When I spotted Leo's smile as he stepped into the room, my heart didn't know whether to slam against my chest or fall to my stomach. The golden eyes I couldn't forget widened as they met mine, draining air from the room and oxygen from my lungs.

Leo was in my hospital. Hell, Leo was in my *town*. How? I never told him that I lived in Kelly Lakes, as the likelihood of anyone knowing where it was usually was slim to none, unless they had to pass through here at some point.

The sight of him made my head spin enough to have to hold on to the counter behind my station.

Albany was a big place, and he had no idea I lived in this random small town. So while it hurt that he didn't contact me to let me know he was here, it was what we'd agreed upon, regardless of any deep regrets about not contacting him myself that I'd wrestled with since.

The town's one fire station was only five minutes away from my house. Wasn't this what I'd dreamed of whenever I thought of Leo? *If only things were different. If only he didn't live so far away.*

Now that dream had somehow come to fruition, and I couldn't get away from him fast enough.

"I'd introduce you, but I think you've already met." Buck's eyes lost the mirth they'd had a minute ago. Now he regarded me with a wary sympathy that made my urge to escape even worse.

"We have," Leo said, his eyes boring into mine as a slow, cautious smile crept across the mouth I could still feel on mine. He was even more gorgeous than I'd remembered, even sexy in blue scrubs. "Hi, Kristina."

"Hi," I said, clearing my throat. "You can bring the patient in. I need to get something in the other ultrasound room."

The other ultrasound room had a broken machine that we never used, but it had air, which I couldn't find in this one, so it wasn't a total lie.

"I'll be less than five minutes," I said, attempting to casually maneuver around them instead of pushing past them in a panic.

I'd deal with this new and shitty life development later. I had a job to do, but I needed to get myself together—somehow—before I had to share such a tiny space with the now-former man of my dreams.

Now, he was a man of my reality, a reality that I had no doubt I'd keep running into.

I rushed inside, shutting the door behind me and grabbing on to the edge of the counter with both hands as I took slow breaths in and out.

What the hell was wrong with me?

I was behaving as if I'd seen a ghost, but maybe, in a way, I had. Leo wasn't a real entity in my life, just someone who'd hovered in the corners of my mind.

I'd be able to tell Nicole I'd finally give up the fantasy because I had no choice, but the loss over it was deeper than any of this should have been.

I dropped my chin to my chest at the creak of the door behind me.

"Buck, I just need a minute. I'll be right out."

"So do I."

My head whipped around to Leo, his jaw tense as he bored his eyes into mine.

"I know what you're thinking."

"I assure you, you do not." I squeezed the back of my neck. "I never expected to see you in my town, never mind in the hospital where I work. I'd managed to..."

I rubbed at the space between my brows, taking slow breaths to bring down the uptick in my pulse.

"I managed to compartmentalize my time in Florida, I guess. And now that you're here" —I sucked in a deep breath and let it drain from my lungs —"I can't do that."

"I never wanted you to do that." His voice was soft, his gaze so fixed on me he barely blinked.

"We have a patient. This is not the time or the place." I stepped to the door and reached for the knob, when he grabbed my wrist, squeezing gently until I peered up at him.

"When is your next break?"

"In about an hour, maybe."

His eyes searched mine, expectant and desperate. My boring night suddenly became more than I knew how to deal with.

"I think mine is in an hour too, but I'll ask to make it whenever yours is."

"Demanding on your first day." I lifted a brow, hating how complicated this already was between us when it had been so beautifully simple in another time and place.

"My first day won't be worth shit if I don't talk to you. I'll wheel the patient in, and I'll see you in an hour."

He opened the door, pressing it open and holding out his arm until I headed out.

When Nicole said she thought things would change for me, I'd had no idea they were about to implode.

TWENTY-TWO
LEO

I wheeled the patient into the ultrasound room, leaving once he was set up, my gaze falling on Kristina punching on the computer keys before I closed the door.

I'd had every intention of contacting her, but everything had moved so damn fast. Once we all decided that the assisted living facility would be the best choice for my aunt and uncle, I put in my notice and prepared to move back up here. My captain helped me get a transfer to the station close enough to where my aunt and uncle would be, and once that all went through, I came up to stay with Gabe until I found an apartment.

The station was small, and I finally had enough time in my schedule to apply for a per diem nursing job. Things fell into place easier and quicker than I'd anticipated.

While my uncle still had a long road ahead of him, he was progressing well, according to his doctors. My aunt's symptoms hadn't worsened much since I'd been back, so we were hopeful her new therapy regimen was working too.

Now that it all seemed permanent, I was finally going to let Kristina know I was close. I'd apologize for the radio silence since the day she'd gotten home, and I'd ask to see her again.

It had been the perfect plan before it'd all gone to shit.

"So, you're Leo," Buck said, regarding me with narrowed eyes as we finished updating charts.

"Yes, I think we established that when I started shadowing you tonight. But I'm guessing Kristina told you about meeting a Leo a few months ago."

"She did." Buck chuckled, still scrutinizing me. "That trip was good for her. She came back with a much different attitude."

I nodded, taking a little pride in how our time together had been good for her. *Had* been good, until she saw me again and couldn't get away fast enough.

I'd come back with an entirely different attitude myself, grumbly and miserable until I finally gave my life a little direction.

While I knew she lived in this state, I had no idea that new direction would lead me straight back to her.

"I think she mentioned you too once, now that I think about it."

"I'm her oldest friend, I should hope she mentioned me." Buck smiled and shook his head. "We all told her to contact you and give it a shot. She's been on all these shitty dates because she won't give anyone else a chance."

"As her oldest friend, won't she be pissed at you for telling me that?" I asked, smothering the wide smile that wanted to rip across my mouth. Even though I hated the idea of her going on dates, despite how it was none of my business, I loved knowing that they didn't go anywhere—and that her feelings for me may've had something to do with that.

"Oh, for sure."

I laughed with Buck until his smile faded.

"As I said, whatever happened between you two seemed to be good for her. But now that you're here..." He sucked in a long breath and let it out slowly. "She's a little blindsided at the moment. I'm not sure how much she shared with you, but she's been through a lot. I'd hate to have to kick the ass of the only other male nurse here."

I smiled and nodded. I'd worried about Kristina whenever I let myself think about her. I was glad she had someone who cared about her enough to threaten me.

"I know she has. You won't have to."

Especially since this surprise may have fucked up everything.

"Can I give you a little advice? It's none of my business, of course, but you'll learn soon enough that everyone around here likes to pry without any remorse, especially when it's about people they care about."

"Good to know." I chuckled as I put away the last of the charts. "And go on."

"Kris has never had anyone fight for her. Prove to her that she's worth it. Yes, she's a little shocked to see you again, and it may be a battle at first. But if you really want her, show her. She's stubborn, but please don't give up on her. That's all I'm saying."

He held up his hands and backed away.

"You can take a break now if you want. I think Kristina is in the break room taking hers."

"You guys hear everything too, I suppose."

I laughed at Buck's innocent shrug.

"I may have lingered outside when you stalked off to follow her to make sure she was okay. Good luck. You're probably going to need it."

I watched Kristina from the doorway of the break room, focusing on the bottom of her coffee cup as she swirled it around. I smiled, remembering how she'd done that with the drinks I'd given her at the bar. I'd wanted to tease her about making sure she'd gotten the last drop, but I was too lost in those green eyes to care about anything else.

She was every bit as beautiful as I remembered, but I hated the guarded stance she took with me now. When she lay naked next to me, she was open, warm, and breathtaking.

She trusted me then. And now, she couldn't get away from me fast enough.

"This seat taken?" I asked and slid into the seat across from her.

"Nope, you can sit anywhere you want." She looked up with a tight smile, both her hands wrapped tightly around the empty paper cup in her hand.

"I wanted to text you so many times. I've looked at that damn photo so often I have us memorized."

She jerked her head toward me, confusion pinching her brow. "I did too. I always thought about you and wondered if you still lived in Florida. Seeing you here, in this tiny little town, is something I never expected."

"Can you hear me out for a few minutes? Please."

"Leo," she said before exhaling a long breath. "I'm fine. Yes, I'm a little weirded out to have you here, but I'll deal with it."

"My uncle had a stroke. My cousin called the night it happened and told me I had to fly back right away. And even though I call every week, I didn't know how sick my aunt was until I saw her."

She brought her hand to her mouth.

"Oh God, Leo. I'm so sorry. How are they now?"

"My uncle has a long road ahead, but he's moving in the right direction. My aunt has Parkinson's, but we moved them both into the assisted living facility in town."

"The one on Maple? That's a great place. Brand-new." Her eyes widened as she gave me a slow nod. "So you moved back up here for them."

"Yes. For all of them. I thought by staying like some kind of despondent nomad, I wouldn't risk caring about anything too much. Almost losing the family I had left finally snapped me out of it."

She'd started to snap me out of it back in July. The main reason I didn't contact her after that day was that I didn't want to get even more attached to her.

I reasoned it was to not disrupt her life or lead her on, but it was my stunted emotions that prevented me from reaching out like I wanted to.

"I'm sure they're glad to have you back. The fire station is within walking distance of my house." Her chest deflated with a long exhale as she shot me a wry grin. "Small world, isn't it?"

"It is." I bobbed my head with a slow nod. "I just started there last week and got the job here on Monday. I wanted to wait until I was completely settled to call you, and I swear to you I was going to. Maybe I didn't know you for very long, but…" I sucked in a breath, fighting the urge to pick up her hand. "You made a very big impression on me."

"Same."

I relaxed at the warm smile tilting her lips.

"Where are you staying?"

"I found an apartment close to my aunt and uncle. The condo complex up the road."

"My sister-in-law lived there when she first moved to town." Her brows knit together as she leaned back in her chair. "You bought a condo? I didn't think they had rentals."

"They do not." I shook my head. "I plan to stay. It's about time, I think."

"That's great. Congratulations."

She flicked her wrist to glance at her watch and stood.

"I better get back." A tiny smile danced across her lips, relaxed and warm like the Kristina I knew, or used to know.

"Listen," I said before I stood and grabbed her wrist, letting my thumb drift back and forth over her hand, that same electricity between us sparking to life. "Since I'm new around here, I could use a friend."

"Friend," she said, a laugh bubbling out of her. "Is that what we are?"

I had to laugh when she used my own words against me.

"I understand either way, but I'd like to be."

Just friends wouldn't be enough for me, but for now, I'd take what I could get.

Earning her trust was going to be a lot harder in her regular daily life, where there would be more to it than just getting her to let loose and have fun on a beach.

"Sure," she said, her reply as nonchalant as mine was when she'd asked to keep in touch.

I let my eyes travel down her profile when she shifted to leave. I lingered on the gorgeous slope of her neck, imagining the freckle on her collarbone that was darker than the cluster she'd gotten from the sun and the moan that had escaped her when I'd traced my tongue over it.

I'd moved here to have a real life, but it already seemed empty if I couldn't have even a small part of hers.

TWENTY-THREE
KRISTINA

"**S**o what's your job like?" Edwin, my date for the evening, asked with a mouthful of tortilla chips. I'd sat through what seemed like hours of him droning on about being a mechanical engineer but had really been probably only fifteen minutes after the hostess led us to our table.

When I'd agreed to this date weeks ago, swearing it was the last one before I deleted this stupid app, I'd mostly complied because he'd suggested the new Mexican place I wanted to try. From what I'd heard, it had great food and drinks and, as a bonus, was a comfortable two towns over from Kelly Lakes.

Edwin was attractive in a Ken doll sort of way. His perfectly coiffed, dirty-blond hair hadn't moved an inch since we'd sat down. I fixated on the part in his hair in almost fascination, which turned out to be helpful when I had to appear interested in what he had to say.

Meeting men on a dating app had turned me into a nasty version of myself that I didn't care for. I was impatient, judgmental, and bored from the beginning, always finding a thousand things wrong with the poor guy I'd agreed to meet because my standards were too high.

Or maybe just fixed on someone else.

And now that the "someone else" lived close enough to high-light all the reminders of why no one else measured up, any dating life I attempted would never work out unless I made an effort at a change in attitude.

Edwin's question caught me off guard as I was deep in thought about what meal would be the quickest to prepare and eat before I bade Edwin farewell.

"I'm a vascular technician. I work in a doctor's office and one day per month in the ER."

"Technology is great, isn't it?" He smiled at me over the edge of his menu. It was a blow-off, but I didn't ask for any details of his job either because I was, most likely, equally as uninterested.

"The drinks look pretty good."

"Yes!" I sank a little in my seat when his head popped up at my boisterous reply. "I've heard the drinks are good, and I peeked at the menu online this afternoon."

"Excuse me," the waitress said, holding what looked like two margarita glasses on a tray. "The gentleman over at the bar sent these." She set down the frozen drinks as Edwin and I looked them over with the same puzzled gaze. "I'll be right back to take your order."

I craned my neck to the bar, and my heart dropped into my stomach when Leo waved at me.

"If you'll excuse me, I want to thank my friend for our drinks." I plastered on a smile as I stood and stalked toward the bar.

"I thought you'd take a sip before getting up to thank me," Leo said before taking a pull from his beer bottle, holding his eyes on mine as he smirked around the top.

"Thank you, but don't you think sending a woman drinks while she's on a date is kind of a ballsy move? And what are you doing here?"

"One of the guys at the firehouse invited a few of us out for his birthday," he said, motioning behind him to the two joined tables. "Those of us who had the night off. I came up to the bar to start a tab and spotted you." He shrugged. "Just as miserable as you were when I first saw you by the pool a few months ago."

"I'm not miserable. It's the first time we've been out together, so it's awkward like all first dates are. Although you probably just turned that up a notch."

"Was it ever awkward with us?"

The smile curving his mouth faded, his brazen gaze now sad as his eyes met mine.

"Aside from how I stammered all over the place when I first tried to speak to you, no, I guess not."

He nodded, a tiny smile pulling at his lips as he spun his stool toward me.

"You were cute. Beautiful. Never awkward."

I rubbed the back of my neck, trying to cool off from the rush of heat over my skin.

"But that doesn't matter. Different time and place."

He stood and took a step toward me. I hadn't realized how close I was standing to Leo until he didn't need to eat up much space between us to close the distance.

"I'm the same guy as I was then. Maybe with a little more of my shit together than I had when we met, but I want the same things now. How about you?"

I swallowed, my mouth parched from our proximity and the palpable need in his voice.

I wanted all the same things too, but I didn't know how we could get that magic back. It already wasn't the same, and I hated to tarnish the memories any more than they already were.

My reaction to him was identical to when he stumbled into the ultrasound room at the hospital.

Instead of leaping into his arms like I'd been dreaming of all this time, I was still running away.

"Kristina, sorry to interrupt."

I cleared my throat and backed away from Leo when I heard Edwin's voice behind me.

"The waitress came back twice to take our order, and it's getting busy."

"Sure, sorry." I pressed my hand to my forehead, so embarrassed and out of sorts I had trouble making eye contact. "I was just thanking my friend for the drinks he sent over."

"Oh, thanks, man. I've never had a lemonade margarita before, but it's not bad."

I shut my eyes and held in a groan. Leo was pulling out the big guns tonight.

"No problem. You both have a nice night."

Leo gave us both a nod and headed back to his table. My eyes followed his retreat, the tight Henley shirt over black pants, his broad shoulders slumping in disappointment.

I turned and didn't realize that Edwin was already at our table. Whether I was into the date or not, getting into a heated discussion with another man wasn't right, nor was fixating on Leo the entire time—even before I'd seen him.

"Sorry about that."

"Don't be. This drink is pretty good." His genuine smile made me feel even worse.

I took a long slurp, the drink not exactly the way Leo had made it at Turtle Bay, but familiar enough to cause a pang in my chest at the taste.

"Ex-boyfriend?" He cocked a brow as he crunched on another chip.

"Something like that." I grabbed my straw for another long pull. "Did you decide on what to order?"

"How about splitting the appetizer special?" He motioned to

the whiteboard behind us. "That way, we could at least taste the food while we're here and then get the check."

I nodded, getting what he was offering, and despite the lack of chemistry or interest before the Leo intrusion, I felt nothing but guilt.

"I'm sorry, I've been really rude tonight."

"You haven't." He waved a hand. "I like a more organic way of meeting people, so I've been on a lot of first dates that have made me wonder why I didn't delete the damn app in the first place. Not that this was one of them, but I think with a more natural way of meeting, it would be easier, you know?"

"I do." I heaved a long sigh. "So, listen, now that we know we're on the same page, we don't have to rush out of here. I've been dreaming of tacos all day. We can have dinner and part ways, with no weirdness or regret. How does that sound?"

He was handsome when he smiled, but I still felt nothing. Dinner wasn't bad after that, both of us laughing at past tales of disastrous dates and quick escapes. Maybe there were some nice guys out there. I just had to find the motivation and desire to look.

And I had none. I'd known that, but I didn't get the significance until now.

"This has been one of the strangest dates I've ever been on, but I have to say one of the best lately."

I laughed with Edwin as he walked me to my car after dinner, stilling when he leaned in as if he was about to kiss me. I exhaled when his lips landed on my cheek.

"I wouldn't mind a dinner with a friend sometimes if you'd be up for it."

"I would like that," I said. "Comparing notes with you tonight made me feel much less alone."

"You know, you don't *have* to be alone. That guy who sent us the drinks was looking our way every time he walked up to the bar, and before I called you, I watched the conversation you were having. You both couldn't take your eyes off each other. Why waste your time with this?"

I chuckled with him, despite the sour churn in my stomach.

"It's complicated."

"Isn't everything? Safe travels home."

Edwin waved before he shifted toward his car.

What I felt about Leo was simple. My fear of ruining it or getting too close only to watch him walk away as he moved on to his next destination was what made it complicated.

TWENTY-FOUR
KRISTINA

"**W**hy are you looking at me like that?" Peyton asked my brother around a mouthful of fries.

Jake snuck me a look, a smile pulling at his mouth as he held up his hands.

"I just remember when you insisted that the burgers here were a once-a-month thing because they were too big, and now you're staring at the double cheeseburger at the next table like you stare at me sometimes."

"I can't help it if your daughter likes to eat." She rubbed circles over her round belly. "Or if things make me hungry." She bit into a fry, holding Jake's gaze long enough to make me a little queasy.

"Ugh, hello," I groaned, raising my hand. "There are people here across the table who don't want to lose their dinner."

Not that Emma was paying attention as she swirled a fry across the puddle of ketchup on her plate.

I liked to tease them both, but the love and longing between my brother and his wife was so obvious, it was palpable. It was impossible not to notice—or be jealous.

"Can I babysit Keely after she's born?" Emma asked,

squaring her shoulders. "I'm six and a half now, so that's like a grown-up."

"Babies are a lot of work. I think you should be a bigger grown-up before you babysit," I whispered as I leaned in.

"You said she would be here next month. I'll be bigger then." Emma crossed her arms and fell back into her seat, her lip jutted out in a pout.

"I think that when Keely gets here, you guys are going to be best friends."

Emma grinned, Peyton's words appeasing her enough to pick up her burger for a bite.

"Chloe missed out. This is the best cheeseburger ever. Can we come back next week?"

I had to laugh at Emma's wide, hopeful eyes.

"You're with Daddy next week. He's taking you guys to the farm and on a hayride, remember?"

"That's right! I can't miss that."

My brother and I shared a tiny smile. For the past few months, Colin and I had been getting along better when he came to pick up the girls, and the tension around his weekends with them had—mostly—dissipated. We hadn't gotten into an argument since he'd called me while I was on vacation, and I'd learned how to smile and shrug when he got into a mood. For the fifteen minutes I saw him on weekends, I could be friendly and—sort of—mean it.

Now when their father stopped by, I didn't catch the usual dread I'd find etched on my daughters' faces as they watched us together. They didn't expect the fighting between us as a given anymore, and I hoped the new pattern would be permanent.

Her sophomore year of high school was busy enough for Chloe to stop fixating on her worry for me. She was out with some new friends from her basketball team tonight, without any nudging from me.

I kept an eye on her but hoped that her asking to go out rather than holing up in her room and watching my every move meant she was turning a corner.

Even though I was able to let go of some of the worries about my firstborn, I had other reasons for losing sleep these days.

Like knowing Leo lived in my town, worked at the fire station I passed each day on the way to and from my house, and the way he'd looked at me when he'd asked me what I wanted.

I'd welcomed the temporary distraction when Jake invited us to get burgers at Salma's with him and Peyton.

"Kristina? I thought that was you."

I almost coughed on a fry when I turned to find Leo standing next to our table.

So much for distractions. It was difficult to get your mind off something that was always right there in front of you.

This was the first time I'd seen him in firefighter mode. He wore a Kelly Lakes Fire Department T-shirt that seemed a size too tight over jeans that hung on his hips the same way they had when he'd tended bar that first night.

"Hey, Leo. I guess you're on shift tonight."

He nodded. "I offered to pick up takeout. I'm told the whole town swears by the burgers here."

Leo's easy smile both enraptured me and pissed me off. Three pairs of narrowed eyes fixed on me when I glanced around the table.

"Leo, this is my brother, Jake, and my sister-in-law, Peyton."

Jake stood to shake Leo's hand.

"Hi, Leo," Peyton chirped, holding out her hand for Leo after Jake sat back down. "It is so nice to finally meet you."

I glowered back at her when she gave me a tiny wink.

"And this is my youngest, Emma."

"Well, it is very nice to meet you, Emma." Leo stepped closer to us. "I've heard a lot about you."

"You have?" Emma scrunched up her nose. "Where did you meet him, Mommy? Wait!" She gasped and pointed to the swirl of ink around Leo's bicep. "He's got the drawings. He's your friend from the sleepover!"

I winced at Leo, his smile still easy and gorgeous as he laughed.

"I met your mom while she was on vacation," he said before I could think of a reply. Emma had dropped it, but now that she'd gotten a reminder, I was going to work on that excuse I couldn't figure out but dreaded, especially when she slipped in front of her sister.

"Oh. I thought you were coming home with her, so I saved you a bagel. But when you didn't come, I ate it."

"I heard." He chuckled, throwing me a quick glance. "That was very nice of you."

She shrugged. "Mommy always says that it's good to share and be nice."

"Sounds like your mom."

A shiver ran down my spine at the husky dip in his voice, his eyes still fixed on me. It was ridiculous to be this uncomfortable around Leo now, considering all we'd shared—and all we'd done—during our short time together.

Maybe it had seemed so easy because we always had a time limit. We didn't know each other long enough to have to worry about anything beyond what we were feeling at the moment.

Those feelings came right back the minute I laid eyes on him again, and I had no clue what to do about them in the here and now.

Kelly Lakes became even smaller when there was someone you were trying to avoid.

"How are you liking Kelly Lakes so far?" Jake asked him, breaking the long silence hovering over our table. "I imagine it's quite the shift from Florida."

"I'm originally from a small town, so while it's a shift, for sure, it's just something I have to get used to again. But ask me again after the first snowfall. I'm sure I'll miss Florida more when I have to shovel."

He laughed, that sexy rumble I remembered too well, and shoved his hands into his pockets. Just like when he'd done that on our movie night, my eyes went to the bulges in his biceps and the ink wrapped around his arm.

I could still taste his skin, sweet and salty under my tongue when I licked all the intricate patterns on his arm and the constellations on his hip.

Getting this flushed and flustered with my family and my daughter watching me was wrong and, when I spotted Peyton's brown eyes dancing, all too obvious.

I tried to blink it away and grabbed my soda for a long slurp, letting the cool liquid coat my parched throat.

The rest of me was still hot, bothered, and confused as hell.

"Are you working at the hospital this week? They set my hours to Wednesdays for now."

"No," I said, not knowing what to do with all the hope in his eyes. "I only do one Saturday per month, rarely more than that."

"Are you planning to go to the festival next weekend? I'm in charge of decorating the truck."

"Yes," Peyton said. "Well, we are." She pointed back and forth between herself and Jake. "It's a big deal around here. My friend Claudia comes in from Brooklyn because she thinks it's such a Hallmark movie thing for a town to have a holiday festival in November. The whole town goes."

They sure fucking did.

"Will they let us go on the truck this year?" Emma's head snapped to Leo. "They said no last year."

"You know why they said no," I told her. "If you go on, everyone will want to go on, then it will get crazy."

"Not if you come early," Leo said, his mouth spreading into the same sly grin as when he offered to pick my drink. "I may know a guy."

Leo's wink at Emma both melted my insides and boiled my blood. I'd forgotten how persuasive he could be, and while I knew he had nothing but good intentions, I resented being cornered into saying yes.

"Can we go early, Mommy? *Please.* I promise I won't be a problem at breakfast that day." Her pleading baby-blue gaze, as usual, rendered me and all of us powerless.

"She eats breakfast very slowly and drives her mother and sister a little crazy, which is why we call her a problem." She giggled at my crinkled nose. I tried to keep it light for my daughter's sake, even though my insides quivered with panic.

Not only did I have to figure out how to be around Leo, I'd have to do it with my kids watching.

"What time would we have to be there?"

"Probably ten since I think everything opens at noon. I wouldn't want to get you off the truck the minute you step on, right?"

"Exactly," Emma agreed with a nod.

"I'll text you to confirm, if that's okay." Leo had the decency to look a little contrite. He may not have meant to use Emma as a means to get me somewhere, but he sure ran with the opportunity.

"That's fine."

"Great," he said before he craned his neck to the back counter. "I think our order is up. Nice to meet all of you. And nice to see you again, Kristina."

"You too," I said, clearing my throat when my reply came out breathy and scratchy.

"Nice to meet you, Leo." Emma kneeled on her chair and waved.

"It was especially nice to meet you, Emma." He flashed her a megawatt smile before he shifted toward the back.

I rubbed my eyes, letting it sink in just how screwed I was.

"He's nice," Emma mused, chomping on her last fry as she plopped back down in her chair. We both glanced over to where Leo was picking up the takeout bags.

"Yes, he is," Peyton said, waggling her eyebrows.

"Aunt Peyton shouldn't be noticing if Leo was nice or not." My brother narrowed his eyes at his wife, only half kidding.

"Oh, relax, babe." She massaged Jake's shoulder. "Be happy for your sister. If she would only give the poor dude a break."

"Happy?" I coughed out a laugh. "I didn't need to bring my kids into this."

"So you admit there's a *this*."

"There *was* a this on the beach when I was living a temporary and very different life."

"He sure thinks there's still a this. He didn't take his eyes off you for almost the entire time he was standing here, but you wouldn't give him an inch."

"I agreed to meet him early on Saturday so Emma could go on the truck, not that he gave me a choice."

Peyton fell back in her chair, shaking her head.

"You know," she said, pushing her empty plate away. "When I picked you up from the airport, you were so sad because you missed him, even though you thought you shouldn't. There's obviously something still between you that may be deeper than you thought, or could be if you gave it a chance."

I had gone to Jake and Peyton's house after I'd left the hospital on Sunday morning and vented my heart to them both for hours, but I was still left unsettled and without a clue.

"It was better when he was back in Florida. Easier anyway. Attempting *this*"—Peyton laughed when I glared at her—"in real life is all kinds of complicated, and I'm not ready for it."

Or to get attached to it when he picked up and left.

"Can I give you some advice?" Jake said as he stretched his arm behind Peyton's chair.

"Order a cocktail since you're driving?"

"You can." He nodded as a lopsided grin stretched his lips. "Second chances are gifts that don't come along very often. And if you want to be with this guy, who cares how long you've know him or if it's complicated? If it feels right, just go along with it."

A laugh escaped me. "So people keep telling me."

"People are wise," Jake said, his brows raised.

"But it's not just me that I have to worry about." My eyes drifted to Emma. "In Florida, things were a lot simpler. I'm a package deal in Kelly Lakes." I sputtered out a laugh.

"I remember someone telling me that when I found the one, she'd be good for both Mike and me." He leaned back and crossed his arms. "It was one of the few times in our lives I was happy to admit you were right."

I nodded, remembering the very night I'd said those words. I was trying to push Jake to take a chance with the woman he wasn't supposed to fall for, while I was still entrenched in saving a miserable marriage for the sake of my girls.

Every date I forced myself on was doomed before it started because they didn't measure up to the idea of Leo. Now that I could have the real thing, all I did was fight it.

Who knew getting exactly what you wished for was so damn terrifying?

TWENTY-FIVE

LEO

"Wow, this is a lot of food," I mused, taking in the tower of various canned goods, boxes of cereal and pasta, and packages of baby food and formula.

"This isn't even half of what we'll get," our captain, Vic, said as we tried to clear a path inside the firehouse through the growing pile. "Kelly Lakes may be small, but we show up for our own, especially on holidays. On Thanksgiving Day, the restaurants donate hot food too. Wait until the festival. All those businesses will fill up the whole damn truck with food."

It wasn't the first fire department food drive I'd been involved in, but Thanksgiving was still two weeks away and we were already receiving donations in droves.

"I guess you've lived here your whole life, too."

Vic laughed. He was in his sixties but was in better shape than any of us. His grandkids stopped by the station all the time.

"I have. It's small enough to get a little claustrophobic at times, I grant you, but I never wanted to live anywhere else. I'm sure it's an adjustment for you."

"I grew up in a small town, a long time ago." I laughed, covering up the pang at how long ago it really was. The strong sense of community here reminded me of the neighbors we used to know.

My parents loved to get involved in all the local events, and everyone would beg my mother to cook rabo encendido. We were the only Dominican family in town, and Mom's oxtail stew was considered a local delicacy.

The entire town had piled into the funeral home to express their condolences and love for my parents. Everything after their death and before I moved in with my aunt and uncle was a blur. Since arriving here, the memories I would always bury before they'd surface hit me from all directions and I couldn't stop them.

The town my aunt and uncle had lived in was small but bigger than where I was originally from. I didn't get to know the residents that well over the two years I'd lived with them, and I was never back long enough after that to create any kind of attachment.

After moving from place to place to avoid attachments for most of my life, I'd ended up in a town built on roots and entanglements.

"I would never have left the Keys," Bobby, one of the other lieutenants, said. "You could have stayed on the beach with no one in your business." He snickered as he piled some of the goods into a cardboard box.

I nodded, not wanting to get into how empty that was after a while, despite how enticing he imagined it to be.

"There she is," Bobby said as he glanced over my shoulder. "The love of my life."

"Ugh, please stop that."

I froze, whipping my head around to Kristina's voice. She

didn't notice me as she carried two large boxes over to the piles of food we were stacking in a corner.

She stood, stumbling for a moment when she noticed me.

"Oh hey, Leo," she said, breathless as she set her hands on her hips. Her chestnut hair was pulled back in a ponytail, the loose strands falling over her face and accentuating her delicate cheekbones. She still took my breath away, and it was impossible to hide it.

"I'm in charge of delivering the donations from Emma's school this year. I'm sure there'll be more, but I don't have the room on my garage floor to keep piling them, so I'm just bringing it all straight here."

"Why didn't you text me to come to help you?" Bobby crooned, the lilt in his voice combined with how he gave her body an obvious perusal when she turned around filling me with a white-hot rage that I could do nothing about.

It wasn't as if she was mine and I could tell him to back the fuck off. That night I claimed her in front of the jerk at the bar flashed in my mind, but if I brought her into my arms and kissed her now, she wouldn't be so pliable and willing.

"I lift weights specifically so I don't need to ask for anyone's help unloading groceries. This was nothing. But thanks for the offer."

"You lift?" he asked, and my fist flexed at my side on instinct from the smirk twisting his mouth. "We can arm-wrestle if you want."

I was about to wrestle him myself until Kristina's face twisted in disgust. I held in a laugh at her exasperated exhale.

"I don't want. Thanks, though." She rolled her eyes. "Vic, I didn't separate anything, but I can do it now if you need me to."

"No need, Kristina. We appreciate it."

"I have two more in the car. I'll be right back." She held up a hand in Bobby's direction. "No need for help, I've got it."

"So stubborn," Bobby said, his lips pursed as his gaze followed Kristina's departure.

"One day, she's going to slug you, and I really hope I'm around for it." Vic narrowed his eyes as he unpacked the boxes Kristina brought in.

"She won't slug me. I'm getting through, you'll see. How do you know her, Reyes?"

"How do *you* know her?" I asked through gritted teeth as I tried and failed to unclench my jaw.

"We went to high school together but could never catch each other when we were single. Now that she finally divorced Colin, I think it's been long enough to make a move."

"Didn't look like she's into your moves."

He stood from the floor, squinting at me as he approached.

"Do you have something going on with her? Because you look like you want to take a swing at me." He chuckled, clueless of how spot-on he was.

"Just hate to see someone embarrass themselves hitting on a woman who is clearly not interested. Small-town brotherly love and all that." I shot him a tight smile and turned away, heading to the parking lot to find Kristina.

I was sure Bobby wasn't the only asshole drooling over her. Now that it was clear that he didn't have a chance, my urge to kick his ass wasn't as blinding, but my current standing with her was no better. Kristina didn't seem to be any more interested in giving me the time of day either.

"If I keep my mouth shut, will you let me help you?" I asked as I came up to where Kristina was digging around in her trunk.

She laughed when she lifted her head, and my chest swelled at her gorgeous smile.

"Thank you. These two are heavier than the ones I just brought in, but I didn't want to ask for help and then not be able to shake Bobby all damn day."

"Even though he called you the love of his life?" I teased as I scooped up the last box in the trunk and grabbed the one she had in her arms.

"After twenty years, he still finds it hard to take a hint." She sighed and shook her head. "You don't have to take both."

We stilled when our fingers brushed as she tried to pull the box from me. Neither of us stepped back at the contact, and I was too lost in those damn green eyes to look anywhere else.

"I don't mind," I said, clearing my throat as I tried to get my bearings. "So, to be clear, Bobby isn't the love of *your* life?"

Her shoulders shook with a silent chuckle, her eyes searching mine with a slow shake of her head.

"Not even close."

"Good," I said, hoisting one of the boxes onto my shoulder. "And I was right, by the way."

"Right about what?" she asked, her brows crinkling as she studied my face.

"That you're impossible not to notice, you just aren't looking. Not that I'm saying you should notice Bobby." She laughed when I jerked my chin toward the firehouse door. "You just need to pay a little more attention."

If only she'd pay attention to *me*.

My feelings for her were deep enough to have paralyzed me these past few months. She was different from any other woman I'd ever known. Special in a way I didn't think was possible and never looked for, but she'd found me.

Instead of saying goodbye to her that day at the airport, I should have tried everything I could to keep her in my life, no matter how hard it would have been.

I'd told her to have no expectations when it came to me and us, when I was the one afraid of wanting more, and I regretted my stupid mistake more and more each day.

Roots didn't scare me anymore, and neither did attachments, not where she was concerned.

She wasn't mine, then or now, but losing her terrified me all the same.

TWENTY-SIX
LEO

"You're the new fireman-nurse, right?"

I put down the string of lights I was winding around one of the mirrors on the truck and turned to an older woman with fiery red hair.

"I am. I guess word travels fast around here." I smiled and held out my hand. "I'm Leo. I'm the new lieutenant, and I work per diem as a nurse in the ER."

"Nice to meet you, Leo. I'm Mary, owner of Mary's Coffee Shop on Main Street. I never knew anyone who did both."

She took my hand, holding it for a few extra beats after the customary shake. Her eyes traveled up and down my body, and I couldn't tell if she was giving me a shameless perusal or sizing me up.

The festival was set up on the main road in town, where most of the businesses clustered together. The long street was blocked by our fire truck on one side and two police cruisers on the other.

The road was lined with vendor booths and Christmas trees. It did seem a little out of place to have a holiday festival in

November, but I'd been told that small businesses ruled this little town.

Every Kelly Lakes resident I'd met so far had been friendly, but more than a handful were just plain nosy. I supposed a new firefighter and nurse from out of town was something different enough to raise interest.

"I guess you must be single, then. If you can work two such demanding jobs."

"For the moment," I said, bracing myself when her eyes lit up.

"My daughter is single too. Recently divorced but not too recent. She's helping me at the booth today if you'd like me to introduce you."

"I get the feeling we may be too busy today to socialize too much."

"Fair enough. But make sure you stop by the shop. I always take care of Kelly Lakes's first responders."

"I appreciate that…" I trailed off when I noticed Kristina over Mary's shoulder, holding Emma's hand, with an older girl lingering behind them. I guessed that was Chloe, as she looked every bit the bored teenager as they got closer.

Even in a winter jacket, Kristina was still gorgeous. The jacket was fitted enough to tease the curve of her hips and trigger the sweet memory of her thighs squeezing my face as she came in my mouth.

Her body had been burned into my brain ever since that night in the pool. It was the memory that rolled around in my head the most, especially on weak nights when I'd wrap my hand around my lonely dick and wish for her.

I'd played a little dirty to get her to the festival early, but I couldn't waste the opportunity for some extra time with her today. After missing her for so long and resenting how perfect we could be together, she was here. *We* were here.

All that time I'd spent restless and unsettled, wanting to jump out of my skin if I stayed still for too long, didn't seem to apply here. I had my family close, a place to live that didn't seem like a glorified hotel room, and—I hoped—a second chance with the one I'd let get away.

"Hi, Mary," Kristina said, her smile tight as she held Emma in place by her shoulders. "I'm sure Emma will be visiting your booth for a cinnamon roll."

"They're the best," Emma told me as she bounced with excitement. "Are you going to keep all the lights on?" She pointed to the fire truck behind me that now looked like Christmas had thrown up all over it with my last touches of lights and garland streaming over the front.

"Just the lights for sirens, sweetheart. It would be hard to drive and get out what we need to when we have a call. Ready for the tour?"

"Yes!" Emma squirmed out of Kristina's hold and grabbed my hand.

"I was just getting to know Leo. Do you know he's a fireman and—"

"A nurse, yes. It's impressive, isn't it?" Kristina shot me a glance, her smile real enough to kick up my heartbeat.

Buck said that I had to fight for her, and I was more than ready to do battle today.

"Yes, it is. Oh, so you've met?"

"We have," I replied to Mary, my eyes still locked on Kristina's. "I offered Emma a quick tour before they opened the festival to the public. And I think she's a little excited."

Emma giggled at my loud whisper.

"I see. Well, if you still want to meet Renee, come by our booth when you have a minute."

I assumed Renee was her daughter, whom I didn't agree to meet today. I had the feeling that was more for Kristina's benefit and took the dirty side-eye Kristina gave the both of us as a great sign.

"So, Mary is peddling her daughter on you." Kristina said as she watched Mary's departure. "That sounds about right."

"I think she was trying to, but I told her no. My interests are elsewhere."

She didn't ask about where my interests were because she had to already know. She nodded without a word, but I caught the hint of a smile.

"This is my eldest," she said, her eyes full of love and pride as she pulled her daughter closer. "Chloe, this is Leo. He's the reason why we're all up an hour earlier today."

"Nice to meet you." I reached out my hand. "You could be your mother's twin."

She took my hand and met my gaze with a shy smile. She had the same dark hair and green eyes as her mother and was almost her height.

"People say that a lot." She shrugged, her eyes focused on the ground.

"You should take it as a huge compliment," I told her, my eyes on Kristina. It was easier to make my intentions clear back at Turtle Bay, where we didn't have an audience, but I couldn't resist pushing a little.

"Thank you." Kristina's voice was a shy whisper, like when we'd first met, both of us lost in our own ways until we found more than we expected.

Today, I would take one little win at a time.

"Leo is Mommy's friend from Florida. They had a sleepover."

Kristina's eyes bulged as Chloe's head whipped around.

I bit back a smile as I lifted Emma onto the truck while Kristina and Chloe spoke in whispers behind us.

"Can we put the sirens on, please?" she asked, her blue eyes wide with her lip jutted out in a pout as she slid her tiny hand against my palm.

"I think if we put the sirens on, people may get scared." I picked her up, my resolve almost wavering a little at her exaggerated frown. "But I can show you everything else."

I craned my neck over to where Kristina and Chloe were standing. "You guys can hop on too if you want."

"It's okay," Kristina said. "We can see you, but we'll wait out here."

"Chloe was once on a fire truck in Girl Scouts, she said," Emma told me with a shrug. "She maybe doesn't want to see since she already did. I was in a police car once! Unca Jake's friend Keith is the chief, and he let us ride with him one day and it was so cool when he put on the sirens." Her eyes darted to the floor and then back to me.

"Nice try, sweetheart."

She bunched her shoulders, gazing up at me with a sweet giggle. I'd bet she didn't hear the word no a lot because she was a cute little conniver.

"Why do you have so much stuff?" she asked, wide-eyed as she surveyed the space and all the equipment.

"A fire truck is like a big toolbox. We never know what we'll have to do for the next call, so we have to be sure we're ready for anything. That's why the hoses are different sizes and we have all those axes and tools."

"Ah," she said, tapping her chin. "Like Unca Jake's toolbox when he fixes stuff. He said sometimes he uses all the tools, and sometimes just one."

"Exactly. You're a smart girl."

"Thank you. A lot of people tell me that."

"I'm sure." I led her into the driver's area, pulling her onto my lap after I sat in the passenger's seat.

"Can I trust you to look out the window and not touch anything?"

She pursed her lips and peered up at me, her brows knit together.

"I don't know, so you better hold my hands." She clasped her hands together and held them up.

I couldn't help but laugh as I enclosed her tiny hands in mine.

"Mommy was nervous about the festival."

"Nervous? Really?"

"Oh yes." She gave me a slow nod. "She took longer than Chloe to do her hair and tried on, like, three different color lipsticks. She *never* takes that long. I was afraid I'd miss the truck."

I sucked my bottom lip into my mouth, holding back the wide grin wanting to break out across my face. I was up a lot earlier than I needed to be today in anticipation of seeing Kristina, just like I had been before taking her out that morning.

I loved thinking that maybe she was having the same problem.

It was hard enough to move on when she left, and it was impossible now that she was close. I was starting to possibly believe in fate, especially with this inside information that maybe Kristina hadn't written me off after all.

Emma was an adorable informant.

"Hey."

As if I'd conjured her up, I found Kristina standing behind the driver's area, a wistful smile curving those plum-colored lips. I loved thinking she was made up for me, but it wasn't necessary. I'd notice her anywhere, and she was gorgeous from the second she woke up.

"Chloe left me for her friends. They asked her to help with

the trees the high school is donating. I thought I'd step on and check it out." Her brow furrowed when she noticed our hands.

"Leo is holding my hands so that I don't touch anything. I asked him to hold me back in case I couldn't help myself."

Kristina's smile widened as she chuckled. "Well, that was very nice of him."

"Could you take our picture? I want to show my teacher I was with a real firefighter on a real truck."

"Sure," Kristina said, digging her phone out of her purse and holding it in front of her. "Smile."

"Yay! Thank you!" Emma threw her arms around my neck when I let go of her hands.

"Thank you for being here early and taking her on the truck."

"My pleasure," I said, Kristina's smile shrinking when our eyes locked. The electricity between us lit up a room, regardless of who else was in it.

"It's hard to tell this one no."

"Tell me about it." Kristina sighed as Emma scampered off my lap and ran to her mother. "So did you have fun being on a fire truck?"

"Yes! Can Leo sleep over like when you were on vacation? He can have my sleeping bag."

Kristina stilled, clenching her eyes shut for a moment. We shared a silent chuckle before she cupped her forehead and dug her fingers into her temples.

"I think Leo is too big for your sleeping bag, but I'm sure he appreciates the invite."

"I do," I said, folding my arms and leaning back against the seat. I'd accept another invitation from her mother in a heartbeat, but I wouldn't push.

"How're your aunt and uncle?"

"Coming along. My cousin is down this weekend and is

staying with them. We take turns so they aren't alone, but he's too far to visit during the week."

"I bet they're happy to have you around."

I shrugged. "I'm happy to *be* around. I should be with the people I care about, and since I made the decision to come here, I'm not so restless anymore. A little, but not my usual distant and detached."

"I'm glad to hear it." A smile broke out on those perfect lips. "Why are you still a little restless?"

"You tell me." I leaned forward, resting my elbows on my knees, and lifted a brow. I spied her chest rise and fall, her eyes barely blinking as they held mine.

"Can we go visit the booths now? Would Mary let me buy a cinnamon roll before they open?"

Kristina blinked as if she were coming out of a trance. Both of us still seemed to be under a spell when we were close, but whereas I was ready to give in to it, she was still trying to escape.

But I was trying to turn things around, and Emma had given me an unintentional glimmer of hope.

"If not, we can find something since you hardly ate any breakfast today." Kristina peered down at Emma with her lips pursed.

"Because you took *so* long to get ready. I told Leo you kept changing lipsticks and doing your hair and almost made us late."

Kristina dropped her head back, shaking her head as she exhaled a long breath.

Emma was my new favorite little person.

"She told me about your extra effort, but it wasn't needed. You're always beautiful."

"Thank you," she whispered, a blush tingeing her cheeks as a shy smile danced across her lips. "I guess I'll see you later."

"I'll be here. Avoiding the booth with the cinnamon rolls."

A smile tore across my mouth at her wide grin. I stood and watched them climb off the truck and head toward the booths cluttered on both sides of the street.

Maybe I wasn't exactly where I needed to be, but I was getting there.

TWENTY-SEVEN

KRISTINA

"**G**od, I love the country."

I laughed at Claudia's audible sigh.

Peyton's best friend lived in Brooklyn, where they were both from, but she loved making the long drive to visit, both to see Peyton and to people-watch in a small town.

Since Claudia had been a city girl her entire life, Kelly Lakes fascinated her. I'd lived here since I was born, so I didn't see the nuance or novelty she seemed to get such a kick out of.

I loved raising my children in a place with the same strong sense of community I'd always known. But I had to admit, the anonymity of a big city that Peyton and Claudia would talk about sounded nice at times.

Neighbors who didn't care when you were coming or going had an enticing appeal.

"I keep telling you, this isn't the country," Peyton scoffed as we walked past all the different booths from the businesses in town.

"No, it's a Hallmark movie set." Claudia snickered, tucking a lock of black hair behind her ear and adjusting her gray knit hat.

"It's not even Thanksgiving, and there are lights and tinsel all over the damn place."

She clasped her hands under her chin and breathed out another sigh.

"One of these days, I'll probably end up living here because I've seen the error of my jaded big-city ways, right after I fall in love with a hot local."

Peyton rolled her eyes when Claudia elbowed her side.

"God bless Hallmark for making small towns seem so romantic." I looked toward where Chloe was across the street, laughing with a group of kids and not looking back to see where I was.

Usually, parents of teenagers felt slighted when their kids ran off with their friends and didn't give them a second thought, but after all this time of her giving me *too* much thought, I couldn't have been happier that she didn't care where I was for the entire afternoon.

"Come out with us tonight." Claudia patted my arm. "We're going to Halman's. We can volunteer your brother to watch the kids."

"You really want to go to Halman's tonight? It's going to be extra packed after the festival today."

"It's the only bar in town, so it's always packed." Peyton nodded. "But I need a night out, even if I can't drink and I only last for a couple of hours. Maybe you can use one too."

"Hey, how was the fire truck?"

I jumped, not noticing Chloe behind me.

"It was so cool. Leo let me sit up front and everything," Emma gushed as she came up to Chloe.

"I heard about Leo," Claudia said, her brows jumping.

"Don't get mad." Peyton squeezed my arm. "I told her because I knew she'd be happy for you too."

"I so am. Is he still on the fire truck?" Claudia swept her gaze over the street.

I craned my neck to where the fire truck was, now surrounded by other firefighters I recognized, but I couldn't find Leo.

"Maybe, I can't tell from here."

"How perfect is that? You meet someone on vacation, and he ends up in this little town. Kind of like it was meant to be." Claudia pressed her hand to her chest.

"Kind of," Peyton agreed, sneaking a smile at me.

"When did you meet him on vacation?" Chloe asked, squinting at me with a sour expression on her face. She'd asked what Emma meant by a sleepover, and I had simply told her that it was nothing. Her friends had called her over before she could press me to clarify, but it was a bullet I wouldn't dodge for long.

"He worked at the resort I stayed at. Having fun?"

"Yeah, Mina asked a few of us to stay over at her house tonight. Is it okay?"

"How many girls? Her mom will be home?" I knew Mina's mother from the doctor's office I worked for in town, and from what I'd seen, Mina was a sweet kid.

"Yes, and she's here if you want to ask her. Only a couple of us. Can I go?"

I'd speak to Mina's mother on the side, but I couldn't say no. I was so proud and relieved to see Chloe come out of the shell she'd barricaded herself in after the divorce, and I was embarrassed about how much trouble I was having lately doing the same.

Except for that one cluster of days when I had no problem opening up and giving everything to someone I barely knew but who had gotten under my skin in a way no one else had.

And now he was here, but I wasn't the Kristina he knew in

the Keys. Kristina in Kelly Lakes had a lot more hang-ups, and she was getting on my nerves.

"Sounds fine if her parents will be there. We'll pack a bag when we go home."

"Ooh, is he the one talking to your brother?" We all turned toward where Claudia was pointing, my eyes finding Leo right away. Jake laughed at something he said, but they both seemed to be in deep conversation.

"We know our next stop," she chirped and took Emma's hand. "We'll go see your uncle Jake and the hottie your mom likes."

"Claudia," I started, but I was unsure what else to say other than stop.

"So, you do like him? I thought so."

I didn't know how to address Chloe's scrutinizing stare, but I couldn't lie to her. I'd had a long talk with her before her first day of high school on feelings and boys and how important it was to be careful. While I hoped she was still mostly innocent where that was concerned, she knew what a "sleepover" meant.

"Would that bother you?"

"No. I mean Dad has a girlfriend, and it's not like the two of you are together anymore."

My brows shot up. That was news to me, but Colin and I didn't share details about our lives other than work schedules and what weekends he wanted to take the kids.

A heads-up would have been nice, especially if he brought her around the girls, but it didn't bother me. Whether or not Leo was sort of in the picture, Colin and I were very over, and I wished him nothing but happiness if he could find it.

"Hey," Jake said, his arm around his wife. "I hear I have the kids tonight."

"Just Emma. Chloe is sleeping over at her friend's house. I'll be home early." I tried not to let my eyes drift toward Leo.

"Where are you headed? The guys want to head to the bar in town after we de-holiday the truck and unpack all the donations."

"Us too." I nodded. "I bet this town won't seem so small to you when it's all packed into Halman's."

He cracked a slow grin at my joke, the same sinful glint in his eyes he'd had right before I'd taken his cock in my mouth.

Focus, Kristina.

"I suppose not," Leo said, his eyes searing into mine. I shifted back and forth, fighting the inclination to squirm under the weight of his stare. Did he get flashbacks from those three days as often as I did?

Instead of longing looks and heavy moments of silence, we needed to talk and figure out if we were on the same page.

Yet I couldn't seem to make that suggestion.

Kelly Lakes Kristina was pissing me off.

"Sounds like a plan," Peyton said as she burrowed into Jake's side. "Even though I've had plenty of peopling for today."

"Me too, sweetheart," Jake said, kissing the top of her head. "But I got a few new customers from this afternoon."

"There are people in this town who haven't dealt with Russo's Contracting yet?" I squinted at my brother.

He was great at his job and the only contractor in town. He used to hold the title of most eligible bachelor here. He'd sworn to all of us over and over again how he'd never remarry, until he fell madly in love with his best friend's niece.

I was reminded of being at this festival only a couple of years ago. Colin and I weren't speaking to each other because of an argument we'd had on the way here and had almost turned back home. Once we'd finally arrived, my brother snatched the girls away from us for the day, both to give Chloe an escape from the obvious tension—Emma was too little at the time to notice anything but the sweet treats on sale—and to keep the women drooling over him at a distance.

This was considerably better, although fraught with a different kind of tension that only I had to suffer through.

"*I* haven't." Leo laughed, his golden eyes holding mine and making me forget where I was or who was watching us.

At this festival, I was the one drooling, and when I spied Claudia gaping at me, I ran my hand over my mouth to check if it was pooling in the corner.

"My place could use a little work, and Jake seems to be highly recommended around here. Since I'm not planning to eventually move for a change, I'd like to make the place I'm living in seem like mine."

"Makes sense," I said, clearing my throat when my reply croaked out.

"I better get back. Hopefully I'll see you later." He shot me a smile over his shoulder and jogged back to the truck.

"You know, Emma could sleep at our house if she wants," Peyton offered. "She could help set up the baby's room a little with me in the morning."

Emma's hands flew to her mouth after she took in a loud gasp.

"Oh please, Mommy. I won't be any trouble. I promise." She clasped her hands under her chin.

"You're never any trouble, pretty girl," Jake said. "If it's okay with you, Kris."

"This way," Claudia began, her grin so wide her cheeks probably ached, "you don't have to worry about rushing home, should you want to stay out longer or if you want to bring a friend ho—"

"Okay, fine. Emma can sleep over at your house tonight. I'll call Nicole and see if she wants to join us."

"Perfect." Claudia clapped her hands together. I turned to where her gaze traveled over my shoulder.

Mary had one hand on Leo's arm and the other on her daughter's shoulder. I knew she wouldn't let the day end without introducing them. I watched as Leo shook Renee's hand and went to leave when Mary pulled him back.

"Why is Mary always so damn pushy?" I groaned and turned away before I saw anything else.

"Oh boy, we may have a rumble in the sticks tonight if she shows up. This place is so much more fun than Brooklyn."

I ignored Claudia's squeal.

"Come on, girls. We have sleepovers to pack for." I took Emma's hand and tilted my chin for Chloe to follow me.

"Yes, you all probably do." Peyton's lips twitched as she waved goodbye.

Knowing something wouldn't last was different from hoping it would last forever and then it didn't.

Leo and I were on a new timeline now—and if I kept stalling, it would run out.

TWENTY-EIGHT
KRISTINA

"You'd think they'd expand this place," Nicole said as she scooted her chair closer to the table to make room for the crowd behind us. "This is why I always hated coming here."

"Maybe one of you should open a bar here to give them a little competition." Claudia arched a brow as she took a long sip from her wineglass.

"Maybe you can make that your segue into small-town life," Peyton teased. "A city bar in the country, that's a million-dollar idea, Claud."

"And when you do, please have swanky couches to sit on." I shifted on the hardwood chair that my parents probably sat on when they came here back when Halman's first opened.

Halman's had been a town staple for as long as I could remember and hadn't had an update since I was old enough to legally come here. Same plain gray tables, black floors, and dull paneling. They'd gotten a big-screen TV a decade ago to replace the tiny one that hung from the ceiling, but that had been the only upgrade in my generation.

Despite the decor, they always had a crowd, although

Halman's attracted older customers in recent years. The local college kids preferred to head a town or two over when they wanted to drink, not wanting their parents to receive a full report of where they were and what they did before the morning papers came.

"That's because you're supposed to mingle, not sit around and stare like we've been doing."

"I've mingled plenty all day long," Peyton said with a chuckle. "I'm good on my uncomfortable seat."

We all cringed at the screech of Claudia's chair as she pushed it back. "Suit yourself. Does anyone want a refill? I'm going to make friends with a couple of locals." Her brows jumped as she stood and strutted up to the bar.

"God bless her," Nicole said, glancing back at Claudia with a grimace. "I want to get away from the crowd, not wade into it."

"When did we get this old?" I sighed, shaking my head.

"You're not old. I don't want to get up either." Peyton laughed over the rim of her ginger ale glass. "I'm out for the company of friends, so..." A frown pulled at Peyton's mouth when she trailed off.

"What? Did Claudia find a friend?" I joked, resting my elbow on the back of my chair as I turned to figure out what Peyton was staring at, my stomach dropping when I found my answer.

For what seemed like the hundredth time today, my eyes found Leo. I couldn't tell who he was chatting with, but his stance was relaxed and his smile was easy, just like the first moment I met him.

I was about to turn back around when I noticed Renee come up to him and curl her hand around his bicep, squeezing it as she leaned in to whisper something in his ear.

Life was passing me by, and if I didn't make a move, I'd never catch up to it. I slammed down my glass of cider as something inside me snapped and I couldn't sit still.

"Excuse me," I muttered as I stood, slinging my purse over my shoulder as I stalked toward the bar.

Although Mary and her nosy ways bothered me, I had nothing against her daughter. *Had* nothing, until she decided to get too close to Leo.

She wasn't doing anything wrong, as he didn't belong to me or anyone else. I had no claim on him, and he could get close to whomever he wanted to.

I'd done my best to write off my feelings, despite the way he looked at me every time we were together and how my body hummed in response. I'd tried to dismiss it all as lust and a visceral reaction to the combustible chemistry between us that sizzled from the moment we'd met.

But while the dirty times we had in Florida popped into my head on lonely nights—which were all of them—that was not what I thought about the most when I let my mind drift to those few but amazing days in the Keys.

It was how he'd hung on my every word those first few hours and encouraged me to open up to him in ways friends and family couldn't. That lost look in his eyes when he'd told me about his past and why he moved around so much made what he'd told me on the fire truck today a huge deal.

He finally wanted to stay.

I played "Crazy for You" on an endless loop when I was alone in my car, reliving that amazing moment when he dropped everything to come back for just one night with me, and how he'd made love to me for hours like I was a treasure he wanted to savor before he had to let me go.

What if that weekend wasn't just a flash in time like I kept saying it was? What if it was a beginning, and in my efforts to downplay something so rare and wonderful as temporary, I was about to blow it all and would only have my own regrets in the end?

"Oh, hey, Kristina," Renee drawled, sounding like she'd been at the bar a long time before I'd noticed her. "This is Leo. He's new here." She pressed her hand against his chest, and I wanted to swat it away. She let it drop but stayed close.

I envied her for enjoying her post-divorce life while I was still figuring out mine.

But I was sure of one thing, even if it scared the hell out of me.

Leo eyed me as he took a sip from his beer bottle. He wore a simple black T-shirt over jeans, just like the time he'd first caught me staring and then admitted he couldn't take his eyes off me either.

I sucked in a breath and came up to him, grabbing the collar of his shirt and pulling him in for a kiss before I lost my nerve. He stiffened for a moment, most likely just as shocked as I was that I was doing this in front of everyone, but after a second, he melted into me, taking my face in his hands and moving his lips gently over mine, going in for more when I inched away.

His lips were just as warm and soft as I remembered and tasted exactly the same, salty and sweet and so damn addictive. I groaned, warm satisfaction bursting in my chest as I savored the craving I tried to forget but could never ignore.

I missed him and I missed this, too much to dwell on whether it made sense.

He slanted his head and brought me flush to his body, deepening the kiss as if we were all alone and not in front of a crowd. The tang of beer hit my tongue as I parted my lips for him, and the vibration of his needy groan shot right to my core.

Time seemed to stop until he backed away with a teasing flick of his tongue against the seam of my lips.

When I opened my eyes, Leo pressed his forehead against mine, a dazed smile ripping across his mouth as he chased his breath.

When I regained a little of my senses, I registered dozens of eyes piercing my back. I met Renee's perplexed gaze and shrugged.

"Yes, I know Leo." I smiled at the confused elation in his golden eyes despite my heart thundering in my ears. "Hi."

"Hi yourself, beautiful." His voice was low and husky as he inched his hands down my arms, goose bumps trailing his touch.

I backed out of his hold and tapped on the bar.

"Shot of tequila please." I slapped down a ten-dollar bill. The bartender was younger than me and new enough to know me by face but not by name. He smirked as he picked up the cash, amused, I guessed, at what I'd just done in front of half the town, as he poured the shot and slid it over to me.

I thanked him and gulped it down, the fire blazing through my chest doing nothing to soothe the one between my legs, and headed back to the table without a word.

"Wow," was all Peyton said as she regarded me with both wonder and caution. "Are you okay?"

"Well, I can't really feel my legs, but otherwise I'm good." I chugged the rest of my cider, the burn of the tequila already muted by the adrenaline coursing through my veins.

"Oh my God!" Claudia squealed as she rushed back to the table. "That was amazing. You should have seen the look on that woman's face. She's still trying to talk to him, but he's totally ignoring her and looking this way."

"I have never seen you do anything like that." I spied Nicole's dropped jaw in my periphery but didn't turn around. "Even during our most drunken days in college."

I shrugged without lifting my head. While I didn't regret what I'd just done, I was clueless as to where to go from here.

"Leo must really be something." Nicole smiled when I finally looked up.

"Or I'm just out of my goddamn mind."

My hands quivered as I hooked my purse strap over my chair. I was about to let my head plop onto the table when my phone buzzed against my back.

Leo: *Get your coat on. We're leaving.*

"What is it?" Peyton reached over to touch my arm. "Are you okay?"

I didn't answer her as I glanced back to the bar. Leo was leaning against the wall with his phone in his hands, arching his brow at me as if he were issuing a challenge.

I turned around and punched out a shaky reply.

Me: *I'm with friends and can't leave.*

Leo: *You should have thought of that before you kissed me. And I think you can. Did you drive here?*

Me: *No.*

Leo: *Good. We need to talk. Now.*

"Would you guys hate me if I left?"

"Is something wrong with Chloe?" Peyton's brow furrowed as she grabbed her phone and checked the screen. "The last I heard from Jake, all was fine. Emma was already sleeping."

"No, it's not the girls..." I trailed off when I found Leo looming over our table.

"Sorry, ladies. Kristina is coming with me." He held out his hand, narrowing his eyes at me until I stood.

"I'll be back," I whispered to Nicole as I shrugged on my coat and grabbed my purse.

"No, she won't," Leo said with a slow shake of his head. He slid his palm against mine, lacing our fingers together so tightly I'd have his fingerprints on the top of my wrist when he let go.

"I'm Nicole. We spoke over the phone."

"Ah, nice to meet you in person. I'd shake your hand, but..." He held up our joined hands and shrugged.

"Oh, that is no problem." Nicole waved us off. "She's all yours for the night."

"See you in the morning," Peyton sang as Leo dragged me out of the bar so fast, I almost tripped twice to keep up with him.

"Look, I don't know what came over me." Leo didn't look back as he led me to the rear of the parking lot. "I just saw Renee with her hands on you, and I didn't think."

He let go of my hand and leaned against the passenger side door of his truck, his arms crossed and leveling me with a piercing and expectant scrutiny that left my mouth parched and my panties wet.

"It's been so hard not to think of you all these months."

After all this time of holding it in, the alcohol I'd tried to calm myself with brought on some liquid courage.

"But I thought I'd never see you again and moved on. Or tried to. Now you're here, in my tiny fucking town where I can't escape you. What if we ruin it?" My voice fell to a whisper. "What if the real me, the mom with two kids and two jobs, disappoints you? Or you get restless and leave because that's what you've always done? Then I lose both the real you and the dream of us."

I pressed my palm to my forehead, grateful for the one flickering light in the parking lot that prevented me from seeing Leo's reaction.

"I'll just go back inside."

Leo caught my arm when I turned around and yanked me back. He grabbed the back of my head and covered my mouth with a scorching, toe-curling kiss that liquefied my knees. His warm tongue curled around mine as I slumped against him, running my hands up his chest and down his arms. I whimpered into his mouth as he grazed his hands down my back and cupped my ass, pushing deeper into me, his hard cock rubbing against my core with delicious and perfect friction.

"Does this feel like you're disappointing me? Since the moment I saw you again, I've only wanted you more. You were beautiful when I met you, but seeing you in action here"—he cradled my cheek, sinking his teeth into his bottom lip, still wet from our kiss—"you are fucking incredible. Like I always knew you were. I'm not going anywhere. Give me a chance, baby. Give *us* a chance. Things happen for a reason."

I laughed, breathless from my heart thudding against my rib cage.

"Are you telling me to believe in fate, too?"

"With us, what else would you call it?"

"I suppose," I relented, burying my head into his chest.

"Listen," he whispered and kissed the top of my head, "I should have reached out, whether or not we agreed to. I was an idiot, because everything I felt for you confused and scared the hell out of me."

He grabbed my arms and pushed me back, dipping his head until I raised my own.

"I didn't want to disappoint you either. Leaving you at that airport was the hardest thing I ever had to do."

He traced the curve of my jaw with his thumb.

"Knowing how good we were together, how amazing we'd be if we could just make it work somehow, it killed me. I was afraid of ruining all the good we had for that little amount of time too. I had the inkling to move back even then, although I know it was a crazy as hell thought, even for us."

A smile tugged at my lips as I fidgeted with the collar of his jacket.

"So, now what, Kristina? You tell me."

I pressed my hand to his chest, my own pulse kicking up when his heart thumped against my palm.

"Do you want to come home with me?"

When I'd asked him the first time, home was the temporary

oasis of my vacation suite. Having Leo in my real home was a big step and one that still frightened me, if I was honest.

But the alternative, walking away and never feeling this way again, always wondering what could've been, terrified me to my core.

"I was about to ask you the same thing."

He pulled me into a blistering kiss, full of slow passion instead of sad desperation.

It was wonderful yet scary as hell when dreams came true.

TWENTY-NINE

LEO

"Wow, you do live close to the firehouse," I said, taking a quick glance at Kristina as I turned onto her street. I was still half afraid she'd jump out of my truck and tell me goodnight once I pulled up to her house.

After that kiss, there was no way in hell I was letting her walk away again. We'd already wasted too much time giving each other space that neither of us really wanted.

What I wanted was *her*—so much that I could barely see straight. To kiss me in a crowded bar, essentially claiming me in front of the whole damn town, was a huge step for her and hot as fucking hell.

If she didn't agree to leave, I would have hoisted her over my shoulder and dragged her out, not giving a shit about who saw or what they'd say.

In fact, the more people who saw Kristina kiss me tonight, the more satisfaction seeped into my veins. I'd claimed her as much as she claimed me on that crowded barroom floor, and if she let me, I'd keep claiming her all night long.

"I do," she finally replied. "Emma loves running to the window to watch the lights and listen to the sirens."

"I owe her sirens. I'll figure out a way to take her for a ride."

"She'd love that."

I studied her face, looking for any signs that she regretted asking me to come home with her, but all I found was an easy smile spreading across her lips.

"You can park behind my car in the driveway. There's room."

I nodded, easing my truck behind her SUV and cutting the engine once I parked.

I shifted toward her and slid my hand over the nape of her neck.

"I'm following your lead. I want you so much, but we'll take it at your pace. I just want to be with you—"

She leaned over the console and cut me off with a kiss, whimpering as she slanted her mouth over mine, all the trepidation and hesitation she'd first come at me with earlier tonight now gone. She pulled me closer, kissing me harder as she drifted one hand down my chest, stopping at my belt buckle. My cock twitched at her proximity.

"You really want to give your neighbors a show? Make sure everyone knows I'm off-limits?" I murmured against her lips.

She pulled back, her eyes hooded and a smile curving her swollen mouth.

"I won't fight you, baby." I took her bottom lip in between mine and let it go with a nibble. "I'm all yours."

She feathered her hand down my cheek.

"Claiming you tonight wasn't my intention."

"Oh yes, it was." I kissed the tip of her nose as she laughed. "Please don't deny it because I loved every second."

"Not a conscious intention, anyway. But I couldn't let her have you."

"And why is that?" I nuzzled her cheek and dusted light kisses over her jaw, smiling against her skin at her soft sigh.

She grabbed my face, fusing her mouth to mine and kissing me with enough passion and possession to make me almost blow in my jeans. As if she read my mind, she coasted her hand down my chest and over where my cock strained against the denim.

"If you want to keep claiming me," I panted after I broke our kiss, "let's take this inside. There isn't enough room here for all I want to do to you right now."

"Don't threaten me with a good time," she said, still breathless, with a sly grin pulling at her mouth. She opened the door and stepped out of the truck, not looking back at me, and headed for her front door.

I almost jumped out of the driver's seat and was hot on her heels by the time she had her keys in her hand. I pulled her back by her waist, brushed her hair off her shoulder, and ran my tongue down her neck until she slumped against me.

"Remember when I told you that you'd feel me all the way back to New York?" I asked as I skated my hand under her jacket and slipped it under her shirt, coasting my palm over the soft skin of her stomach before I dipped it inside her panties. "Did you?"

I muttered a "fuck" and dropped my head into the crook of her shoulder. She was warm and wet and already dripping all over my fingers.

She nodded, moaning as she pressed her hand against the door and swayed her hips in tandem with every tiny circle I traced around her clit.

"So wet," I growled into her neck as I moved my finger up and down her slit. "Maybe I'll make you come out here. And when you do, you can scream my name, so everyone knows I'm yours."

"Jesus, Leo," she croaked out as her keys dropped to the ground with a soft jingle. She clutched the top of my hand resting on her waist as I moved my other hand between her legs. I slid two fingers inside her, circling the hard and swollen bump again when I inched them out.

"Don't stop, please." Her voice was barely a whisper as she leaned forward, spreading her legs wider as I thrust my fingers deeper inside.

"I'm not stopping until you come. Then once I get you inside, you're going to ride my face until you come again all over my tongue. Fuck, I miss how you taste."

I groaned, my own breathing ragged and my cock ready to burst through my zipper. "And then I'm going to fuck you so hard, every time you move tomorrow, you'll remember that you belong to me."

She slammed her hand against the door, pulsing against my fingers before she cried out. I turned her head toward me, covering her mouth with mine to swallow her whimpers as her climax ripped through her.

She fell back, laughing as she scrubbed her hand down her face.

"I seem to lose track of where I am when it comes to you." She craned her neck and peered up at me, her cheeks flushed as her green eyes glimmered. "You're a blinding distraction."

"Back at you, baby." I brushed her lips with a quick kiss, holding her gaze as I sucked my fingers into my mouth.

"*So* fucking sweet."

"What are you doing to me?" She dropped her chin to her chest and shook her head, still pressing her hand to the door as she chased her breath.

I bent down to grab her keys.

"Once we're inside, anything you'll let me."

She slid the keys from where I dangled them on my finger,

narrowing her eyes despite the dazed smile coasting across her swollen mouth.

I dropped a kiss on her shoulder and wrapped my arms around her waist.

"I missed you so much."

"I missed *you*." She looped her arm around my neck and tilted her head back to kiss my cheek.

I followed her inside and locked the door behind me.

"Feels a little surreal to have you here. In my house, not my vacation suite." She came up to me and wrapped her arms around my waist with a gorgeous and relaxed smile that I hadn't seen since her last night in Florida.

"Feels weird to be here. Weird in a good way." I rubbed her back. "After all those nights of me wondering where you were and what you were doing." I pressed a kiss to her forehead.

"I'm glad you're here," she whispered into my chest.

"I'm glad you let me in."

I meant that in every way. From the time she'd kissed me tonight, everything had felt real and familiar between us.

And right—so damn right.

"This is a big house to have all to ourselves."

She burst out laughing when I waggled my eyebrows.

"Don't get used to it." She huffed out a laugh. "I'm never alone. At least not usually. Being with me is being with my girls most of the time."

"That's more than fine with me. Why would you think it wouldn't be?" I squeezed her shoulders until she lifted her head.

"That was part of my hesitation. When we met it was a lot of"—she nodded to the front door—"that. I'm not saying the connection wasn't real, but things were a lot easier and more fun when it was just me. Now I come with all this." She let out a sad laugh.

"Why would you think I would consider that a deal-breaker?

I want the girls to know me. I think I'm good with Emma already, but with Chloe, I get the feeling I'm going to have to work at it." I took her face in my hands. "And I'm happy to rise to the challenge. Because I want you—all of you. I thought we had that settled."

"We did, we do." Her mouth quirked into a smile. "Being this happy makes me a little nervous. Not used to it."

"Well, get used to it. I'm not going anywhere."

She pressed her lips to mine, smiling into the kiss before she backed away. "Take your jacket off, and I'll give you the tour."

I shrugged off my jacket and hung it on the rack by the door. Every inch of wall space heading up the stairs was filled with a picture of her and the girls. My eyes landed on a framed photo on an end table. Kristina held a baby wrapped in a pink blanket, and a younger Chloe sat on a man's lap next to her.

"That is the only photo left in this house of Colin," Kristina told me when she caught me staring. "And it's only there because Emma won't let me take it down because it's of her original birthday." She picked it up, gazing at it with a sigh. "Chloe's tried to move it a few times, and Emma gets upset." She shrugged and placed it back on the table. "I usually keep it more hidden, but Emma likes to take it and stare at it sometimes."

She chewed her bottom lip as she studied my face.

"I think Emma likes it so much because her parents in one place and not arguing is a fascinating anomaly to her."

"Is he still being a dick?"

Rage had run through me the night he'd called her in Florida and after everything she'd confessed to me about how he treated her, all that she didn't tell friends and family. They'd probably want to kick his ass as much as I did, and I'd have to keep myself in check when we eventually crossed paths.

"He has a girlfriend now, or so I hear. When I came home, I found it easier to ignore him so we don't fight in front of the girls anymore. Or at least, we haven't for the past few months. I finally realized that maybe I wasn't such a shrew and he was just a jerk." She shrugged. "Although when tonight gets back to him, I bet he'll have something to say."

I backed her against the wall and slid my hands down her arms. She shivered against me as I laced our fingers together and pinned her hands above her head.

"Then, he'll have two of us to deal with if he does. But you aren't going to worry about him—or anything else." I slanted my mouth over hers, smiling as she fought against my hands. I kissed her slowly enough to drive us both crazy.

"Let go of my hands so I can touch you."

I laughed against her lips and dropped her hands. "If this is our only night alone here, we should make the most of it." I lifted her shirt over her head and threw it behind me.

"Tan lines faded," she whispered as she ran her thumb back and forth along her bra strap. The swells of her breasts pushed against the lace of her black bra, and I couldn't resist hooking a finger inside each cup and dragging them down until she spilled out.

I sucked a nipple into my mouth and traced around the rigid peak with my tongue. She dug her fingers into my hair as she arched her back, pushing those perfect breasts against my greedy mouth.

"My favorite freckle is still here." I peppered kisses along her collarbone as I unclasped her bra, sliding the straps down her arms. "You're so fucking beautiful."

I grabbed the back of her neck and hauled her close, plundering her mouth as she slid her hands under my T-shirt. Goose bumps pebbled along my chest as she scratched her nails down my torso.

I peeled off my shirt and dropped to my knees, unbuttoning her jeans as I held her gaze.

"*You're* so fucking beautiful. I still think I'm dreaming." Her hooded eyes raked down my body, the hungry look in her eyes making the blood roar in my veins.

"I'm real and all yours, gorgeous. Now, step out for me." I glided her jeans down her legs, dropping kisses along her thighs as she lifted one leg at a time.

"Leo," she said, her voice trembling. "I'm still sensitive—*holy shit.*"

I sucked her clit into my mouth through her panties, now so wet I could see through the silk. I moved them to the side, the same way she'd offered herself to me by the pool that night, and devoured her, clutching her hips to bring her even closer and snake my tongue deep inside.

She screamed my name, her legs already shaking as she bucked her hips against my mouth.

"That's it, baby. Ride my face and come in my mouth." I sucked and licked every inch of her slick skin, high on her sweet taste and every tortured noise that fell from her lips.

She dug her nails into my shoulders, stilling against my tongue until I slapped her ass with a loud smack.

She thrust forward, screaming my name at first then repeating it like a plea and a prayer until she almost slid down the wall. I caught her, hooking my thumbs into the waistband of her panties and dragging them down her legs.

I unbuckled my belt and unfastened the button on my jeans, grabbing my wallet out of my pocket before letting my clothes drop to the floor and stepping out of them.

"Ever make love against a wall?" I asked as I rooted around in my wallet for the foil packet I was looking for.

"Not here."

I froze right before I rolled the condom on.

"Is that so?"

I was never possessive about any woman, part of my aloof

way of life, but fucking her against the wall for the first time in this house, knowing her ex had lived here, kicked up my heartbeat enough for it to thunder in my ears.

Old me would have run for the hills at this point, but the man I was now reveled in it too much to stop or ever let her go again.

"Wrap your legs around me, baby," I said, my voice a low growl as the caveman I never knew I had in me took over. I thrust inside her as soon as she did. Every thump against the wall grew louder as I went deeper, our mouths crashing together in a mess of lips and tongues and sweet fucking relief.

I held off as much as I could until she clenched around me. I slammed my hand against the wall as I emptied myself inside her, this time really giving her all I had and already eager for her to take more.

"For the second time tonight, I can't feel my legs." She laughed and held on, her arms tightly wrapped around my neck. "The first was when I decided to kiss you."

I chuckled and set her down, brushing her lips one last time as my pulse and the rest of me came back down to earth.

It was too early to say, "I love you," so why was it on the tip of my tongue? I swallowed it down, hating holding it back but scared of ruining our first perfect night since Florida.

She broke me out of the lifelong funk I'd been in and opened my eyes to all I'd missed. I'd come to right after she'd almost slipped through my fingers, and I'd never leave her again.

It was too soon to think she was the one, but it'd been too soon for so many things since we'd met. She had to be it because I couldn't picture my life with anyone else, and the thought of her with another man made me want to engulf the world in flames.

Maybe the big moments in life weren't supposed to make sense.

THIRTY

KRISTINA

It had been a long time since my sleep was so restful and dreamless that I didn't know where I was when I woke up. Gray light filtered into my bedroom as the wind rustled through the bare branches of the trees in my yard, the faint whistling sound breaking through the morning stillness.

I buried my head back in the pillow when I read the time on my alarm clock. It was barely eight thirty a.m., and there were no children in the house to drag me out of bed for pancakes, or no *child* since Chloe didn't unearth herself from her room until ten if she didn't have school or a good reason.

I stretched out my legs and let out a groan. Muscles all over my body screamed at me as I tried to curl myself into a ball and go back to sleep. I sank my teeth into my bottom lip at the sting between my legs each time I tried to adjust my position.

I prided myself on being in decent shape, but I wasn't built for a night of sexual athletics on every surface of my living room and up my staircase. The tension between Leo and me was combustible enough to explode, and it did—all over my house. I had a trail of clothes to clean up and pictures to rehang on my wall.

"Where do you think you're going?" Leo grumbled as he looped his arm around my waist and pulled me back.

"Since I can barely walk, nowhere fast."

He chuckled against my shoulder and ran his lips over the nape of my neck. I smiled at the scratch of his stubble as he dragged kisses down my back.

"None of that," I protested despite squirming at the scrape of his stubble against my skin. "We have a living room to clean up."

"None of that? What about this?" He skidded his hand up my thigh, gliding his fingers across my stomach until they settled at my core.

"Leo, please," I begged into the pillow as my hips followed the swirl of his fingers.

"I can clean up." He dropped kisses on my shoulder as he slid one finger inside. I groaned at his slow entry, my body sore from last night's repeat invasion but still hungry for more. "It's the least I can do since I'm the reason you can barely walk."

My legs went rigid when he pressed his thumb into my clit. I'd thought my nerve endings would be burned out after last night, but I was still a live wire when it came to Leo. Sex was never like this with Colin or anyone else, and until Leo and I met, I hadn't thought sex was like this, period.

During a terrible argument a month or so before he moved out for the last time and we started "dating," Colin had called me frigid. He'd apologized right after, realizing he'd gone too far, but I'd never forgotten that. Each time we had sex after, I could never relax enough to enjoy it, always wondering what I was doing wrong or if Colin would be upset if I didn't appear into it enough.

With Leo, I could let go and forget all the hang-ups that stemmed from old insecurities. Like everything else when we first met, I'd tried to write it off as the rush of something forbidden and temporary.

The almost all-night marathon we'd had and the destruction we'd left in its wake had proven me wrong.

What had always drawn me the most to Leo wasn't the bedroom eyes, the muscles, or the sexy lines of ink on his perfect body. It was how, from the second we met, he made it clear that he just wanted to be with me—as I was. I didn't have to change for him or try harder to be anything other than myself.

The inhibitions I'd fought so hard to shed were finally gone because I was finally with the right person.

He burst out laughing at my exhausted sigh into my pillow.

"You're going to break my vagina if you keep doing that."

"Nah, I think you're both up for the challenge."

I turned my head, warmth spreading in my chest at his wide grin.

"Good morning, gorgeous."

"Good morning," I replied in a gravelly whisper, still recovering from the early morning aftershocks he'd just given me. "I'm glad you're here."

"Me too, babe." He pecked my lips and stood. "My clothes are all downstairs too, so before the girls get home, let me get dressed and clean up."

"Wait." I shot up, sucking in a breath at the new sting blazing through my core at the change in position. "I'm not totally sure if the curtains are closed, which is something that should have dawned on me last night. Let me get a robe on, and I'll bring you your clothes."

"It's not like the neighbors are right on top of you like they are at my condo. The next house is almost halfway up the street." He tilted his head to the side and laughed. "Are you afraid a deer is going to see my dick?"

I shrugged into my fuzzy robe, holding his gaze as I came closer.

"My eyes only, babe."

"Fuck," he hissed and pulled me back on the bed. "I love you possessive."

I moaned into his kiss, running my hands up and down his back as I willed my heart to calm down. The rush from hearing him say I love you and the inclination to say it back, even if out of the right context, was so overwhelming I was afraid to tear my mouth away from his for fear it would slip out.

If I added up all the time I'd known him, minus the months of lonely pining, it only amounted to weeks. Too soon to be in love with someone, no matter how intoxicating the passion was between us.

Colin and I had some good times together before everything started to go bad, but I didn't recall a time when things were as intense between us as they were between Leo and me.

The crazy lust was probably doing things to my brain, but when Leo broke the kiss, staring down at me with so much more than just heat, it sure as hell felt real.

I couldn't blame a time limit for trapping us into a powder keg of emotions anymore. We were both here in this town to stay, at least I hoped, as that was still a fear I needed to shake.

But when I was with Leo, even though I'd just gotten him back, I didn't want to be anywhere else.

"Last night seems...almost like it didn't happen." I cuddled next to him when he drew me into his side. "I mean, other than not being able to move."

"It happened, all right. The way you grabbed me and kissed me like that, in front of everyone, I've never been so turned on in my life. That moment is going to roll around in my head for a long time."

"I'm sure we're going to *hear* about it for a long time. A good way to start over, I guess," I said, skimming my finger along the grooves of his abs.

"We aren't starting over, we're starting back."

"Starting back?" I pushed off his chest and squinted at him. "What's the difference?"

"Well, starting over means that we were doing things wrong. Starting back means we were interrupted. All that good from when we first met still counts. We don't have to do anything over, just keep going." He cupped my chin, his wide and easy grin stealing what was left of the air in my lungs. "Without worrying about when we have to stop or when one of us has to leave."

If I wasn't fully in love with this guy yet, the free fall was soon and inevitable.

"You're kind of romantic."

"I thought I was suave."

"That too," I said, scratching my nails along the longer bristles of stubble at his chin. "But as much as I enjoy having you naked in my bedroom, let me get your clothes."

"Fine." He exhaled a long sigh as I pushed off the bed. "If it makes you feel better, you can go pick up my clothes. I'll wait up here."

He sat up, one hand behind his head as he leaned against my headboard.

"What?" He lifted a shoulder in feigned innocence when he caught me staring. "You're the one making a big deal about getting my clothes when you could just stay naked with me for another hour."

I shook my head, a smile rushing across my mouth as I walked down the stairs.

Our clothes were strewn across the whole living room, and I would have to explain why two pictures crashed off the wall in the hallway.

We'd managed to stop pawing at each other long enough to sweep up the glass, but I needed a better reason for why they broke other than Leo plowing me against the wall.

My shoulders rolled with a sexy chill at the recent memory.

"I think that's all of it," I said as I plopped the ball of clothes onto the chair next to my bed. "Enough that if we have to go downstairs for anything left behind, we won't shock any wildlife peeking through the window."

Leo lounged on the bed in the same sexy pose as I'd left him. He scooted under the sheets and crooked a finger at me.

"So, come back to bed." He grabbed my hand and yanked me back until I fell on top of him. "While there's still no one around to hear all the noise you make."

"I don't make that much noise," I said, propping my elbow onto Leo's hard stomach and resting my head on my hand.

I scowled at him when his brows popped up.

"So all that screaming for *harder* and *deeper* was my imagination?"

I swatted his chest as it rumbled with a laugh.

"You know what I was thinking?" He dragged his finger up and down my back. "I don't even know what your favorite food is. I've never taken you out anywhere."

"That's not true. What about that seafood place on the coast?"

He shook his head. "That doesn't count. I mean a place where our meal is on a plate, not in a basket. As far as we've come and how fast we got here, there's still a lot we need to do."

"So," I started, studying his face for a minute. "You want to date me now?" I chuckled, but his mouth stayed a hard, flat line.

"When I ran into you when you were on that date, at a table sitting across from another guy, I almost lost it. Not only because *I* wanted to be at that table with you, but because I never had the chance to take you out on a real date."

"And I guess that's why you sent drinks over," I teased, cocking a brow. "The same drink you made for me the night we met. If I weren't so mad, I would have appreciated the sentiment."

"You weren't mad. Flustered, frustrated, maybe." He sat up, leaning in to brush my lips. "Nothing changed between us, the only difference was that I admitted it before you did. I heard you were stubborn."

He swept the hair off my neck and painted a trail of tiny kisses down my shoulder. I shut my eyes as that side of my robe drooped down to my elbow, savoring the wet warmth of his lips as he sucked a nipple into his mouth.

"Who told you that?" I asked in a scratchy whisper, grasping the back of his head as he dragged openmouthed kisses across my chest.

"Everyone who knows you." He slid the other side of my robe down my shoulder.

"You can date me if you want," I joked, my eyes popping open when Leo weaved his hand into my hair, latching on to a fistful and tugging my head back.

"Let me be clear." Heat rushed between my legs at his low growl. "Only *I* date you. No more of these tools from the app, no more of anyone but me. Got it?"

"I never wanted anyone else, that's been my big problem since I came back." I straddled his lap and let the rest of my robe fall away. "Same goes for you."

His hooded eyes widened as he burst out laughing.

"By now, all of Kelly Lakes knows I belong to you. And I'm very glad they do."

I took his face in my hands and slanted my mouth over his. The kiss was slow and deep as Leo groaned against my lips.

I backed away, running my thumb over the bristles of stubble covering his jaw.

"Italian is my favorite food. Probably because that's what I mostly grew up with. But tacos are a weakness and the only reason I agreed to that date you saw me on." I smiled at the low moan escaping him when I wrapped my legs around him.

"Then I'll take you for Italian next, and maybe after that, we can go back to that Mexican place where I can actually enjoy the food this time because you'll be across the table from *me*, where you belong." He drew me closer, skimming a callused finger up and down my spine, goose bumps breaking out along its path from both his touch and the possessive burn in his gaze.

"Those kinds of nights will be rare. When I go out to eat, I usually have to check the menu for chicken fingers and French fries because I have two picky eaters who don't allow me much variety."

"I am very into chicken fingers and French fries, so all that sounds perfect to me."

I sat back on my heels, squinting at Leo's serene smile.

"You sure about that?"

"I'm sure about you," he said, sliding his hands under my hips and pressing me closer to his chest. "Any time I can get with you, that's perfect."

THIRTY-ONE
KRISTINA

"Where are you going?" Emma asked from my bed while she lay on her stomach, her head resting in her hands as she observed me in the mirror.

"I'm going out to dinner, nothing big." I smiled at her reflection as I coated my lashes with mascara.

When she scrunched her nose at me in reply, I couldn't blame her for being confused.

When I met my dates from the app, the girls were with their father and had no idea what I was doing while they were gone. And even if they were here, I did not put even close to this amount of effort into how I looked.

Leo and I had plenty of sex, but he'd brought up a great point about not knowing the little things about each other because we didn't have the time—and never expected to last past our hot and heavy beginning.

While I was sure everyone was still whispering about the kiss at the bar, I was thrilled to give confirmation to whoever we saw tonight about whether we were really together.

I wore a green sweater dress, just tight enough to highlight all of Leo's favorite places, and went a little heavier than usual on the shadow to play up my eyes.

On the first few "dates" with Colin during our failed last-ditch effort to save our marriage, I'd tried to bump up my appearance like this but stopped when it was obvious that he didn't notice or care. He'd said I "looked nice" once or twice, but with none of the emotion or the reaction I was looking for, which only made me feel worse.

There was no desperation in trying to look my best tonight, only excitement as dressing up for a man who would appreciate it was an exhilarating kind of fun.

"Where?" Chloe asked, her arms crossed over her torso as she studied me. She'd shrugged it off at the festival when I'd admitted that I liked Leo, but watching me get ready to go on a date with him seemed to put her on alert.

"Dino's," I told her as I fastened my earrings.

"You're getting *that* dressed up for Dino's?" Chloe lifted a brow as she leaned against the doorjamb. Dino's had been a family favorite ever since I was a kid. They had the best Italian food, but we'd never dressed up to go there. We'd stopped by last week after Chloe's basketball game in sweats.

I was dressing for the person, not the place, but I was leery to put too much emphasis on that. This new phase Leo and I were heading into was exciting but still new. I was sure enough about him for it to frighten me a little, but if we wanted to make this real in the long-term, we had to move slowly, if only for the girls' sake.

"It's not a crime to want to look nice." I tapped Chloe's nose. "I wear scrubs at work and leggings everywhere else. This dress still had the tags on it and deserves a night out of the closet."

I spun around with a dramatic flair, hoping to make them laugh. I was rewarded with a giggle from Emma but could only pull a weak shrug out of Chloe.

Leo was going to be around a lot—I hoped. While Emma would be all in without much convincing, I knew Chloe would have a hard time. Leo had said that he was up for the challenge, and I prayed that seeing me happy would help her acclimate to Leo and me sooner.

"You look beautiful, Mommy!"

"Thank you, Emma," I said, raising a brow at Chloe. When she moped away, I stifled a frustrated sigh.

Leo and I had already pulled back on each other plenty of times for no reason other than fear, only to be miserable in the end. Tonight was a beginning for all of us, and like all beginnings, some things and some people would be uncomfortable.

Trying to protect my girls from change hadn't helped any of us. I would reassure them as best as I could, but as far as I was concerned, there was no other direction for Leo and me than forward.

"Don't you look beautiful." My mother brought her hand to her chest and sighed.

"See?" I turned around to where the girls had followed me down the stairs. "Grandma doesn't even remember the last time I dressed up, so I think it was about time."

Mom was staying the night with the girls so that Leo and I didn't have to rush back. There would be no "sleepovers" tonight, but we could enjoy each other's company without a time limit, and that was good enough for me.

"Well, yes, I love the dress, but I was talking about the way you're lit up from the inside," she whispered as she clasped my arm. Her emerald eyes shone as they searched mine, her wide and relieved smile squeezing my heart. "I like Leo already."

"Me too!" Emma said as she hugged my waist. I smoothed the loose hairs from her ponytail back while the innocent happiness in her features scratched at the back of my throat.

I inhaled a long breath through my nostrils and smiled

down at my youngest. Tonight was a happy night, not one to get all blubbery and ruin my makeup.

"He's here!" Emma yelled at the chime of the doorbell.

My mother grabbed Emma's hand as she raced for the door.

"Why don't we both let him in since you're still too young to answer doors by yourself." Mom gave Emma's ponytail a playful tug before she took her hand and unlocked the door.

"Leo, come in, it's freezing," Mom said as she pulled him inside with Emma still latched on to her waist.

"Thank you, Mrs. Russo," he said, taking both of Mom's hands in his. "I'm so happy to finally meet you."

"I am thrilled to meet you too." Mom shot me a glance over her shoulder, her eyes widening for a moment before she turned back to Leo.

While he spoke to my mother, I gave his body a shameless perusal. His gray jacket clung to his torso and tapered waist, and I was looking forward to the view from the back when he turned around in those black pants.

My mother's reaction was spot-on. The man was beautiful— and all mine tonight.

"Wow," he breathed out, a slow grin spreading across his lips when his eyes met mine. "You're gorgeous." His eyes flicked down my body for a quick moment before he straightened, clearing his throat.

"Sorry," he said to my mother with a sheepish smile.

"Oh, don't be sorry. She *is* gorgeous." Mom squeezed his arm. "We'll go into the living room so you can say hello."

"Hi, Leo!" Emma wrapped what she could of her tiny arms around his muscular thighs.

"I didn't mean you." Mom chuckled and held out her hand.

"It's all right," Leo said and picked Emma up. "We're old friends right, chiquita?"

"Yep," she said and swiveled her head to my mother. "He

took me on my first fire truck." Her brows snapped together as she turned back to Leo. "That's not my name."

"It means 'little one' in Spanish. *Special* little one."

"Like when Mike calls you pipsqueak, but a little nicer," I tried to explain, holding back a laugh at her slow nod.

"So, I'm special?" she asked, her little forehead creased as if she were mulling it over.

"Very," Leo said, drawing a giggle from Emma when he tickled her side. As I looked between them, my heart squeezed so hard it ached, grateful for my daughter's pure and open heart.

"Oh, okay. It was really cool, Grandma. Leo showed me *everything*," she said, craning her neck back to my mother.

"I heard. The one year I miss the festival, all the good stuff happens." Mom's brow popped up when she glanced at me over her shoulder. I hadn't told her about the kiss in the bar, but I didn't have to. She wasn't a Kelly Lakes resident anymore but her over-fifty community a town over was close enough. When she was overly thrilled to see me the following day, I was certain she'd been filled in by one of her former neighbors or a member of my traitorous family.

"But no sirens because he said we couldn't scare people."

"I can see that. Why don't we let them head out, and we can choose a movie for tonight?" Mom lifted Emma out of Leo's arms and set her down. "You had dinner already, and Leo and Mommy are probably really hungry."

"But he just got here." She peered up at us with a deep frown.

"He'll be back. I promise," I said, sneaking a smile at Leo. "Maybe he can come here for dinner next time, and we'll bake him dessert." I crouched in front of her. "Now, give me a kiss goodnight since you'll be way into dreamland when I get home."

She threw her arms around my neck and squeezed. I kissed

her cheek, my heart sinking when I scanned the living room and what I could see of the kitchen.

Chloe was nowhere in sight and had most likely retreated up to her room. I'd leave her alone for the moment but would speak to her in the morning to remind her about manners for guests in this house, no matter what her feelings were.

"Good night, Leo." Emma stepped in front of him and held up her arms. "I'm little, but you're really tall. Can I see if I can touch the ceiling?"

"You sure can," Leo said, lifting her up as if she were nothing but a feather and holding her over his head by her waist while she stretched her arm toward the ceiling.

"I got it!" she said, flashing us a wide grin when she dropped her hand.

"Sweet dreams." He kissed her forehead and set her down.

I wrapped my arms around Leo's waist after Emma scurried into the living room to join her grandmother.

"Hi."

"Hi yourself, beautiful." I laughed as he kissed my forehead, remembering the same breathless greeting he'd given me after our kiss at the bar.

"You're beautiful too." I coasted my hands down his chest. "I wish you could come back and stay, but—"

"Hey, baby steps." He tapped my chin with his knuckle. "I'm just happy I can take you out. The right way. Where's Chloe?"

"Hiding in her room. She needs to get used to this, and she will. I hope sooner rather than later."

He nodded, cupping my cheek as a smile pulled at his mouth. He leaned in and brushed my lips, his grin deepening with every lingering kiss.

"I'll be here, either way."

THIRTY-TWO
LEO

"Kristina!"

The hostess's eyes lit up as soon as she spotted us. When she ran up to Kristina and pulled her into a hug, she barely came up to Kristina's shoulders. She reminded me of my aunt, tiny with every short gray hair in place as she looked us over with kind blue eyes.

"You act like you didn't see me last week, Connie."

"I didn't see you with your new friend." She smiled as she looked between us. "I'm Connie. You're the fireman-nurse, right?"

Kristina flicked her gaze to mine, a smirk curling her red lips.

"No secrets in this town. Yes, I'm Leo." I held out my hand. "Nice to meet you."

"Very nice to meet you, too. I've known this beautiful girl since she was this big." Connie rested her hand on her knee.

"I haven't been a girl in a long time, but thank you."

Connie waved a hand at her and grabbed two menus from the front counter.

"Vera, my granddaughter, has class, so I'm the hostess tonight."

"I can't believe she's in college already," Kristina said as we followed Connie.

The customers at the other tables all looked familiar, although I was still learning the names of some. Between both my jobs, I'd met or seen most of the people in town.

And judging by all the heads we turned as we made our way through the space, there weren't many who hadn't heard about what happened between us at Halman's. A man I recognized from the bar that night averted his gaze when I made eye contact.

I kept my hand on the small of her back all the way to the table to clear up any confusion about whether we were together.

"We can't believe she's in college and graduating in June. Where did all the time go?" Connie exhaled a long sigh and handed us our menus when we sat down. "Your girls are getting big too. The older one looks just like you. I wish Tommy could see."

Connie frowned and shook her head.

Kristina nodded, a sad smile curving her lips. "I like to think he does."

Connie squeezed her arm before she headed back to the front.

"Tommy was my father," Kristina said. "He was very good friends with Dino and his wife for as long as I can remember, so Jake and I have grown up in this restaurant."

"I like to believe that too. That they still see, even if you can't see them. Although, I hope they don't see it *all*."

"Ah, yeah. There are some things I'm very grateful that he wasn't here for." She scoffed, nodding a thank-you when the busboy filled our glasses with water.

"But I hope he sees Jake and me now. I like thinking maybe

he had something to do with the unexpected good fortune my brother and I stumbled upon." Her brows jumped as she took a sip of water.

"That's funny because I thought meeting you was *my* good fortune."

She narrowed her eyes at me as her lips twitched.

"Always so suave."

"When you're good at something, it's smart to stick with it."

Her shoulders shook with a laugh as she nudged my foot under the table.

"I never stood a chance, did I?"

I was the one who never stood a chance, who was so captivated by a woman on sight that nothing was the same after. I was still getting used to the fact that we were both here to stay and I wouldn't have to give her up at the end of the night.

I'd memorized every curve and sensitive spot on her body, but this kind of together was what I'd been craving all along, even if I didn't understand it at first.

"Hey, I thought that was you."

We both turned our heads to the familiar voice behind us. Keith McGrath, the Kelly Lakes police chief, smiled as he came up to our table.

"Another one who doesn't recognize me out of scrubs or sweats," Kristina joked as she stood to give him a hello hug. "On duty tonight?"

"I am, just stopped in for some takeout." He craned his neck toward me. "Hey, Reyes, right?"

"Yes, nice to see you, Chief."

I rose from my seat to shake his hand. I'd met Keith during my first week at the firehouse when he'd stopped by to speak to Vic. The guys had told me that between the two of them, they made sure to know everyone and everything that happened within the town limits.

This wasn't my first time living in a small town, but it seemed as if the degrees of separation between everyone in Kelly Lakes were much fewer than anywhere else.

Keith nodded, smiling at Kristina when he dropped my hand. "I heard you guys were a thing. Good for you, kid."

She rolled her eyes when he jabbed her arm.

"I'm in my forties with two kids. I think you can stop calling me 'kid.'"

"Nah, no matter what you do in this town, you're still my best friend's baby sister." He looped an arm around her shoulder and turned back to me. "You two have fun. I have a shift to finish, then I'm kicking your brother's ass in handball tomorrow morning."

"It's amazing, isn't it?" Kristina breathed out a long sigh as she sat back down. "No matter how old you get, some people never let you grow up."

"It's nice when you think about it. In New Hampshire, everyone knew me and my parents. It was a good thing to have extended family everywhere, although not when you were doing something you weren't supposed to be and wanted to stay under the radar. Then it wasn't so great."

"Ugh, yes, not that I ever rebelled too much or was even able to, thanks to my brother's quest to be my father's extra set of eyes."

"I forgot you had mentioned the chief and Jake were best friends, before I knew who the chief was."

Her eyes widened as she nodded.

"They've been attached at the hip since high school. Keith was the same big-hearted pain in the ass back then as he is now."

I laughed when her lips pursed.

"I hear he's a good guy. Keeps the town safe, a big family man. And anytime I've seen him, he knows everyone in the room." I nodded to where Connie was handing Keith a large bag while the waiters hung on his next word with rapt attention.

"He's a very good guy." She nodded, her smile shrinking a bit. I was about to ask what was wrong when the waitress came up to the table.

"Hey, Kristina!" she chirped and dropped a bread basket onto the table. "Do you know what you want, or do you want to hear the specials?"

"I haven't even looked. I figured I'd just get what you get." I reached across the table and draped my hand over hers. If there were rumors swirling around that we were a *thing*, why not make it crystal clear for all the heads still swiveling in our direction?

"Is Chicken Marsala okay with you?" Kristina asked as she flipped her hand over and laced our fingers together. She was claiming me right back—and I loved it.

"Sounds good to me," I said as I drifted my thumb back and forth over the top of her wrist.

"So, two Chicken Marsalas, and please ask Dino if he's doing potato croquettes tonight."

"He is. I'll ask him for two. Anything to drink?"

"I'm good with the house white if you are." Kristina arched a brow at me.

"Anything you want, mi corazón."

A wide grin split her mouth as she shook her head.

"A bottle of the house white, please. Thanks, Missy."

After the waitress left, Kristina leaned in closer to the table.

"Laying it on a little thick tonight, no?"

"Don't pretend like you don't love it," I lifted our joined hands and brought them to my mouth. "Where did you go just now?"

"What do you mean?" Her brow crinkled as she tilted her head.

"When we were talking about Keith being a good guy. You seemed to drift for a minute."

"Oh, it just made me think of something. Between Connie mentioning my dad's name and thinking about what he sees..."

She tore a piece of bread from the loaf and set it on her plate, picking at the crumbs.

"My father had a heart attack while he drove home from watching the Yankees game at his friend's house. They said it was massive and immediate, which I hope it was since he crashed right after." She took in a deep breath and leaned back. "Keith was on duty at the time and told everyone not to call the family until he said. He drove out to my brother's house, then they picked me up, and we all went to tell my mother. He didn't want any of us to be alone when we heard."

The waitress came back to the table to fill our wineglasses. Kristina didn't add anything else before she took a long sip.

"Sorry, that's not good date conversation. Sometimes the memories just hit you, you know?"

"Don't be sorry. The whole point of taking you out is getting to know you better." I reached for her hand again, squeezing until she gave me a smile. "I mean, I do know you *pretty* well already, but..." I lifted a brow, smiling when her shoulders shook with a chuckle. "I'm sorry about your father."

She nodded, her green eyes glossy when she lifted her head.

"I'm sorry about your parents too. You were young, but I would think the same thing happens to you."

"Why do you think I've never been back? My mother's best friend keeps in touch with a Christmas card, even though I kept changing addresses."

"Why don't you visit? I'd come with you."

"We'll see," I said, lifting a shoulder. "My father once told me how afraid they were to move up there."

"Afraid?" Kristina's brow furrowed. "Why?"

"He and my uncle took night classes to get their electrical engineering degrees for a promotion, but when they couldn't get one, they started looking for work outside the city. My uncle found something upstate, and my father took a job in New Hampshire. Both places were a huge change from New York City, but they wanted Gabe and me to live where we could have big yards to play in."

I was allowing the memories of my parents in more than I ever had, and that was a big step.

"My father said the town, at the time we moved in, wasn't very diverse, so he wasn't sure what to expect. The day we moved in, the neighbors all swarmed us with pies and welcome casseroles, plus gifts for me. I was still a baby, so I don't remember any of it, but I grew up with huge parties and barbecues, always going back and forth to neighbors' houses. They were all like our family."

"Kind of like how it is here."

"We had the decency to wait until December to celebrate Christmas, but yes."

Kristina burst out laughing, the sweet sound distracting me from the ache in my chest.

I never talked about New Hampshire, but again, something about Kristina made me want to tell her everything, the good and the bad that I'd kept locked up until now. But talking about my hometown was one thing. Actually going back there, seeing where we'd lived and the people we used to know who may have been left seemed like more than I could handle for now.

Kristina's smile was warm and sweet and still drew me all the way in. She was a balm to all the cracks in my scattered soul.

"If and when you're ever ready, my offer will still stand, okay? I bet you still have friends there. Probably some brokenhearted girls, too."

I laughed when her brows shot up.

"Are you saying that you want to make out with me in bars out of state too? That does offer some incentive. And I know, babe," I whispered, grabbing her hand again. I'd spent so many years mourning the life I was supposed to have that looking forward to my life now was still a strange feeling.

Dinner seemed to go by so fast, and before we both knew it, three hours had passed. The customers at the tables around us had thinned out, and when I swept my gaze around the rest of the dining area, we were the only ones left other than the waitstaff.

"We better get the check before they throw us out," I joked after I swallowed my last mouthful of cappuccino.

"They close in a half hour, and they won't. The girls are probably sleeping." She glanced at her phone before shoving it back into her purse. "Well, Emma is. Chloe is probably on her phone or playing something. Either way—" she shot me a sly grin "—no need to rush anywhere."

I already hated taking her home tonight, but this was a beginning, not the start of something we knew we couldn't finish. Still, my chest pinched with disappointment once the check came and we headed to my truck.

"I don't think I've seen your condo yet. I mean, I've been to the complex when Peyton lived there, but it would be fun to stop by to check it out."

I laughed at her innocent shrug as she fastened her seat belt.

"It would. But on our first date, I don't want the girls to catch you coming home when they're waking up. I'm trying to make a good impression here." I squeezed the back of her neck.

"I said I just wanted to see it, not stay the night. Presumptuous aren't you, Lieutenant?"

I took a quick glance around the empty parking lot and grabbed the back of her head, pressing my mouth to hers in a bruising kiss. I dug my hands into her hair, slanting my mouth over hers to go deeper, taste more of her. I swallowed her whimper as my tongue curled around hers, my self-control dwindling when she hooked her finger into the waistband of my pants to yank me closer.

Her head fell against the inside of the passenger door as our lips kept moving, each of us going in harder when one of us would try to back away, until I finally tore my mouth from hers and ran a thumb over her swollen, wet lips.

"That is why you can't just *stop by* tonight. I'd peel your clothes off and make love to you until the sun comes up, never stopping long enough for air, never mind driving you home." I pressed my forehead against hers, both of us trying to catch our breath. "As fucking gorgeous as you look tonight and how much I *always* want you, I need to take you home." I kissed her cheek and dropped my head into the crook of her shoulder. "Believe me when I say how painful this is for me right now."

She chuckled and wrapped her arms around me, pressing a light kiss to the side of my head. "Maybe when you have dinner at my house, we bake in a sleepover."

"You're sure?" I asked when I lifted my head. "You...They'd be ready for that?"

"I have recently learned"—she sucked in a breath and let it out slowly—"if you wait until you're ready, nothing happens. And you and I, we're happening, and they'll get used to it. We'll be as gentle as we can easing them into it, but I'm not going back."

She pressed her lips to mine with light, lingering kisses, smiling into the last one as she feathered her hand down my cheek.

"Not again."

THIRTY-THREE

LEO

"Thanks for coming with me." I took Kristina's hand and laced our fingers together on the elevator ride up to my aunt and uncle's apartment. "I know it's a busy day."

She tilted her head to the side and smiled. "It's a day for family, and I'm happy to meet yours." She kissed my cheek. "It's been a while since I met my boyfriend's family for the first time." She grimaced before leaning against the elevator wall. "I'm actually a little nervous."

I laughed, pulling her to me by the waist as my heart seized. It was still surreal that Kristina was mine, not a dream or a yearning I couldn't have. I'd never brought anyone to meet my family before because I was never interested in a woman long enough.

I was nervous too, but not because I was afraid they wouldn't love Kristina as much as I did, but because bringing her here meant how much *I* loved Kristina. It had only been a couple weeks of actually being together, but from the second I'd met her, I was sure.

I was also scared out of my mind, but I hoped I'd eventually get used to both.

"You have absolutely nothing to be nervous about." I gave her a quick kiss after the elevator dinged on their floor. "You're easy to fall for. Trust me, I know."

"Still so suave," she whispered, sliding her arm into the crook of my elbow and cuddling into my side.

"You just called me your boyfriend."

Her head snapped up from where she'd rested it on my shoulder.

"I did," she said, searching my gaze. "Although, can I say boyfriend? I'm in my forties, and it seems silly to call you a boy," she teased, squeezing my bicep.

"Nice of you to notice." I flexed the muscle and pressed my lips to her forehead. "You can say boyfriend. I like it." I kissed her cheek, giving her earlobe a quick nibble before I took her hand and led her down the hall.

My aunt and uncle seemed to be settled in and doing well, all things considered. The new meds and additional therapy for tía Lucia seemed to be helping. Her voice wasn't so strained, and now that she was able to make weekly trips to a salon in the facility, she sounded *and* looked like herself again. With her illness, we all learned to take things day by day, but seeing her smile again was enough for me.

Tío Joe's speech was coming back but still slurred enough to frustrate him when he tried to speak. The side affected by the stroke was weak, but he'd been learning to move a little more each time I'd seen him.

When I'd stop by after work, we'd often just sit in silence watching the big-screen TV Gabe and I bought them as a new home gift. Conversation wasn't needed as I was happy to just be with them as much as they wanted me there. The years-old shards of grief from losing my parents and the life I'd had as a kid had finally begun to heal. I'd felt my share of guilt once my eyes were finally open, but I was grateful to have the time to make it right.

Since July, I'd realized that certain things in life were meant to be, and fighting them or running from them, as I'd done both all of my life, was exhausting and pointless.

"Anyone home?" I called out as I knocked on their apartment door. Downgrading from an entire house to a one-bedroom apartment was an adjustment, but as they couldn't take care of the upkeep anymore, their sadness over moving was mixed with a lot of relief.

With their living room and bedroom furniture in place, the spirit of the old house was there. They still had the plastic-covered couch that my aunt could never part with, and my uncle's recliner remained in the same spot on the far end of their living room next to his walker and wheelchair.

"Leo!" My aunt opened the door and pulled me down for a hug. I'd been two heads taller than her since middle school, but each time I'd seen her lately, she seemed tinier.

"Happy Thanksgiving, tía!" I kissed her cheek, the whiff of her perfume floating up my nose reminding me so much of my mother, I tightened my hold around her.

When you finally stopped avoiding the memories of the most important people in your life, they were everywhere.

"Come in, come in." She gestured inside and shut the door. "You must be Kristina."

She took Kristina's hands in hers, shaking more than usual. We'd have to watch that, but for today, I'd try to write it off as excitement.

"We are so happy to meet you." She turned her head toward me, a wry grin tilting her mouth. "Took you forty years to finally bring someone to meet us, mijo."

"Took me that long to find someone special enough to

bring." I held up my hands. "These things come in their own time."

"I can see she's special," tía said, beaming at Kristina. "And beautiful." She brought her quivering hand to Kristina's cheek.

"Thank you. I'm so happy to meet you." Kristina held up a bag. "My girls and I made cookies. I hope chocolate chip is okay."

"That's Joe's favorite. And all we wanted was you." She squeezed Kristina's shoulders.

"Excuse me," I said, clearing my throat.

"Oh. Him, too." She smiled at me as she wrapped her hand around Kristina's arm. "Come with me. My husband is having a good day today, and he's been excited to meet the woman who finally got to our nephew, too."

Kristina glanced at me over her shoulder, her wide grin flooding my chest with even more warmth. If she only knew how much she'd gotten to me from day one.

"Joe, Kristina is here," she said as she led Kristina to my uncle's chair. He was a big man, but his recliner was high enough to hide the top of his head.

"And Leo too, but I guess I'm not that important."

I laughed when tía waved a hand at me.

"It's so nice to meet you, Mr. Reyes," Kristina said, leaning over to take one of his hands in both of hers.

When he met my gaze, the corner of his mouth curved up as the weak side of his lips twitched. The joy and pride from both —for me—scratched at the back of my throat.

My uncle stirred in his chair, pushing up on his good elbow as he slowly brought her hand to his lips.

"Que belleza."

His speech was still slow, but my eyes watered at the first clear words I'd heard him speak since his stroke.

Kristina turned to me with a furrowed brow, probably wanting to respond to what he'd said but unsure of how.

"He said que belleza, what a beauty," I said, squeezing her shoulder. "I couldn't agree more, tío."

"Thank you," she said when she met my uncle's gaze.

He nodded, the smile faded on his lips but still evident in his eyes, and fell back in the chair.

"For some reason, even though he's lived here for sixty years, it's been easier for him to speak Spanish in therapy," tía told us. "Thankfully, his therapist is fluent, so she said whatever comes easiest for him first." She shrugged. "Where are your girls?"

"They're at my brother's house, helping their aunt with pies for later. I'd like to bring them next time if that's okay. Chloe is fifteen and quiet, but Emma is six and may drive you a little nuts."

"Emma is the best. You'll eat her up, tía."

Emma loved me and hung all over me whenever I'd visit, but Chloe still looked me over as if I were a walking disease. She was polite, but I couldn't get more than a nod or a one-syllable answer from her, and never any eye contact.

I was hoping I'd break through the ice with her soon, or at least eventually.

"I know you can't stay long, but look," tía said, pointing to the dish of butter cookies on the coffee table. "Mantecaditos. His therapist picked them up from a bakery in Queens." She shook her head. "There were never any Dominican bakeries up here, at least, not any I could find. Which I never minded when I could make what I wanted myself." She held up her hands. "They're almost as good as mine used to be."

"Maybe when I bring the girls over, you could tell us what to get and what to do. They love baking, and it would keep Emma busy while she's here."

Tía's eyes lit up as she grabbed Kristina's arm.

"I would love that. Our kitchen hasn't been used except to reheat something. My son and daughter-in-law tried my old recipes but..." She trailed off as her lips twisted in disgust. "Don't tell him I told you that."

I cracked up when she pointed a shaky finger at me.

"I won't, tía. Knowing that is enough."

My uncle didn't try to speak again for the rest of the time we were there. He'd nod, sneaking a smile at me once or twice as tía broke out the family albums from under her coffee table.

"And that baby is Leo. Such a little doll with all that curly hair," my aunt gushed as she pointed to one of the pictures.

"Look at those cheeks," Kristina squealed as she lifted the album off tía's lap to get a closer look.

I peeked over her shoulder, my heart sinking a little when I spotted my father's face.

"Is that your father? Wow, you could be his twin."

"Especially now," tía said, a tiny smile spreading on her lips. My nose burned when I realized what she meant. My father was around my age when he passed away.

My blood ran a little cold, but not because of the comparison. I'd come so close to wasting the second half of a life my father never got to have. Kristina was a gift, and despite the ghosts of the past swarming around me, I felt lucky and blessed in a way I never had before.

We kissed them both goodbye, promising to make a date for Kristina to bring the girls over very soon. Tío gave my hand an extra squeeze before we left, as if he knew the epiphany I'd just had on his couch.

"So, how hard are Dominican cookies to make?" Kristina asked me after we climbed into my truck. "I've always been good at baking, but I feel pressure to beat your cousin and his wife now."

After she buckled her seat belt, I grabbed the back of her

head and covered her soft mouth with mine. Things had moved fast between us since we'd met, yet they never seemed that way. At that moment, all the love I didn't think I should feel so soon for the woman in my arms swelled inside me, kicking up my pulse enough to leave me breathless. I kept my hand on her nape, a groan rising from my throat as my tongue tangled with hers, the passion we could never explain always igniting easily enough to blind us both. Instead of pulling her onto my lap like I wanted to, I tore my lips away before we never made it back to her brother's house or out of my truck.

"Wow," she panted, roping her arms around my neck. "That was...wow."

I laughed, dropping kisses down her cheek and along her jaw.

"Sorry, I couldn't help myself." I traced the tip of my finger down her cheek, loving the dazed gloss in her eyes, and pressed my forehead against hers.

"Que belleza."

"Seriously?"

I laughed at her frustrated sigh.

"I have to go see my family and my kids now, and all I want to do is climb into the back seat with you."

"We could make time for that later, mi corazón." I pecked her lips and started the engine, laughing as she glared at me in my periphery.

"That means 'my heart,' right? I know a little Spanish."

"My heart or could mean sweetheart. My father used to call my mother that."

"I'm sure no one could resist you once you called them that." Her brows jumped as a smile danced across her lips.

"That I couldn't tell you since I've never called anyone that but you." I grabbed her hand and brought it to my lips. "But if I did, you're probably right."

I cracked up when she shoved my shoulder.

Home was a strange concept that had never meant anything to me since I'd lost my parents. I'd run from making one most of my life, but I'd never felt the need to—until now.

I'd lost the inclination to move from place to place because when I found my home, it was a person.

THIRTY-FOUR

KRISTINA

"**S**ay cheese!"

Emma pointed her new camera at Peyton and me after she rushed into the kitchen. My mother had given my nephew and the girls one early Christmas present each for Thanksgiving Day. Chloe was upstairs with Mike, playing their new video games and steering as clear of Leo and me as she could.

I'd been trying for patience, but I couldn't give her a pass any longer, especially considering how hard Leo was trying with both my daughters. Emma adored him already, but I couldn't understand what Chloe's issue was.

When I'd tried to talk to her and find out what her problem was with Leo, she insisted that she didn't have one, despite the constant questions over the past couple of weeks about where Leo took me on the nights we'd go out and when he was coming over again.

I'd thought we'd gotten past the days when she worried over every move I made, and I'd hoped that seeing me happy would finally put all that to rest.

I was over the constant wait for the other shoe to drop, and

I'd booked an overdue appointment with a therapist for all of us to finally dig into what was really bothering her all this time.

I leaned in closer to Peyton, now nothing but belly as she entered her ninth month, and smiled. There was so much to be happy about today, and I would do my best to set aside my guilt and worry over Chloe until the weekend.

"Here it comes," Emma chirped as she waited for the picture to print. The camera was a smaller digital version of the Polaroid my father had loved to break out on holidays. I could still imagine him shaking the picture in his hand and the excitement in his crystal-blue eyes as it developed.

The kids were a good distraction, but there would never be a holiday when it didn't seem like a big part of all of us was missing.

"Wow, your belly looks really big in this one, Aunt Peyton." Emma eyed the picture in her hand with a wide gaze.

"Emma, what did I tell you about that?"

Peyton laughed and squeezed my shoulder. "It's fine, my niece is very observant." She waddled over to Emma, bending slowly to kiss the top of her head. "And it comes in handy." Peyton caressed her stomach, moving her hand in light circles. "Like when I won't be able to sit close to the table and I can balance my plate on my stomach."

"Will the baby be here by Christmas?" Emma's eyes danced. She was already fascinated with her baby cousin, and although we'd have to make sure she gave the baby space, I was glad not to spot any jealousy yet over losing her title as the youngest in the family.

"God, I hope so." Peyton glanced at me with a chuckle. "Why don't you go into the living room and take more pictures of Leo and Uncle Jake?"

Emma nodded and scampered away.

Chloe had been almost ten when Emma was born, and she'd

approached being a big sister with trepidation from the time I'd started to show. I'd always made sure to give her extra love so she didn't feel left out, and I was relieved when she adored Emma on sight. She still did, even if her little sister grated on her nerves at times.

"Sweetheart, enough," Jake said as he came into the kitchen and took Peyton's hand. "Come sit down."

"I'm fine, babe." She rolled her eyes with a low groan. "I can't let your mother and sister do everything when we invited them to our house for Thanksgiving."

"You can." My mother came up behind her, grinning as she patted her stomach. "It's all done anyway, so rest while you're able to, honey."

"Exactly," Donna, Peyton's mother, said as she strolled into the kitchen. "The table is all set up, and there is nothing for you to do but sit and eat, which is going to be a rare luxury very soon."

Donna shared Peyton's dark hair and eyes but was a head taller with a booming voice and no-nonsense attitude. She had a big heart and less of a filter than my six-year-old. Peyton and her mother bickering back and forth was a constant every time they were in the same room, but poor Peyton was too pregnant to argue today.

"Come on," Jake crooned and wrapped his arms around Peyton. "Listen to your mother. You can put your feet up until dinner is ready."

She grumbled before burying her head into his chest. Mom smiled when my gaze slid to hers, both of us thinking the same thing. Jake was happier than we'd ever seen him, even when Mike was born.

I was always thrilled for them both, and my usual jealousy was tempered by a second chance of my own.

"Look!" Emma barreled back into the kitchen with Leo. "We

took a selfie," she said before shoving the picture at me. He had Emma in his arms as one stretched far in front of the camera. I'd have to steal this one and keep it with the photo she'd made me take of them on the fire truck.

"Okay, now the three of us could take one."

Leo laughed when she pulled on the hem of his shirt.

"We've learned it's easier to just comply," Jake joked, with his arms still around his wife.

"Oh, so have I," Leo said before scooping Emma into his arms. "You'll have to take it this time." He turned the camera around and set her finger on the button, shooting me a wide grin before looping his arm around my waist and drawing me to his side. "Ready?"

"I can take it," Donna said, holding out her hand for Emma to give her the camera. "That way, I can get all of you." She tapped Emma's nose.

"Okay, cheese!" I winced as Emma screamed in my ear.

The camera clicked just as Leo planted a kiss on my cheek.

"That should be a good one," he said when his eyes caught mine.

"Yes, it should." Donna smiled, her brow lifting when she found my gaze. "It's coming out already." She turned the camera to show Emma where the picture was printing.

"Okay, let's see." Emma tapped his chest for Leo to set her down.

"You're a patient man," I said, brushing my lips against his cheek.

"Happy to be her servant for the day." He pressed a kiss to my forehead.

Donna snuck a smile over her shoulder as she shifted toward the dining room. "Peyton, take off the apron that doesn't fit you and come sit down. Now."

Peyton groaned, lifting the strap over her head, hanging it next to the back door, and following her mother.

"Is the apple cider open?" Mike grumbled as he yanked on the refrigerator door.

"It is, but why can't you wait until dinner?" Jake asked.

Mike responded with a grunt.

"He's mad because he lost," Chloe taunted, a sly grin splitting her mouth as she crossed her arms.

"It's a hard game to figure out," he said, glaring at her when he set the bottle of cider on the counter.

"Wasn't that hard for me." She shrugged, laughing until her gaze stumbled on Leo and me.

"Nice work," Leo said. "Beating my cousin in *Street Fighter* was the best part of all my holidays."

Mike poured a half glass of cider and stomped into the dining room.

"The best part was how pissed he'd get," Leo told her in a loud whisper.

Chloe nodded, a tiny smile drifting across her mouth so quickly that if I blinked, I would have missed it.

"Is dinner almost ready?"

"In a few minutes," I said, studying her face and wishing I could do something to melt all this ice between her and Leo, but her half-second smile gave me a sliver of hope.

"Why don't you go into the living room with Emma? Let your cousin nurse his wounds and let her take a few pictures of you."

She padded into the living room without another word.

"I'm sorry," I told Leo. "Our first appointment is next week, so I'm hoping—"

"Stop. It's okay. And I think I got a little smile from her just now, if I'm not mistaken, so we're getting there. I tend to grow on people, whether they like it or not." I smiled when his brows shot up. "I'm happy to be here with all of you, so don't worry about that today, all right, babe?"

It was too soon to be so in love with this man, but here I was. The kiss in his truck after we left his aunt and uncle's apartment still had my head spinning, but my worry over my daughter took my high down a few notches.

"Can I help you, Mrs. Russo?"

"You can help Jake take some of this into the dining room." She motioned toward the steaming bowls of side dishes and handed him a pot holder. "Thank you, Leo."

Leo squeezed my hand and grabbed a bowl before he headed out.

"Mom still runs Thanksgiving," I joked as Jake and I shared a laugh.

"You're damn right I do," she said, pretending to scowl at us until a wide smile stretched her lips. "I haven't been this happy on Thanksgiving Day since..." She looked between Jake and me. "Since a while." Her throat worked as she reached for our hands and pressed them against her cheeks.

"Christmas is already better too. But, go." She tilted her chin toward the bowls of side dishes on the counter.

This was a big change from the dark cloud that had hovered over me for the last few holidays, and it was as wonderful as it was unexpected.

My nephew loaded up his plate, plowing through his Thanksgiving dinner and unbothered by his loss to Chloe right before. Chloe seemed quiet, but I hadn't caught any odd looks in our direction, even when Leo stretched his arm across the back of my chair. I was so excited to have Leo here today, but by the time we finished dinner, it was as if he'd always been there.

I supposed things just clicked when they were right, unlike my past experience of discomfort when I thought sighs and huffs of frustration were an unavoidable part of holidays.

"Is Keith stopping by?" Mom asked as we finished dinner. "Poor kid has to work on Thanksgiving. I'll make him a plate."

"That *kid* is the chief of police, so sometimes he doesn't have a choice but to work," Jake said, shaking his head. "Nice to know at almost fifty, you still think of us both as kids."

"I am sure my brother will eat very well on shift today. The police station gets overloaded with pies every year, and everyone is always so happy to feed the chief." Donna sighed as she leaned back in her chair.

Chloe and Mikey were already yelling upstairs, engrossed in their rematch.

"Aunt Maya took the boys to her brother's house, so Uncle Keith said he was heading up there after work tonight." Peyton groaned as she gingerly rose from her seat. "Excuse me for a minute."

"Are you okay, sweetheart?"

She nodded at Jake as she ambled toward the stairs. "Your daughter doesn't let me rest for too long without kicking my bladder. Sorry if that was too much information, Leo."

"I remember those days," I sighed as Peyton trudged toward the bathroom.

Jake stood, mumbling an "excuse me" before following his wife.

"Jake, your wife can go to the bathroom alone. That's another treat she won't have for much longer," Donna called out to Jake, rolling her eyes when he didn't answer.

"So, wait a minute," Leo leaned in to whisper to me. "Chief McGrath is Peyton's uncle?"

I nodded. "You didn't know that?"

"No. I knew he was your brother's best friend, though. So..." He clicked his teeth with his tongue. "That must have been interesting."

"Oh, it was," Mom answered for me.

"That's for sure," Donna said, taking one more forkful from her plate before standing. "I'm sure you've met my brother at the firehouse. He's good friends with Vic, so they both stop by to visit each other and compare town notes. It's cute." Donna stacked empty plates without looking up.

"I have a few times. I just didn't connect the dots."

"There are nothing but dots in this town, honey. You'll learn."

Mom laughed as Donna headed for the kitchen. "Did you have enough to eat, Leo?"

"I did, thank you, Mrs. Russo. Can I help you?"

"Call me Rose, please. I'm glad you had off from both jobs to join us today. Sit with Kristina. Donna and I will clean up."

"Mom, I can help—"

She shook her head. "Stay with your guest." She beamed at us before shifting back to the kitchen. "Plus, Donna probably already has it half done anyway."

"Can you come back home with us tonight?" I slipped my hand into the crook of his arm. "The girls should be in enough of a food coma to pass out once we're home."

"I don't have work until tomorrow afternoon. I can come back for a while." He tucked a lock of hair behind my ear. "Thanks for having me today."

"I'm happy to have you here. Really happy," I said and pressed a quick kiss to his lips. "If you don't have to go in until the afternoon, maybe you could stay until the morning? We usually have a big breakfast the day after Thanksgiving."

"You're sure?" His brows pulled together. "They won't be weirded out?"

He'd slept over before but was gone early the next day. Having Leo at the breakfast table with us in the morning seemed significant. We were going at warp speed with so many things, but I wanted him to be a part of our daily life when he could, and even though things between us had always been quick, it seemed like it was time.

"Emma will be thrilled, and Chloe will get used to it."

"As long as they're okay with it, yes, I'd love to stay over tonight."

"You're sleeping over?" Emma gasped and climbed onto Leo's lap. "Tomorrow, we're having a big breakfast. Bacon *and* sausage."

"Both?" Leo widened his eyes. He leaned back when she bobbed her head in a slow nod. "Wow, that is big."

"I guess I'm still not allowed in the kitchen." Peyton took a seat next to us. "Someone should check on Rose and make sure my mother isn't rearranging everything."

"They're both fine." Jake came up behind her and rubbed her shoulders. "You need to relax."

"Leo is sleeping over at our house," Emma said, bouncing in Leo's lap.

Jake and Peyton both glanced at me, the same smirk curling their lips as they looked between us.

"If we open the couch in the basement, I think that will be better for you."

"Why do you say that?" I asked, my chest tightening as I tried to figure out where Emma was going with this.

"Because," she began, her big blue eyes narrowed at me. "The last time he slept over, I heard him tossing and turning like Chloe does when she can't sleep. I heard the bed hit the wall just like when she keeps moving around. I think it's because your bed may be too small and his legs are really long."

Peyton burst out laughing, while Jake scrubbed a hand down his face.

"But don't be scared," Emma said, wrapping her arm around Leo's neck. "That weird noise is just the boiler, like Mommy said."

"That's very nice of you. Thank you," Leo said, trying and failing to stifle a laugh. I wanted to melt into the carpet and thanked God my mother was too busy in the kitchen to hear.

"Is dessert out yet?" Chloe asked, her eyes darting away from where Leo was laughing with her sister.

"Soon. We'll call you when it's out. The kitchen is a little crowded right now."

She nodded, her mouth angled down in a frown as she turned to go back upstairs.

Leo brushed a kiss on my shoulder and squeezed my knee. As much as I tried to put it out of my mind for the holiday, I couldn't fully enjoy my life until I figured out how to make my daughter enjoy hers.

THIRTY-FIVE
LEO

"So, do you leave here today and go be a fireman tonight?"

I held in a laugh at the question I'd been asked what seemed like a thousand times every hospital shift I'd worked for the past month.

My per diem days ranged from one to two per week. I didn't sacrifice days off in my new small-town life because I actually *had* a life here—a life with a woman I couldn't get enough of and was always dying to see.

I spent as much time as I could with her and the girls, although having a conversation with Chloe was still hard work for a one-syllable reply or a nod—if I was lucky. But I was fine with that. I didn't mind earning her trust, but it concerned me why it was so broken when it came to someone being with her mother.

"Not today, Mr. McCormick," I said as I adjusted his position in the bed. He was a man in his early eighties, but no one could convince him of that. His panicked wife brought him in almost every week for a fall or deep cut he'd suffered from attempting something he shouldn't have.

Kelly Lakes Hospital hadn't seen a lot of action in the ER since I'd been here, at least compared to the hospitals I'd worked with as a firefighter in other places I'd lived. Some falls and broken bones and a few nasty viruses were all I'd seen here so far.

"Today, this is my only job. How's the headache?" I nodded to where the ice pack lay across the bump on his forehead.

"Oh, fine." He waved me off. "Joanie panics."

I couldn't help but laugh and shake my head.

"A fall off a ladder is enough to raise a little concern."

"I always put the star on the tree. I just didn't realize the one we picked up this year was so damn high."

"Don't take this the wrong way, but I'd like a shift or two without having to treat you for an injury."

He chuckled as he held the ice pack against his head.

"That would be nice."

"Leo, can you come over here when you have a minute?" Sonya, the attending doctor on call today, asked me as she peeked inside the curtain. "We have a sports injury from the high school."

"Sure," I said, checking Mr. McCormick's ice pack for a moment. "I'll be back."

"Eh, help the ones who need it. I'm fine."

He sat up and fell back again, holding on to the sheets to steady himself.

"We'll see about that," I said, easing him back on the bed. "Stay here."

"What happened at the high school?" I asked, following her. She was new to Kelly Lakes like me—or at least wasn't a lifer here, as was the case with most of the people I'd met in town.

She'd come here from New York City, and on our first shift together, we'd discussed the horror cases we'd seen compared to what we'd dealt with lately here. Being a firefighter, I'd had

270

medical training, but I'd had a lot to learn when I entered the nursing program in Florida. My only advantage from the fire department was a stronger stomach for trauma during my clinical hours.

Nothing had tested that here yet, and I hoped that continued.

"We called her parents but haven't been able to get in contact with them or anyone else on her emergency contact list. The coach showed us the waiver allowing us to treat her, but she's a little shaken up."

When Sonya pulled back the curtain, my eyes landed on Chloe. Her chest heaved up and down, her eyes clenched shut as she held the blood-soaked towel to her knee.

"Hey, Chloe," I whispered and draped my hand over where she clutched the towel. "What happened?"

"Practice got a little intense."

I turned my head to the man in the chair beside her with a red baseball cap on. Sympathy pulled at his features. "She tried to make a shot over her opponent's head and crashed to the floor after she jumped. Her knee was torn up enough to get her here as fast as I could."

"Mom's at that tech conference," she croaked out as she opened her tear-filled eyes. "That's why she's not answering. I guess my dad is at work, but I'm not sure."

"I remember," I said as I dug my phone out from my pocket and shot Kristina a text. "She's probably on her way home, but let me try."

Me: *Hey, babe. I know the school called you, but I'm here with Chloe in the ER. I'll stay with her until you get here.*

"Yes, you're going to need a few stitches. Can you bend your knee?" Sonya asked and pressed the towel back on her knee.

Chloe winced as she bent her knee and slowly extended it back.

"I know that hurts, hun. It's a bad scrape, but we'll fix you up."

"How many stitches will I need? Can you wait for my mom to get here?"

"After I couldn't contact your parents, I worked my way down the list. I spoke to your uncle, but he's working two towns over and wouldn't be able to get here for another hour at least," her coach said, eyeing Chloe with resigned sympathy. "Your aunt would have been the easiest since she works at school, but she took off for a doctor's appointment according to Principal Swift, and her phone goes right to voice mail."

"It would be better to stop the bleeding now," Sonya said. "It's in a tricky place for healing, but you'll only need a few stitches."

She straightened and grinned at Chloe as she tightened the rubber band around her ponytail of braids. "I don't like to brag, but my stitches *rock*," she told her in a loud whisper. "You'll be all fixed up by the time one of your parents comes to get you. Leo will help me get you nice and numb, so you won't feel a thing, I promise."

Chloe nodded after Sonya left, turning her glossy gaze to mine.

"Are you going to stay here?" she asked me, her voice shaky and timid.

"Of course. I'll help the doctor and stay with you until one of your parents gets here." I picked up her hand to give it a squeeze. "I've had stitches on both knees, one knee from basketball, as a matter of fact. My contact with the concrete was brutal."

"She made the shot, though," her coach said, smiling as he rose from his seat. "You must be the fireman-nurse. I'm Dale," he said, standing to offer his hand. "I guess you've already met Chloe."

"He's my mom's boyfriend," Chloe said, without making eye contact with either of us.

"Yes to all of that," I joked, taking his hand. "Let me help the doctor gather all the supplies we need, and I'll be right back." I craned my neck and glanced at Chloe, holding her gaze until she gave me a tiny nod.

"I'll give her the lidocaine injection before the stitches," Sonya told me on the way back to Chloe, shooting me a quick smile over her shoulder. "Not that I don't trust you of course, but it's hard to do that to one of your own."

I didn't know how to answer that as I took the tray of supplies and followed her, her comment making more sense than I expected it to.

"Okay, take a deep breath," Sonya whispered. "This is just a needle to numb you up."

Chloe shut her eyes, fisting the sheet next to her with one hand and grabbing my wrist with the other. I turned my hand around and slid my palm against hers and squeezed.

Her eyes fluttered open and met mine.

"It's going to be quick, I promise. She really does rock at stitches." My chest swelled when I spotted a tiny smile drift across her mouth after I winked.

Sonya really was—thankfully—quick as she closed the wound. Chloe relaxed halfway through but kept hold of my hand the entire time.

"Until this heals, I'm afraid you're going to have to ride the bench for a while. Stitches on knees take longer to heal, and I wouldn't want you to tear them if you hit the court too soon, okay?" Sonya said as she peeled off her gloves.

"Noted," Dale said. "We want her healed for the big games in a couple of weeks."

"Great," Chloe mumbled, sitting up and dropping my hand. I took any and all wins where Chloe was concerned, and the one moment when she not only acknowledged me but let me be there for her was significant enough to feel like a victory.

"If you're going to stay with her, let me go see if I can get one of her parents on the phone."

"I'll stay with her. I already told her mother I wouldn't leave until she got here."

Dale nodded. "I'll just be outside for a few minutes."

"You did great. I'll tell the desk to get your discharge papers ready, and Leo will take care of all that by the time one of your parents comes to pick you up." Sonya smiled and patted Chloe's foot, sneaking a smile at me before she left.

I pulled the visitor's chair up to the bed and took a seat.

"How's it feel now?"

"Weird," she said, scrunching her nose at me. "Sore but tingly."

"So how high did you jump that you came down this hard?" I lifted a brow. Another rush ran through me when she chuckled.

"Too high, I guess." She grimaced as she sat up, shifting on the bed toward me. "It's not that I..." She trailed off, her gaze dropping to the floor. "It's not that I don't like you—"

"Chloe, we don't have to talk about that now. And I know that. Just take it easy until your mom gets here."

"He used to make her cry a lot. My dad."

I froze, tension shooting across my shoulder blades as I straightened in the seat.

"After they'd fight," she said before I could ask her when. "Mom didn't think I saw. I'd watch from the steps when they'd fight in the kitchen, and he would slam the door after he left. I guess to go in the yard or something. But the next day, she'd never look like she'd cried or even like anything was wrong. It was like I dreamed it up or something." She shrugged.

"That must have been hard to see."

She averted her gaze again with a tiny nod.

"Mom told us not to be upset about the fights they had since they weren't about us. I could never really hear what either of them said, and Mom would always look like she was backing off at the end, but he kept going until she cried. And it wasn't only once."

She raked a hand through her hair and exhaled a long breath. I said nothing and let her continue, all the while pushing down my own rage that this douche kept making my girl cry in a house with kids watching.

"I only visit my dad because if I didn't, Emma wouldn't either, and that would start another fight. I'm tired of fights. I guess he's trying, but I'm still so mad at him. He never yelled at us like that, and I haven't seen him yell at Mom in a long time. She never looked like anything was wrong and just kept telling us she was fine. But she wasn't fine. And I don't trust her anymore when she says she is."

"That..." I pinched the back of my neck, trying to think of the right words to say to make her feel better and not tip off my own rage. "That is a lot for someone to carry around. Thank you for trusting me enough to tell me, but you should tell your mom about what you saw or maybe bring it up to the therapist next time."

Kristina told me Chloe had been tight-lipped in their sessions together, and next week Chloe was scheduled to see the therapist alone. Kristina said she hoped maybe then Chloe would be more open, but perhaps the therapist wasn't asking the right questions. I wouldn't have guessed this was the root of what was bothering her either.

"I understand now why you worry about her, and I think if you talk to her, she will too."

I squeezed her wrist until she lifted her head.

"Sometimes fights get heated, and people get frustrated. But

I think you should talk to your parents about what you saw. Maybe they can explain it, or at least be aware of it."

"I guess. I just didn't want to tell her and then bring it up to my dad and have them fight all over again or have anyone else hurt her."

"I love your mother. I would never hurt her, and I'd be just as upset as you if I ever saw her cry. She's safe with me—you all are. I promise."

I was about to tell her that she shouldn't have to make allowances for adults at the expense of her own feelings when we both turned to the curtain opening behind us.

"Good news," Dale said as he approached Chloe. "Your mom should be here any minute, and I found your dad."

"Hey, what happened?"

I recognized Colin from the photo at Kristina's house. He looked about the same. His dark hair was grayer on the sides and his frame was a bit stockier. The idiot caveman in me liked that I was a full head taller than he was when I stood. His eyes darted from me to Chloe, but I kept my gaze on her to gauge her reaction to her father.

"I tried to make a shot over someone's head and landed on my knee."

"Ah, you made it longer than your old man without stitches." He smiled when she lifted her head. "Did you make the shot?"

She nodded, wincing as she tried to push up on the bed.

"Attagirl," he said, squeezing her shoulder. "No more hook shots while you heal." His gaze slid to mine. "Her coach said you were staying with her until one of us got here. Thank you, sorry if you have other patients waiting."

"It's no problem."

I wondered if his smile would be that easy once he knew who I was to his ex-wife, but I'd let Kristina explain once she got here.

"Chloe?" Kristina ripped the curtain open and raced over to her daughter. "Coach just explained it all to me." She kissed her cheek and rested her chin against the top of her head. "I love that you're enjoying basketball, but let's be careful at practice so as not to give me another heart attack on the way back from a conference."

Chloe smiled and gave her mother a slow nod.

When Kristina straightened, her grin shrank as she looked between us.

"So, you've met."

"I just thanked him for sitting with her until one of us got here."

"Well, then let me introduce you." Kristina came up to me and slid her arm around my waist. "Leo, this is my ex-husband, Colin, as you probably guessed. Colin, this is Leo—"

"Mom's boyfriend," Chloe finished for her.

Colin's brows popped up as he scrutinized the both of us.

"Nice to meet you," I offered, extending a hand as I draped my other arm across Kristina's shoulders. It lingered for a second before he took it, squinting at me as if he didn't know what to make of us.

"Emma told me about a Leo on the fire truck but not a nurse." He gave my hand a quick shake, his eyes narrowed to slits.

"He's a firefighter, too," Chloe offered as she leaned her head against Kristina's arm.

"I know, sweetie. You had a rough day. Good thing Leo was on today to sit with you until one of us got here." Kristina swept the hair off Chloe's forehead.

"Yeah, good thing," Colin muttered and shook his head. I almost sympathized when I caught the flash of hurt in his features and would have if I didn't have the image of him yelling at Kristina as she cried burned into my brain.

I understood all of Chloe's frustration, worry, and anger, but I had to find a way to keep mine in check.

"Your mom is here to take you home, so I'll head back to work. I'll pick you both up on Saturday morning if you're feeling okay."

"I'm fine," Chloe said, groaning as she sat up and swung her legs over the bed.

"I'll call you later," Colin said and planted a kiss on the back of her head.

"Bye, Dad." Chloe's reply was a soft whisper as Colin left, not glancing at Kristina or me on his way out. From what she'd told me and how she acted, she was mad at her father but afraid to show it. I didn't want to break her trust, but the kid had made herself suffer enough.

"Don't get up yet," I said, grabbing her shoulder. "I'll get your paperwork, and you can go home with your mom once she signs everything. Just sit for one minute, and we'll be right back."

She nodded and peered up at me with wide, grateful eyes.

"Thank you." I was rewarded with my first real smile from her. It felt like a gold medal.

"Anytime, kiddo." I tapped her chin with my knuckle and motioned Kristina to follow me.

"I am so sorry about Colin," Kristina said as she took my hand. "You both had to meet eventually, and I knew he wouldn't be all that friendly—"

"I don't care about any of that. What I wanted to talk to you about was Chloe."

"I thought she had simple stitches."

"She did. She told me that she saw Colin make you cry a few times, and then the next day you acted as if nothing happened, so it's hard for her to believe you when you say you're fine. I hate breaking her trust, but I thought you should know since this is probably why she's always so worried about you."

Her hand flew to her mouth. "I knew she heard too much. The sad thing is, I can't even pinpoint the night she'd seen that since so many fights ended up like that." She rubbed her eyes, letting out a long sigh before she lifted her head. "I'm glad she told you."

"I am too. She's also mad at her father over it but goes to see him because she's afraid of starting another fight. I think you both need to talk to her. Just please don't tell her I said anything."

I glanced back at the curtain where Chloe was waiting.

"I don't want to ruin the nice moment we had after fighting for one this long."

Kristina grinned when I flashed her a smile.

"I'm glad you had a moment. I wish she would have told me, but this finally makes sense." Kristina pecked my lips. "Thank you."

"Anytime," I said as I rubbed her shoulder. "You can wait with her while I get all this together and get you both out of here as soon as possible."

Her chin quivered for a minute as she nodded.

"Okay." She sucked in a breath as her throat worked. "I'll let Chloe choose whatever takeout she wants tonight. Can you join us after you get off from work?"

"I can," I whispered and kissed her forehead. "Go back with Chloe and stop tempting me to kiss you in front of everyone."

"How am I doing that?"

"You don't have to *do* anything. You're here."

The way she was looking at me didn't hurt either. Maybe I was a little spooked by what Chloe had just told me since it explained a lot about her mother too. Why when we'd first met simple kindness and consideration had confused her.

I was both tempted to pull her into my arms and kiss all of it away and run after her ex to punch his lights out.

I resolved, at least for today, to be a lover and not a fighter.

I watched Kristina go back to join Chloe, the wind knocked out of me when I realized how far I'd come since I'd moved here.

I'd been in love with Kristina for a long time, but I'd told her daughter before I told her.

I'd fallen for Kristina fast and hard enough to be used to it, but I didn't realize how much I'd been falling for all of them.

THIRTY-SIX

KRISTINA

"**A**re the girls ready?" Colin asked the second after I opened the door. On any other day, the absence of a greeting wouldn't bother me, as I'd come to think of us as coworkers, not exes or even friendly acquaintances.

Today, it irked me, but my anger was at myself, not him. Even if we were not inclined to be nice to each other anymore, we should never have forgotten who was watching and the lessons we didn't want to teach.

"They're with my mother. I told her to bring them here at twelve-thirty so that we could talk." I nodded toward the couch.

"Okay," he said slowly, eyeing me with a crinkled brow as he ambled into the living room, taking his usual seat on the far end of the couch. "This must be serious if you're asking to speak to me for an entire hour."

The sad truth of that joke was the entire reason this conversation was overdue.

"You know that Chloe is struggling."

"Chloe took sides pretty early." He scoffed.

"Colin, take your ego out of this. It's not that she took sides."

"No, it's that my firstborn kid can't stand the sight of me." He barked out a humorless laugh. "And won't tell me why even though I've asked her a million times."

"She's upset, by things she's seen and heard. Emma was too little to really know what was going on, thankfully, but Chloe was old enough to take in too much. She saw more than we thought."

"More than we thought? What do you mean?"

I sucked in a long breath, trying to hold my cool and keep my tone even. Despite our history, I did sympathize with the hurt and frustration pulling at his features.

"On the nights before you moved out and the fights between us were at their worst, Chloe would watch us from the bottom of the staircase. You would storm out the back door right when I'd start to cry."

The color drained from his face as his jaw dropped.

"I had no idea she heard all of that."

"It's not so much what she heard, it's what she saw. This is why she's been so worried about me all the time, because every morning after, I acted like nothing was wrong. She doesn't trust me to tell her everything is fine anymore."

I'd cried for so many different reasons on those nights. Sometimes I'd be so furious that the anger and frustration consuming me at that moment would come out in tears. For others, it was the hopelessness of what we'd become and knowing we couldn't fix it, and what we'd do to the girls when we'd eventually go our separate ways.

All my daughter saw was my devastation that seemed to be caused by her father. After I'd left the hospital, I'd felt like the worst parent alive. I'd foolishly thought I could love her out of the funk she'd settled into for longer than I could stomach to think about, when there was a bigger issue I didn't think about or even realize.

"My God," Colin whispered, resting his elbow against his knee and rubbing his eyes. "She must think I'm a monster. Did she tell the therapist that?"

"No, she told Leo that. In the ER after her stitches."

"Of course," he muttered under his breath.

I shut my eyes, trying to empathize with him instead of calling him out for being petty.

"She hasn't been giving him an easy time either. She's been wary of him since the beginning because she's afraid of anyone hurting me."

He nodded, dropping his gaze to the floor and raking a hand through his hair.

"Have you spoken to her about it?"

I shook my head. "I wanted to do that together. I'm glad she's seeing a therapist now because this is going to take time for her to work through, but worrying about me and being angry with you has drained her enough. We need to do better by her. By them *both*."

"I agree." He nodded and lifted his head toward me. "I'm not proud of what happened to us."

"Neither am I." I leaned back against the couch cushion and crossed my legs. "We went from growing apart to setting each other off every time we were in the same room."

"I sometimes wish we would have ended it when Chloe was small, but then..." He trailed off.

"Emma. Yes, I'm right there with you."

"We shouldn't have tried so hard to love each other when we didn't."

I stiffened at his words. They weren't laced with malice, simply laid out like the fact it was.

What Colin said wasn't a revelation, as I'd known that for a long time, but from someone I'd cared enough about at one time to want to marry, it stung to hear out loud.

"I guess arguing about everything with you and blaming you for pressuring me was my way of denying that. But there's no excuse for how I acted sometimes."

"No, there's not." I expected him to argue with me, but when his gaze met mine, it was still contrite. "But we've rehashed everything between us so many times that I don't have the strength to do it again. We owe it to our girls to truly get along, not talk as little as possible so one doesn't set the other off."

"You're right. And I'm sorry, Kris. Truly sorry for everything."

"Me too."

Love was supposed to last no matter how tough things were, but it was more difficult to consider us never really in love than simply falling out of it.

Dwelling on that wouldn't change the end result. All we could do was go forward.

"So, you and Leo have been together a while?"

I almost laughed at his lifted brow.

"Officially not too long, but he's a really good guy."

Colin's eyes widened at the smile blooming across my face. I hadn't told Leo I loved him yet, but I'd known it a long time ago, maybe even back in Florida when we'd first met. I never had a second when I didn't feel loved and appreciated and wanted when I was with Leo.

After forcing it for so long, the way things were so natural between us from the beginning was still a weird novelty, but I couldn't imagine being with anyone else.

Loving someone as much as I loved Leo was a fantastic feeling, if a little terrifying.

After everything, I still wished that for Colin too.

"The girls told me you're seeing someone too."

"Casual," he said, waving a hand. "She met them by accident when she stopped by. I haven't met anyone that I want to introduce them to."

"I hope you do," I told him honestly. "And I hope that after all this—" I motioned around the living room "—you know when it's worth fighting for."

"I guess you do," he said, a hint of a smile on his face.

"I do." I nodded, another smile tugging on my lips. "Now."

THIRTY-SEVEN

LEO

"**H**appy birthday, primo!"

I winced at my cousin's loud greeting in my ear. I'd answered the phone without looking, and after passing out from a double shift at the firehouse, I had no idea what day or time it was.

"Thanks." I cleared my throat after I croaked out a reply.

"I guess you had a double shift if you're only just getting up?"

I squinted at the phone, trying to get my eyes to focus and make out the time on the screen.

"Shit, it's two already."

"Yeah, half your birthday is already gone."

I smiled at his snicker in my ear.

"I'm forty-one, not a milestone or a big deal."

I hadn't truly celebrated my birthday since I was sixteen. I'd kept people at enough of a distance that it was never a real issue if I did or didn't celebrate since I never told them when it was.

I preferred to go about my day and forget about it. My family would still call, but I never had the heart to tell them to stop. If they wanted to acknowledge it, I wouldn't take it away from them or upset them when I requested they ignore it. Waking up with the day already half gone was a relief.

"Forty-one is why a double shift has you on your ass, old man."

"I'm as fit as I ever was. At least I don't qualify for your senior's discount yet."

"Fuck off, birthday boy. Why don't you stop by this weekend? Lona and I will make you some dinner, you can bring Kristina. I promise I won't mention your birthday once."

"We'll see. Thanks for the offer, but—"

"Yeah, I know. Love you, cuz, even if you're a mopey pain in the ass."

"All of that right back at you, primo." I laughed and swung my legs over my bed. "And thank you."

I stood with a yawn and headed to the kitchen to turn on my one-cup coffee machine. My condo was more like an apartment than any other place I'd ever lived, but even after Jake laid new flooring to replace the cracked tiles in the kitchen and installed ceiling fans in the kitchen and bedroom, it still screamed bachelor pad as my newly painted walls were still bare.

I had some food stocked in the fridge, but I usually ate whatever I could pull out of my freezer and shove into a microwave. The only pictures I had on display were the ones Emma had taken of us on Thanksgiving that I'd stuck to my refrigerator door next to my work schedules.

I spent half my nights at Kristina's house, the other half wishing I were there.

The receptionist at the fire station had wished me a happy birthday when I clocked out. I wasn't sure if anyone heard after I thanked her and left.

Gabe was right. Every year on this day I was a mopey pain in the ass.

I picked up my phone and scrolled, surprised I hadn't heard

from Kristina yet. I was about to call her when a loud knock followed by three chimes of my doorbell filtered down the hallway.

I lumbered over to the door, still not that awake yet, and found Kristina, Emma, and Chloe when I peeked through the window. When I spotted the balloons, I realized they'd been tipped off.

"Happy birthday, Leo!" Emma barreled into me, her hand still white-knuckling the balloon strings. "I bought the balloons!" She held up her hand, the shiny string tangled around her little fingers.

"I love them, thank you," I said as I scooped her up and kissed her cheek. "You bought them for me yourself?"

"Yep, I gave Mommy the money from my piggy bank. You can't have a birthday without balloons."

"We contributed the rest," Kristina called out behind her. Her cheeks were red from the frigid air as she cracked a wide smile. Even Chloe shot me a grin as she shivered around the large containers she was holding.

"Come in, it's freezing," I told them, leaning against the open door with Emma still in my arms. "I guess someone told you it was my birthday." I arched a brow when Kristina's eyes met mine.

"Your aunt," Kristina said as she set down two large shopping bags and peeled off her coat. "And she also said that you don't like to celebrate, but we decided to try to convince you."

"Yeah." I had to laugh at Emma's narrowed blue eyes. "Everyone should have birthdays and birthday cake."

I set her down and unwound the string from her hands.

"How about we tie these to one of my kitchen chairs?"

"I thought you'd have more than just this by now," Kristina said as she swept her gaze over my living room. "More than just a kitchen table and chairs, a couch, and a TV."

"That's all the basics," I teased. "I have a bed and a working bathroom. You know I don't need much."

Her brow furrowed as she craned her neck back and forth. She opened her mouth to say something when Emma ran between us.

"After we tie the balloons up, we can have cake."

"Anything you want, chiquita." I kissed her forehead and wrapped the string around my hand. "These are great balloons."

"I knew you'd like them even if you don't like birthdays. How could you not like your birthday? That's why we brought extra presents and cake to change your mind."

I crouched down in front of Emma, her baby-blue eyes searching mine.

"Because when I was young, my parents went to heaven. And I missed them too much to have my birthday without them."

"What about having new birthdays with us? Maybe you'll like them again?"

I couldn't look at that sweet face and refuse to celebrate my birthday, especially when her wide smile faded into a deep frown.

"I like any day I can spend with all of you." I stilled when I noticed all the containers Chloe had dropped onto my kitchen table. "How many cakes did you make?"

"Tía Lucia told me how to make the butter cookies, but the coconut ones seemed complicated." Chloe scrunched her nose as she popped off the tops of each container. Emma rushed over to kneel on one of the chairs, ready to pounce.

"She said when I had more time, I could come back and try."

"Come back?" I turned to Kristina. "When were you there?"

"All day yesterday. Well, maybe not all day." She stepped up to me and looped her arms around my neck. "But definitely most of the afternoon. She said Chloe was a natural and her cookies were better than Lona's, but we aren't supposed to tell anyone."

She pressed a long kiss to my lips. Sweet and chaste since we were in front of her kids, but the wicked glint in her eyes as she eased away made it dirty enough. "Can I even say happy birthday, or is that not allowed?"

"It is if you say it like that." I pulled her to me and pressed my mouth to hers while the girls were distracted. "How about this. Since I just woke up and haven't eaten, why don't we order something to eat before we go on a sugar high? As long as you ladies don't have any other plans," I said, drawing Kristina into my side.

"Nope, I'm free!"

Kristina and I smothered a laugh at Emma's reply.

"You just woke up?" Chloe asked. "Don't you want breakfast instead of dinner?"

"Breakfast for dinner is awesome!" Emma said. "Especially pancakes."

"I think I have the stuff to make pancake batter, and there's a bottle of syrup in the fridge. I can make us pancakes if that's what you want."

"It's your birthday, you can't cook." Emma reared back, her nose turned up in disgust.

"We brought enough sweets and carbs for dessert. So instead of what you *think* you have, we'll order dinner before dessert." Kristina's smile was wide and full of so much love my chest ached.

"How much dessert is there?"

"Cookies and that cake you told me about that your aunt tried to make for you but it wasn't the same? She told us about the bakery in Queens that your uncle's therapist went to. She hoped they made it differently since she knew you didn't like hers." She pinched the collar of my T-shirt between her fingers.

"You went all the way to New York City? When?"

"Today. We left early this morning and just got back now. I didn't mean to take so long, but traffic was brutal, and you were sleeping anyway." She chuckled, scratching at the longer stubble on my chin.

"That's a three-hour drive each way. For a cake."

"Well, seven hours total when you consider traffic. But yes, for a cake, for you."

"We went on a road trip," Emma said as she burrowed herself between us.

"You've never made a home for yourself, or tried to, until now. This cake probably isn't the same either, but maybe it's something close enough. I hope." She cinched her arms around my waist. "You may not want to celebrate the day you were born, but I do. So, we'll order dinner, have dessert, and you'll find a way to tolerate it when we light candles and sing."

My vision blurred as her eyes held mine, a lump poking at the back of my throat blocking anything I could say in reply. The cake was a beautiful gesture, but she was what made this place home for me. From the second she'd come into my life, I never wanted to be anywhere else but right next to her.

"Did I just make you speechless?" She kissed my cheek.

"Something like that," I managed to say before bringing her closer and resting my chin on the top of her head. "You're fucking incredible," I whispered into her hair.

She sighed and cuddled into my chest. "So are you." She lifted her head and grinned. "You can change out of your PJs if you want. I know we caught you off guard."

"I thought me in gray sweatpants would be a present for you too," I teased and kissed her forehead.

"What's so great about gray sweatpants?" Emma asked, scrunching her nose.

Kristina's brows jumped before she stepped back to crouch

in front of her. I needed to do a better job of remembering the little ears around us and how they heard every single thing.

"Why don't you get out the plates and the banner we bought today?"

"Plates and a banner?"

"Birthday plates! We even found ones with a fire truck!"

"You did?"

Kristina turned back to me, the corners of her mouth twitching.

"Emma insisted when we bought your balloons. You're having a *PAW Patrol* birthday, and you are going to love every minute."

I burst out laughing but caught the hurt in Emma's gaze when I looked down.

"*PAW Patrol* is perfect, chiquita." I scooped her up again. "You are a very thoughtful little girl."

I relaxed when a slow smile stretched her lips. She flung her arms around my neck, almost making me cough from the impact.

I rubbed her back when she rested her head on my shoulder. I was never that close with Gabe's kids since I only saw them a couple of times a year. Emma was a ball of energy and love and was just as easy to fall for as her mother.

"Let me take a quick shower, and you all can decide on dinner."

"And we could set everything up by the time you're done." Emma tapped my arm for me to set her down and raced toward the bags.

"This is all great. Thank you."

Chloe smiled at me as she scrolled through her phone. She still wasn't all that talkative, but I attributed most of that to her being a teenager.

The tension between us had dissipated, but every smile she

gave me still felt like a win. I loved the idea of her spending the afternoon with my aunt just to learn how to bake cookies for me.

"We can have pizza or burgers. Both say they deliver here."

"Pizza!" Emma flung her arms in the air.

"It's not your birthday," Chloe told her, rolling her eyes.

"Pizza sounds great to me. Order whatever you want." I slid my palm against Kristina's. "Can I talk to you for a minute?"

Kristina nodded, her brow furrowed as I led her into my bedroom and shut the door.

"I know I probably overstepped." She winced when I turned around. "But maybe if you don't think of today as your birthday so much as all of us wanting to—"

I pulled her to me and cut her off with a kiss, backing her toward my bed until she fell onto the mattress.

The need to touch her and claim her was visceral. My blood roared in my veins as I hooked her leg over my hip, so keyed up to take her right here and now, but I had to find a way to stop with her daughters awake and only a couple of rooms away.

I tried to make every stroke of my tongue and thrust of my hips count until we could be alone. She ran her hands up and down my back, her light touch sending chills along my spine until she dipped her finger into the waistband of my sweatpants.

"Sorry," I panted as I tore my mouth away from hers. "I needed my mouth on you before I lost my mind, but we can't go *there* with company."

She laughed, her swollen mouth spreading into a dazed smile.

"I know," she sighed as she drifted her hand across her lips. "Not used to the extra stubble. It's hot."

"Is it?" I rubbed my hand along my jaw. "Noted." I pressed my hands against the bed and lifted myself up, hating to hover instead of being right on top of her.

"I don't like my birthday for the same reason I never liked

talking about my life before my parents died or staying with anything long enough to get attached. But today, as birthdays went before I started ignoring them"—I cupped her cheek, gliding my thumb back and forth across her cheekbone as her eyes held mine—"this one is already one of the best, thanks to all of you."

Her eyes watered as she sank her teeth into her bottom lip.

"I'm glad," she said in a shaky voice.

I kissed the corner of her mouth and pushed off the bed.

From the second we met, it felt like I'd found something I was too scattered to know I was looking for. I wanted to tell her that, and that I loved her more than I ever imagined I could love anyone, but I could never find the right words.

Kristina was a miracle in so many ways. I wasn't thinking about my next destination, because for the first time in my life, I felt like I was right where I was supposed to be.

THIRTY-EIGHT
KRISTINA

"I'm not used to having you here on a weekday and in the daytime," Buck mused as we ate lunch in the break room.

"Dr. Baker closed for the week, so I offered to come in if they needed a tech. Sorry to cramp your style now that you're on days," I teased and took a bite of my sandwich. "Plus, now I can sneak off to the nursery on breaks, so it's perfect timing."

Baby Keely had finally come into the world last night, a week overdue. I made sure to get in a half hour early so I could head over to see her and Peyton. Visiting hours started at ten, but no one stopped me, thanks to my hospital ID.

Keely was as gorgeous as her mother, and Jake had been a mushy puddle of love when I'd left them this morning.

"Imagine going back to the baby days?" Buck winced. "Don't get me wrong, I loved being a new dad, but now that Mackenzie and Noah are older, I'm not sure if I could do it again. Doreen and I were talking about that the other day. We're too old."

"My brother is almost fifty, and he'll be as hands on with his new baby as he was with Mike because he doesn't know another way to be a father. You're as old as you feel."

"And I feel old." Buck chuckled. "At least for all the diapers and around-the-clock bottles."

"There, I feel you," I agreed. "I couldn't see doing that again, and Emma's little enough for me to remember exactly how exhausting it was."

"Not even with Leo?"

My head jerked up. "What do you mean, even with Leo?"

He chuckled and shook his head. "If you make this permanent, does he want kids of his own?"

I chewed my bottom lip and shrugged. Leo was great with my kids, but he'd never mentioned wanting to *have* kids. He'd just settled somewhere for the first time in his life, so I doubted he was there yet.

"Shit, Kristina. I didn't mean to make you panic." Buck snapped his fingers in front of my face. "Snap out of it and stop worrying. That was dumb to even say because I'll bet this is going to roll around in your head until you clock out. If you're worried, just ask him."

"It's not that. I'm sure he's getting used to settling somewhere if that's what he's still doing."

"What do you mean, still?" Buck pressed, tapping my ankle with his foot under the table when I didn't answer.

"Everything has been pretty perfect up to this point, which scares me a little. He keeps saying he feels like he's home, but when we surprised him at his condo for his birthday, it still looked like he'd just moved in. Nothing on the walls and barely any furniture besides a small kitchen table and chairs. He can still pick up and leave without much of a hassle if he wanted."

"Doesn't he work two jobs? I'm sure he doesn't feel like decorating on his days off. I know I sure as hell don't—and probably wouldn't if Doreen didn't insist. Just because he hasn't hung up a picture doesn't mean he's looking to move."

"I guess, but I still wonder if he's going to get antsy to move on since that's all he's ever done. Winters up here won't help when he's so used to a warm climate."

Buck exhaled an audible sigh and shook his head. "I've seen how he looks at you. I'm sure a little snow and ice aren't going to make him bolt. He's not a temperamental ass like your ex-husband. He leaned back and crossed his arms. " Seriously, Kris, where is this coming from?"

I took in a long breath and let it drain from my lungs before lifting my head.

"I love him, Buck. More than I've ever loved anyone else, and while it's wonderful, it's so damn scary. I know he came here to be near his aunt and uncle and said he didn't want to leave, but I still can't stop worrying."

My heart hadn't been in it with Colin, at least toward the end, so it didn't shatter when it was over. My heart would disintegrate if I ever lost Leo. Love like this was as paralyzing as it was exhilarating.

Buck reached across the table and draped his hand over mine. "Besides babies, know what else I think we're too old for?"

"What?" A chuckle slipped out despite the churning of my stomach.

"Panicking when all you need is a simple conversation. Talk to him." He flicked his wrist and glanced at his watch. "Go see your niece for a half hour and get your mind off things."

I threw out the remnants of my lunch and headed to the nursery floor. I found Jake leaning against the glass of the nursery, his eyes glossy as he peered through the window at his new daughter.

"Hey, big brother."

He smiled, swinging an arm over my shoulder while focusing on the pink bundle behind the glass. "The nurses just gave her a bath. Peyton is still sore and wiped, so I came out here while she slept a little."

"If she's wiped now, I feel bad for her when you guys go home." I snickered and poked his side. "She really is beautiful, Jake. Congratulations."

"Thank you. That she is." We both laughed when Keely's tiny mouth stretched in a wide yawn as the nurse gently brushed her wispy brown hair. "I never thought I'd be here, you know?"

"Meaning what? Being a father again?"

He shrugged. "That. And loving someone this much, now. I figured if it didn't happen already, it wasn't in the cards for me or maybe it didn't exist. I never believed in a great love until I found one."

I nodded, Jake's words resonating so much, my vision clouded and my hands shook. I'd never expected a great love to come along either at this point in my life or after a difficult divorce. Buck's advice made sense. If I was having doubts about what Leo's plans were, instead of stewing about it and making myself sick, all I had to do was ask him.

Was instinct or fear causing all this uncertainty? I wasn't sure, but it was beginning to cripple me all the same.

"Kris, what's wrong?"

"Nothing," I said, waving him off as I took a step back. "Emotional times. I'm easily weepy around newborns, you know that." I kissed his cheek. "Tell Peyton I'll see her later."

"Okay," Jake said, eyeing me with suspicion as I backed away. "You're sure that's it?"

"Sure," I whispered, not wanting to give away the quaver in my voice.

Jesus, what was wrong with me?

I headed down the long hall, taking in slow breaths to calm down enough to go back to work. Once I had my bearings, I pressed the button for the elevator and was surprised to see Gabe after the doors opened.

"Hey, Gabe. What are you doing here? Is everything okay?"

Gabe smiled and gave me a quick hug hello after I stepped onto the elevator.

"I forgot you work here too. My father's cardiologist wanted to do some tests here today to send his new doctor the latest results."

"New doctor? Why are you switching?"

"Leo didn't tell you? A new facility opened near us. Full assisted living and only an exit away. They like the one in Kelly Lakes, but my mother misses her friends, and with the kids missing them both, it's easier to have them close to us. I'm grateful my cousin took a break from his travels to help us out." He squeezed my arm when the elevator chimed on his floor. "Good to see you."

I nodded, forcing a smile after Gabe made his way off the elevator. I got off on the next floor and stalked to the nearest bathroom. I slipped into a stall, sat down, and let my head drop between my knees.

Leo didn't say anything about his aunt and uncle moving to be closer to Gabe. Gabe's mention of Leo's break from traveling fed into all my fears. Yes, he'd bought a condo, but condos could be sold, and he had two jobs that allowed him to transfer to any location he wanted.

He'd told me that this was his home, but would he feel that way if his family wasn't included? He moved here for them, not me.

He'd done nothing but show how important I was to him, but was I important enough to keep him here? Maybe my marriage left me with just enough emotional trauma to always believe I wasn't worth staying for, and that was what was pushing me down this miserable spiral.

The residual insecurities still gnawed at me, the question of whether I was really enough so loud in my head it was deafening.

I stifled my tears, patted cold water on my face, and went back to work.

We were overdue for that simple conversation now, and I needed to know if his home was still here if only *I* was here, even if I didn't know if I was ready for the answer.

THIRTY-NINE
LEO

"Hey man, congratulations!" I spotted Jake leaving the hospital's main doors just as I was coming in for my shift.

"Thanks," he said, shaking my hand. He looked like a happy kind of exhausted as he shot me a tired smile. "I'm heading home to get Mike, and Peyton strongly hinted at maybe picking up a burger on the way back."

"Kristina sent me a picture of the baby. She's gorgeous."

"Thanks." His smile faded as he studied me. "About my sister, did something happen with you two?"

"What? No, why do you ask that?"

My stomach fell at his deep frown.

"When she came by to see us today, she seemed off, upset."

"No, I spoke to her early this morning when she was heading into work, and she was fine. I haven't had the chance to speak to her after that, so I don't know if maybe something happened on shift." I shrugged, rubbing the back of my neck as an uneasy feeling settled into my chest.

"I never felt the need to make the 'hurt my sister and I'll kick your ass speech' to you. I didn't make a mistake on that, did I?" Jake quirked a brow as he took a step closer.

"You did not. I'd never hurt Kristina. I couldn't."

He nodded, still not appearing too convinced with a deep frown pulling at his mouth. "Then when you see her, talk to her. Maybe she'll tell you what's bothering her." Jake shifted, giving me one last glance before heading toward the front parking lot.

I stepped through the doors and jogged to the ER. I headed for the ultrasound room before I clocked in and found her inside, making notes in a folder.

"Hey, babe," I said and leaned against the doorjamb.

The ominous feeling in my gut only worsened when she gave me a fake smile.

"I just saw your brother. He thinks you're upset and asked if he should beat me up." I chuckled, the pang in my gut twisting when she didn't laugh with me. "Talk to me. What's wrong?"

"We can talk later," she said, tucking the folder under her arm and heading for the door behind me.

"Or we can talk now. Tell me what's wrong."

"Not at work," she said, avoiding my gaze even when I grabbed her arm.

"Baby, you're scaring me. Please just talk to me."

"I'm fine." She finally turned toward me and kissed my cheek, resting her forehead against my jaw before backing away.

Something was definitely wrong, and it would kill me to wonder what it could be for my entire shift, but she was leaving me no choice.

"I need to give this report to the doctor before I clock out. Have a good shift."

All I could do was watch her leave, even though I was tempted to make up an emergency excuse not to have to work tonight so I could run after her.

I made it through the first hour, wanting to text Kristina on my break to check on her, but I had a feeling she wouldn't respond, which would only make me feel worse. What the hell could have happened in less than a day?

I was pouring a thick cup of muddy coffee from the break room when my phone buzzed in my pocket. My heart sped up, hoping it was Kristina, but dropped when I spotted Gabe's name on the screen.

"Hey, what's up?"

"Hey! Can you stop by Dr. Keller's office in the morning? He called to say that the receptionist forgot to give us back Dad's insurance card. They open at seven tomorrow if you wouldn't mind stopping by on your way out."

"Sure."

"What's wrong? You sound like shit. Bad shift?"

"No, I wish it were that. I mean, I don't wish, but that I could deal with. Kristina is upset and I have no idea why, and she was leaving when I was coming in, so I couldn't ask her."

"She did seem a little off today when I saw her."

"You saw her? When?"

"She was on the elevator after I took Dad to the doctor. I had to leave while they were doing the tests, and I saw her when I headed back up. She seemed to be surprised that we were moving Mom and Dad to a facility near us."

"Surprised? What do you mean? What did you say?"

"I told her that we were moving them closer to be near us and the kids, and I appreciated you taking a break from traveling to help."

Shit.

"I think that may explain it." I scrubbed a hand down my face.

"Why? What am I missing?"

"I think she's afraid that I'm going to pick up and move again. I keep telling her that this is my home now, but it never looked like it sank in. She probably thinks now that tío and tía are moving by you, I have no reason to stay."

"That makes no sense."

"I told her when we met I didn't like to stay in one place for too long, and I guess I haven't convinced her otherwise."

I leaned against the wall, letting my head fall back with a thud. I wasn't the same guy she met at the bar, other than being so drawn to her I couldn't fight it or stay away. After everything, she still believed if my family left Kelly Lakes, there would be nothing else keeping me here.

"I'm sorry I said that. I didn't know it would upset her, and I thought you would have told her already."

"This was just decided, and when we were together this weekend, it'd been a few days since we'd seen each other so we really didn't *talk* about any—"

"I get it." His chuckle annoyed me. "Answer me this, did you ever tell her how you feel about her?"

"Yes, from the beginning I said I wanted to be with her. She shouldn't have jumped to conclusions so quickly."

"So you told her you loved her?"

"Yes. I mean, not exactly, but she should know that."

"And not exactly means no, right?" I shut my eyes at his heavy sigh. "Some people need to hear the words. Yes, I agree actions are worth more, but if you love her, you should tell her. Spell it all out so there isn't any doubt. I knew she was it for you the second you mentioned her, but maybe she doesn't. Don't be a total guy, like Lona always says to me."

Buck had said I had to fight for her, show her that she was worth it. I thought I'd done that, and that after all this time, she knew how much she meant to me, but maybe after all she'd been through, she needed the words.

Like Buck had told me from the beginning, she needed to know that she was worth fighting for.

And the second my shift was over, I was heading to her house so she'd hear it all, and I wouldn't leave until she finally believed it.

FORTY

KRISTINA

I stared into my coffee mug, my eyes heavy, but if I tried to close them, sleep wouldn't come. I'd tried for hours and may have drifted off for a few minutes of restless sleep before my eyes popped open.

The girls were off from school today and I had nowhere I needed to be, but tossing and turning in sheets that still smelled like Leo wasn't conducive to sleep.

I'd been up early enough to get some chores done, but all I was able to muster the energy for was starting a pot of coffee.

There had been no mistaking the anguish in Leo's features when he'd said I was scaring him. The feeling was mutual. My feelings for him were so palpable they were frightening.

It was already eight, and I'd been obsessing since at least four. I needed to find the motivation to do something other than mope all day.

I'd managed to pretend all was fine for my kids so many times, you'd think I'd be able to turn it on and off like a light switch. But frustration was much different from bone-deep sadness and next to impossible to mask.

Was I doing a disservice to my kids by always pretending

306

everything was fine? It was hard to give myself permission to grieve anything when they were watching, but if Leo did leave, I wouldn't be able to disguise the hurt in front of them or anyone.

I fixed the knot of hair on top of my head into a ponytail and headed to my basement to drown my potential sorrows in the laundry. I'd only gotten to the second step when my doorbell rang.

When I got to the door, I found Leo, still in scrubs, tapping my railing with irritated impatience.

"What are you doing here? You just got off work, you should be heading home to sleep."

"Sleep?" He barked out a humorless laugh. "I could barely function tonight. We're talking. I'll sleep later."

I lifted a shoulder and moved to the side so that he could come in, and I followed him into my living room.

"I'm sorry I distracted you at work." I sat on the couch, wringing my hands in my lap. This was the conversation we needed to have, and I still had no clue where to begin. "That's why I said we'd talk—"

"Later. Right. And now, it's later." He took a seat next to me. "I spoke to Gabe. He told me he saw you and what he said, so I think I may know why you're upset."

"I was just surprised you didn't say anything."

"That's because we only just decided to do this, and it's going to take us time to move them back. And they aren't moving across the country, just to another county. My days of making my family nothing but a once-per-week phone call from thousands of miles away are behind me, which I thought you knew. I have no intentions of going anywhere."

"That's good. I know you want to be close to your family."

He heaved a loud sigh and stood, shaking his head as he knelt down in front of me.

"I want to be close to where the woman I love is. That's you. I may have come for them, but I'm staying for you. You're the love of my life, the love I never thought existed until it came to see me at the bar. I took it for granted that you knew, and I should have told you a very long time ago. I'm so sorry if that created any doubt." He took my hands in his and brought them to his mouth. "You are everything to me. I. Am. Staying. For. You. Am I getting through yet?"

I swallowed, trying to will back the tears that escaped down my cheek. "Then why does your condo look like a hotel room? Like you don't plan to stay?"

"I will grant you, I didn't fix up the condo like I said I would, because when I'm there, I just want to be here. This, with you and the girls—*this* is home. My condo is where I sleep when I can't see you. I'd rather be with you than waste time hanging up a picture there."

"So I panicked for no reason?" I squeaked out, wiping my wet cheeks with the back of my hand as a laugh bubbled out through my sobs.

He cocked his head to the side, the corner of his mouth curving up.

"More or less, but I should have told you I loved you rather than assume that you knew. I've never been in love before, so I guess even at forty-one, I'm pretty clueless about a few things. But you are the one thing I've always been sure about. Even if it's been like five minutes and you haven't said it back."

He arched a brow, tapping his finger on my knee.

"I love you so much it frightens me. And apparently makes me act like an emotional mess. I've always been afraid that you're too wonderful to keep."

"Well, you need to stop doing that, because I belong to you." He slid his hand under my hips and lifted me off the couch and onto his lap. "My home is wherever you are, mi corazón." He brushed my lips, painting kisses across my jaw and down my neck. "Because you're my heart. How long do we have until the girls get up?"

"Chloe still has a couple of hours... Ah, right there." He dove into my neck, biting at the sensitive skin behind my ear after I lolled my head to the side. "Emma was up late watching TV, so we may have another hour or so. Do you want to have kids?"

He stilled and lifted his head.

"That was an odd segue. Are you trying to tell me something?"

"No, not that." I searched his gaze for relief or disappointment, but all I saw was confusion. "I don't want any more kids, but we never talked about if you do. I don't know if you want to miss out because—"

He pressed his finger against my lips.

"Are you asking if I want to give up the woman I love for an imaginary baby I may or may not want to have?" He stroked his hand up and down my back as his shoulders shook with a chuckle.

"Here is another looming question that has basically the same answer. I want *you*. And with you, I already have kids. So, it's a non-question type of question. Now"—he draped his hand behind my neck and yanked me closer with his other arm—"before I take you upstairs, lock the door, and sink as deep inside you as I can until a kid wakes up, is there anything else we need to talk about?"

"No," I whispered, too overwhelmed by the cascade of emotions to find my voice.

He smiled and pressed his lips to mine, soft and gentle until he traced the seam of my lips with his tongue. My mouth opened with a relieved groan, all the panic and doubt I'd tortured myself with pouring out and into that kiss. He loved me and he was staying—for me. From the moment I met Leo, I'd doubted that he was real or that I was enough to make someone want to change his life just to be with me.

I'd managed to push it to the back of my mind, but all it took was a second of uncertainty to make me question it all again.

Leo fell back onto the carpet as the kiss caught fire. We rolled back and forth as I pawed at his shirt and his hands slipped inside my jogging pants.

"Please, baby," Leo pleaded as I kissed down his neck. "We need a locked door for what I'm about to do to you." He swatted my hip. "Up."

I laughed and stood, turning to head upstairs when he lifted me up and put me over his shoulder.

"What are you doing?" I grasped the back of his jacket as he climbed the stairs, adjusting me in his arms at the top.

"Cutting down on noise, one set of footsteps." He plopped me on the bed and locked the door behind him.

"Are you crazy—"

My words trailed off when he peeled off his jacket and shirt. He was too perfect in so many ways. I'd memorized every sinew of muscle and line of ink with my hands and mouth, yet the sight of him stole the air from my lungs every single time.

Great loves came in their own time, and I knew without a doubt that Leo was mine.

"Instead of staring," he said, a wicked grin stretching his mouth as he hooked his thumbs into the waistband of my sweats, "off."

I lifted my shirt over my head as he slid my pants down my legs.

"Fuck, look at you," he said, his gravelly voice drenched with need.

I held his eyes as I reached behind me to unclasp my bra and let it slip down my shoulders before tossing it aside.

"Lie back."

I scooted back on the bed, already breathless with anticipation. This seemed different, significant, and permanent. It always was, but nothing stopped me from believing it this time.

"I wish I could take my time. Make-up sex isn't supposed to be rushed, but I get the feeling we're on a limit." He tore off my panties, almost ripping them as he looped them over my ankles and threw them onto the floor next to the heap of clothes. "Certain things I can't skimp on." He ran his mouth up my thigh until he settled at my core, sucking my clit into his mouth before running his tongue all over me. I pressed a pillow into my face, fighting the urge to scream. I dug my heels into the mattress when he slid two fingers inside, curling them as he inched them out.

"Shh." He tapped my thigh when I let go of a loud whimper. "It's too hard not to make noise."

He chuckled as he dragged kisses along the inside of my thigh, taking his fingers deeper and working me over again with his mouth. He swirled his tongue around my clit before sucking it so hard I had to bite the inside of my cheek to halt a scream.

When he moaned, the vibration shooting down my legs and curling my toes, I lost it. I grabbed the pillow again as I came hard, white dots bursting inside my eyelids as I bucked my hips against his mouth.

"Now hold on," he said after tearing the pillow away from my face. "This may be quick whether I want it to be or not."

I gasped when he filled me with one thrust, looping his arm around my waist to pull me closer and clutching the headboard with his other hand.

I'd been on the pill since the week after that kiss in the bar, and I loved having no barriers between us and nothing to hold us back from giving in to our crazy need for each other that intensified every time. "I was so scared," he said, grunting as he

311

moved harder and faster. "I lost you once, never again. Fuck, I love you so much."

"I love you too, so much. Leo, I—"

My body stiffened from the waist down as I shuddered against him. He groaned in my ear as he pulsed inside me, shaking until his body relaxed on top of mine.

"So." He rolled next to me and tugged me into his side. "We're good?"

I laughed and dropped my head against his chest.

"Yeah, I think so." I brought my hands under my chin and peered up at him. His hair was damp from the sweat beading on his brow. "I'm sorry."

"Just promise me you're not going to doubt this or us again." He smoothed the hair off my sticky forehead. "And if you do, talk to me. I know someone gave you a reason to doubt how amazing you are because they took you for granted for so damn long, but I love you too much to ever do that. You're my heart. Got it?"

"I do," I said, my voice cracking. I pressed a kiss to his chest, my eyelids finally heavy enough to close.

"Think we have time to get some sleep?" Leo asked and pulled the comforter over us.

"Maybe a few minutes." I smiled when Leo's eyes fluttered shut.

Leo wasn't the only one who finally felt like he was home.

EPILOGUE

LEO

Six months later

"Wake up," Kristina whispered and brushed a kiss on my cheek.

I grumbled back at her. After a double shift, I usually let my eyes pop open whenever they wanted, and I was too tired to change that rule for today.

"Babe, I'm exhausted. Give me another hour or two."

"It's already noon. What can I do to convince you?" she crooned, drifting her hand up my leg and coasting it over my stomach. I still had trouble opening my eyes, but my dick was all too happy to greet Kristina's palm.

"If you want to crawl under the sheets and wake me up with your sweet mouth, I may consider getting out of bed."

"Oh yeah?" She dragged kisses down my arm, dipping her head under the sheet to run her lips across my chest. I groaned and turned on my back, still wanting more sleep but unable to resist this amazing way to get up.

"We have breakfast for you downstairs." She pressed her lips to mine and popped off the bed. "We can put a pin in that for now."

"That was mean." I sat up, trying to glare as my eyes were still half closed.

"You'll forgive me, I promise. When that goes down"—her eyes flickered to where I tented my boxers—"you can meet me downstairs."

She blew me a kiss and fluttered out of the bedroom. As I had no choice, I stood from the bed and searched for a tank and shorts after my cock and I moved past our disappointment, and I trudged down the stairs.

"I thought you'd never wake up," Emma said as she rushed over to me, hugging my legs so hard that I couldn't move.

"Sorry, chiquita. I was extra tired." I bent to kiss the top of her head and stilled. "Why is there so much food on the table already?" I rubbed my eyes, and when I opened them again, I spotted eggs, pancakes, a tray of mantecaditos, and donuts.

"It's a special day." Kristina shrugged and handed me a cup of coffee.

"Why?"

"It's like an anniversary, I guess."

"Anniversary?" My tired brain was too frazzled to figure out what happened on this date since I wasn't sure what today even was.

"Today is July fifteenth, the day I went to the Florida Keys all by myself and a bartender took me to see a movie on the beach. And you know, other stuff."

My eyes widened as I shook my head. How could I have known Kristina for a year already? Some days it felt like I'd known her for my entire life, and others it was as if we'd just met. As I was basically living in her house and only went back to my condo to get my mail or extra clothes, I couldn't remember life before her and definitely couldn't fathom one without her now.

"Wow, I'm sorry I didn't realize. But" —I motioned toward the girls—"that's more of a you and me anniversary," I whispered. "We did too much dirty stuff on that day to celebrate with the kids."

She laughed, a blush running up her cheeks as she shook her head.

"Yes, while that's true, we wanted to give you a big present, and today's date was a good excuse."

"Big present?" I narrowed my eyes and took a long sip of coffee. "I feel like I should be giving *you* a present today." I looped my arm around her waist and tugged her close. "After that *awesome* gift you gave me by the pool—"

"What did you give Leo by the pool?"

"A noodle. Go eat." Kristina turned Emma around and gave her a gentle push toward the table. Emma was like a tiny ninja. You never heard her coming.

"Wow, this is a great way to wake up." I sat down and glanced at Chloe across the table. She had a devious smile pulling on her lips as she piled her plate with pancakes.

"We thought you never would," Chloe said with her mouth full. "Emma had five cookies while we waited."

"Save some for the next time we visit tía." I set down my coffee next to my plate and noticed a small gold box.

"Open it!" Emma squealed through a mouthful of eggs.

"Am I allowed?" I arched a brow at Kristina.

"I guess I shouldn't hold back *every* present today." Kristina's eyes watered as she chuckled. "Go ahead."

I lifted the lid off the box and found a gold key.

"What's the key to? Is it like the escape room we did and it's to a safe or something?"

"It's a key to the house."

"I *have* a key to the house. Is it to like a secret passageway?" I teased. Chloe and Emma laughed while Kristina wiped her eyes with the back of her hand.

"Why is your mom crying?" I asked the girls as I kept my gaze on Kristina.

"We're asking you to move in with us," Emma said, squinting at her mother. "I don't know why she's crying, though. Maybe she changed her mind."

"I didn't," Kristina's eyes were wet, but a wide smile shot across her mouth. "We all had a little meeting and agreed that we want you to live with us. Keep your clothes here, get your mail here, and stop wasting money on a mortgage for a condo you don't use."

She sat next to me and picked up the box. "I guess the key is more symbolic. You belong with us."

Now it was my turn to get choked up. I blinked the wetness out of my eyes as my gaze drifted to the girls. "Is that true? Was it a unanimous vote?"

"What's that?" Emma's brow knit together. "We just all said we wanted you to live here."

"All of us said yes," Chloe said, smiling as she glanced at her sister. "That's what unanimous means."

"Then, yes. I'd love to live here with all of you. This is..." I scrubbed a hand down my face, not sure if I wanted to laugh or weep like a baby. "This is the best present I've ever gotten."

"Yes!"

Emma rushed over to me and jumped on my lap. I stood, wrapping my other arm around Kristina's waist and dipping my head for a quick but searing kiss. "I love you all so much. I'm sorry. I never would have been such a crank when I got up if I'd known this was waiting for me."

Chloe came up to me after I put Emma down.

"I'm glad you said yes," she whispered.

"As if I'd ever say no to my girls." I pulled her in for a hug. Even though the days of her looking me over with nothing but distrust and disdain were behind us, Chloe's smiles still felt like rewards, and a hug this tight from her felt like winning the grand prize.

The tears streaming down my cheeks were the good kind, but I hadn't let myself cry at all since I'd lost my parents. I'd spent more than half my life feeling like I was in some kind of in-between because I'd lost my family and the life I was supposed to have.

On a beach, at a bar, one year ago today, I stepped into the life that was meant to be.

BONUS EPILOGUE

KRISTINA

One year later

"How do people keep these on?" Chloe fluttered her fake eyelashes at me. "They feel so weird."

"Leave them alone," I said, cupping her chin. Nothing showed how fast time flew than seeing your daughter in a prom dress and a full face of makeup. It was only her junior prom, but a big enough deal for her family to come to see her off.

"Hey, sorry I'm late," Leo said, blustering into Chloe's room. "I had to leave some notes for the next shift for the lieutenant, and... Wow." He came up to Chloe, exhaling a long breath. "You're gorgeous. Who's this guy you're going with again?"

"Jonah is a friend from school. This isn't a date-date, so it's not a big deal."

"He may change his mind once he sees you. And if he tries anything—" he glanced down at Chloe's feet "—those shoes could probably take out a toe if you step hard enough."

"Wow, look at your cousin, Keely," Peyton whispered as she bounced her daughter in her arms. "She's so beautiful."

"Thank you," Chloe said, waving at Keely. The baby squealed and reached for her.

"Sorry, sweet pea." I scooped my niece up. "Chloe has too much glue and pins keeping her together to hold you."

Chloe's hair was twirled in an elegant knot on top of her head, and her knee-length green dress brought out her eyes. She looked so much like me at her age, although I'd always felt she'd surpassed me in beauty when she was a little girl.

She was a knockout now, and I kind of hoped she'd remember Leo's comment about the shoes, even if I'd known Jonah since he was in kindergarten with her.

"I guess we're all crowding in here."

Jake's deep chuckle drifted in from the hallway. "Look at my beautiful niece." He ambled over and took her hand. "Who's this kid you're going with?"

"Jonah Egan," I answered for her. "You did work on his family's yard last year."

"Good, Chloe can remind him that I know where he lives."

"I'm going downstairs to wait for Jonah. You're all crazy." She wobbled a little in her heels before walking down the stairs.

"I didn't feel it this much when Mike went to his prom." Jake chuckled at her departure. "I guess it's all different when it's one of your girls."

"For sure," Leo agreed. "Where *is* this kid's house?

"Stop it." I looked between them. "Both of you."

"At least she's going to her prom," Peyton mused. "My first prom was at thirty-three. I was a chaperone, but it still counts." She craned her neck toward Jake, exchanging the same wistful smile. "I doubt hers will end the same way, though."

"Better not," Jake growled, taking his daughter out of my arms. "We can't scare this kid from up here, so I'll wait with Chloe downstairs."

"Right behind you," Leo called out, rushing behind Jake.

"They're so ridiculous, but it's cute." Peyton laughed at their departure.

"I'm excited for the day Keely dates. That may finally be my brother's undoing."

"And Mike's," she chuckled. "They bicker over her, but her brother is her everything. Is Colin stopping by?"

"He's working, but I told him I'd text him a picture."

Colin and I actually got along now, not just pulling our punches in front of the kids. He saw them every other weekend and had even taken them for a three-day trip. But for all intents and purposes, Leo had become their full-time father figure. It was a role he came into easily, even if I was a bit jealous when Chloe went to him with her problems before me.

My eldest would always be protective of me, and I'd never stop feeling guilty over it. But with therapy and finally getting everything out in the open, she'd blossomed into the mostly happy kid I always knew was somewhere in there.

"You guys have a good night," Leo told Jonah and Chloe when he picked her up, shoving his hands into his pockets to flex his inked biceps. He shot Jonah a tight smile after he shut Chloe's passenger door and came back to our front porch.

"You're ridiculous," I whispered.

"I was Jonah once and know how he thinks." Leo chuckled. "We all need someone to scare us to keep us in check. Let me do my job."

He raised a brow before going back inside.

I waved at Jake and Peyton after they piled Keely into her car seat in the back of Jake's truck and drove off. Emma was at a friend's house for the day but hadn't left until Chloe came back from getting her makeup done and had her dress on.

Emma's new school year had brought her a ton of friends. She still gave out cuddles, but only in private. She was the class social butterfly, and I received almost-weekly emails about how she talked too much in class.

I told her to stop, but I loved her spirit. I prayed she stayed happy and free of all the burdens her mother and sister struggled with.

"What did Peyton mean when she said Chloe's prom wouldn't end like theirs did?" Leo asked after I cuddled next to him on the couch. "I know what usually happens at the end of a prom, which better not happen tonight, but it looked like there was more to it."

"Jake proposed that night. She'd taken him as her date and then bolted right after he gave her a ring." I laughed and rested my head against his shoulder.

After my divorce, I'd learned that a ring and a license were no guarantees for a happily ever after, and as far as I was concerned, Leo and I were already there. He loved me, he loved my girls, and that was all I'd ever wanted.

Still, I caught myself thinking of how I would sign my Rs if I ever became Kristina Reyes or what I'd say in my vows. Although, as I was reduced to a blubbering mess when I'd asked him to move in, I could most likely only manage *I do*.

I'd want to sneak off somewhere, maybe an island or back to the Keys or even Vegas. I'd had the huge wedding with bridesmaids and a tiered cake, and I had no desire to put on another show for anyone if I married Leo. He was all I needed and all I'd ever want.

"So, since we're kid-free, let's go out to eat. Somewhere with fancy food and good cocktails." I elbowed his side when his gaze drifted toward the wall.

"What's wrong?"

"That's actually kind of funny, they got engaged on prom night."

"Well, they were thirty-three and forty-eight. These are high school kids. I would hope no one is getting engaged tonight."

He nodded, his mouth curving into a slow smile when he turned his head.

"Are you sure about that?"

My heart hammered into my rib cage when he got down on one knee.

"I know this is just a formality since we're basically married already, but I want it on paper that you're mine, that I belong to you for the rest of my life. You and the girls are the best things to ever happen to me. I need you to marry—"

"Yes, so much yes."

"I didn't finish asking you—"

I slid to the floor, crushing my lips to his as the waterworks I knew I couldn't stop cascaded down my face.

"I know you said you didn't want to change your name from Webber for the girls' sake, and that's okay—"

"I want to be Kristina Reyes, and I want to marry you in the Keys. Can we make that happen? Is that a yes?"

A gorgeous smile broke out on his face.

"That's a *fuck* yes."

ACKNOWLEDGMENTS

I always try to keep this brief, but there are so many hands that go into making a book, it's hard to stay short and list them all.

To my husband James and my son John, my reason and my purpose and my biggest fans, all I do is for you guys, and I hope I make you proud.

To my mother, who still hasn't read a book of mine, thanks for supporting me in making this crazy endeavor my livelihood.

To Ann Marie, for the medical advice (both from you and David, your very gracious fireman-nurse co-worker), for helping come up with the whole idea in the first place, and for being my found family.

To Jessenia, thanks for picking me up when I was in the dumps on our walks back and forth to school. Your support and enthusiasm helped bring this story to life.

To my betas: Jodi, Rachel, Bianca, Lauren, Lisa, Karen, and Michelle. Thank you for loving the story and helping me make Leo and Kristina the best they could be. I'm so lucky to have each and every one of you.

To Johanna Vargas, thank you for taking a last-minute sensitivity read request and helping me make sure that Leo's Dominican heritage was shown respectfully and accurately.

Jodi, my PA, alpha reader, and family member at this point, thank you for your amazing guidance, your math skills, and your friendship. I wouldn't be able to function as a writer or person without them all.

To Rachel, I have no clue what I did to deserve you, but I'm not giving you up. For reading chapters at all hours, for your beautiful designs, and for being the awesome person that you are, I can't thank you enough.

Karen, The Wise One, for the voice messages that greet my mornings, the awesome advice tempered with so many laughs, and the beautiful graphics you make with the lousiest direction from me. I hope you know how much you mean to me.

To LJ and Kathryn for being the best hype friends ever, to Melanie for being a wonderful friend and author idol, and all the author friends on this journey with me. With one sprint at a time, we'll get there.

To Lucy, who will forever be Santa Claus to me, and Tim, I can never repay you for all you've done for me by asking me to join TWSS. 2022 was a year of dreams coming true and thank you will never be enough. To Dan, Rick, and everyone at TWSS responsible for putting this beautiful book into your hands, please know how much I appreciate all of you.

To Kari, for a beautiful cover that captures Leo and Kristina so perfectly.

To Lisa, for a beautiful editing job and not making me feel too badly for not knowing enough different words. I love working with you and hope you keep me forever.

To my awesome readers group, the Rose Garden, your support and excitement keeps me going. To Ari and my street team roses, thank you for all your hard work each and every day.

To all the bloggers and bookstagrammers who took a chance on a girl from The Bronx who wanted to write, thank you so much for showing up for me and my people every time. It means so much.

Thank you for reading *Starting Back*. I hope you loved Leo and Kristina's story.

And if you enjoy visiting Kelly Lakes, I may take you back there one more time next year...stay tuned.

AUTHOR'S NOTE

I've always found it fascinating how stories and characters come to me in different ways. Some need lots of planning and plotting to figure out their trajectory, and some carve their way into your brain when you aren't looking and then won't shut up until you put them on the page.

From the minute Kristina had dinner with her brother in An Unexpected Turn, I knew I had to give her a story. With her dry sense of humor and straight-shooting attitude along with that undercurrent of sadness from her disintegrating marriage, she needed a great HEA. Some thought I would write a reconciliation, but even before I dove into crafting her story, I knew there was more to her struggles with her husband than what she was saying. *Starting Back* was one of those stories that just poured out. I sort of knew where I wanted to go, but Leo and Kristina told me how they'd get there when I'd sit down each morning. As I said, some books you need to pull out of you more than others, but this one was the fastest and one of the most fun I've ever written.

And for many reasons, I was grateful.

While I've always loved to write, for the past eight years of publishing, I kept it as my side gig. Eventually, I wanted to at least downgrade my day job to part time, but I never considered making writing my full-time profession. Until, one day in July, I was laid off. It was a business decision and they were kind and gracious, but I was blindsided without warning. I went to the pool the day after with my son and had a crazy idea. Maybe the universe was trying to tell me something, and God shifted me toward a direction that I didn't expect but possibly one that was meant to be.

For the rest of the summer, I woke up with words as my main goal. That saying if you find something you love to do, you'll never work a day in your life? I finally got it. I looked forward to Leo and Kristina every day and was grateful for the privilege and opportunity to make a living doing what I always loved to do, but never thought of as a real job.

I'm here to tell you that it very much is. In fact, it can be even more taxing than a 9-5 at times because you're never really off. When you're not writing, you're thinking about writing, or if you're in the thick of the story and can't stop, you sit there until your legs are asleep and your neck aches because the words on the page are the most important things in your life at that moment. I did enjoy my job, and do miss it at times, but getting in the zone there and immersing myself in something I'm passionate about are very different things.

I was scared if I made this my full-time career, the creative part of my brain would close up like a clam, but I was thrilled to see the opposite happen. I know not every story pours out this fast, but even the ones that will be a challenge excite me. It's new enough to still be a daunting aspect if I'm being honest, but writing truly feels like where I'm supposed to be.

This means a 2023 with a lot of words from me—currently

planning three releases this year for the first time—and a new path I never planned on but excites me like nothing else.

I hope you loved *Starting Back* and am so grateful to all of you for being on this journey with me.

Much love,

Steph

ABOUT THE AUTHOR

Stephanie Rose is a badass New Yorker, a wife, a mother, a former blogger and lover of all things chocolate. Most days you'll find her trying to avoid standing on discarded LEGO or deciding which book to read next. Her debut novel, Always You, released in 2015 and since then she's written several more—some of which will never see completion—and has ideas for hundred to come.

Stay in touch!
Join Stephanie's Rose Garden on Facebook and sign up for Stephanie Rose's newsletter at www.authorstephanierose.com

Follow Me on Verve Romance @stephanierose

BOOKS BY STEPHANIE

The Second Chances Series
Always You
"Always You is the debut novel for Stephanie Rose and I have to say she knocked it out of the park."- *Jennifer from Book Bitches Blog*

Only You
"Paige and Evan's story was beautiful yet so very sad - stunning in its romance, love and friendship. -*Jenny and Gitte, TotallyBookedBlog*

Always Us, A Second Chances Novella
"Alpha daddy Lucas is a sight to behold...damn, I love that man!" - *Shannon, Amazon reviewer*

After You
Some books make you wanna shout them from the rooftops. After You is that book. - *Paige, A is for Alpha B is for Books*

Second Chances Standalone Spinoffs

Finding Me

"What a gorgeous book. Five whole-hearted stars." - *Emma Scott, author of Forever Right Now and A Five-Minute Life*

Think Twice

"Four people, two love stories, one amazing book." *Melanie Moreland, New York Times and USA Today Bestselling author*

The Ocean Cove Series
No Vacancy

No Vacancy is undoubtedly the feel-good romance of the year. Stephanie Rose has all your needs covered in this delectable love story - *Marley Valentine, USA Today Bestselling author*

No Reservations

"No Reservations is *"second chance" GOLD!* Tragic, heartfelt, sensuous, touching and romantic......This is your next 5 star summer read!" - Chelè, 4 the love of books

The Never Too Late Series
Rewrite

"Rewrite gripped me from the start and never let me go." - *Award-winning and Bestselling author, K.K. Allen*

Simmer

"A slow-burning romance about friendship, family, love and the true meaning of home. I absolutely adored this book." - *Kathryn Nolan, Bestselling author*

Pining

"One of my favorites! Comics, and steam, and redemption. It doesn't get better than that! Five stars!" - *Award-winning author, A.M. Johnson*

Standalones

Safeguard

Safeguard, a standalone novel in the Speakeasy series in Sarina Bowen's World of True North

Just One Favor

"Just One Favor by Stephanie Rose is heartwarming, panty-melting perfection." - Brayzen Bookwyrm

An Unexpected Turn

"An Unexpected Turn was a single dad and age gap delight. I ate this small town and slow burn romance up." - Ness Reads